Of ...

Tuhin A. Sinha is an author, scriptwriter and columnist based in Mumbai. He studied at the Loyola School in Jamshedpur and Hindu College, New Delhi, before joining the National Institute of Advertising. Tuhin is best known for his best-selling novels, *That Thing Called Love* and *22 Yards*. Both these books have been translated into several regional languages. *Of Love And Politics* is his third novel.

Appreciation for *That Thing Called Love*

'Tuhin A. Sinha weaves a contemporary story of a bunch of well-etched out characters, exploring expectations, disillusionments and fragility in relationships.'

Indiantelevision.com

'..the book touches several social issues and deals with them in a manner that has hitherto not been dealt with before.'

Screen

'A subject, currently explored in films, coupled with flowing language and generous use of the first person, makes this book an exciting read.'

Afternoon Dispatch and Courier, Mumbai

'A journey of discovery through disparate spectrums, Tuhin waxes eloquent on the choices that lie before the typical urban Indian male and in an odd way strikes a chord that is unmistakable.'

The Sunday Indian

Appreciation for *22 Yards*

'Setting the cats among the pigeons, *22 Yards* steers dangerously close to uncomfortable facts surrounding cricket today.'

Financial Express

'The book is the first of its kind – it embarks on a course that is based on some real life incidents in Indian cricket.'

The Hindu

'The plot is extremely interesting and would find favour with all cricket lovers. The writing is swift and lucid.'

The Statesman

Of Love and Politics

Tuhin A. Sinha

hachette
INDIA

First published in book form in 2010 by Hachette India
An Hachette UK company

Hachette India
612/614 (6th Floor), Time Tower,
MG Road, Sector 28, Gurgaon-122001, India

Typeset in Aldine 10/13
Mindways Design, New Delhi

Printed in India by Manipal Press Ltd., Manipal

To
The sense of spirited chaos that makes
India the world's most robust democracy
&
My parents who carefully enshrined the same
virtues of democracy in my upbringing

Acknowledgements

Of Love and Politics marks my most ambitious work till date. A lot has gone into its writing and I would be failing in my responsibilities if I do not duly acknowledge the contribution of the people who have been instrumental in making this book happen.

I'm grateful to Ramyani – whom I was seeing when I started writing this book and who is my wife now. Ramyani has been a pillar of strength throughout, helping me out with the research, with the ideating, with reading proofs, and with publicity.

I wish to thank Namrata Goswami, Associate Fellow, Institute for Defence Studies and Analyses, for providing me with some rare insights into issues concerning terrorism.

I owe a debt of gratitude to Nandita Aggarwal, Editorial Director, Hachette India, for her conviction in an unconventional subject like mine. The entire team at Hachette has been wonderful to work with.

To acquaint myself with the history of the Naxal movement in India, I referred at times to *The Naxalite Movement in India* by Sohail Javed. The book was of great help and I wish to express my sincerest gratitude to its author.

I'd also like to mention here some renowned writers whose works, especially on recent Indian history, have been an inspiration and learning for me. They include late Shri. P.V. Narsimha Rao (*The Insider*) and Shri. L.K. Advani (*My Country, My Life*). Another book I found very useful was

Great Speeches of India (published by Random House, India) and some of the writings of Ramachandra Guha.

Finally, thank you Akashaditya Lama and Mahua Majumdar for your enthusiasm in helping me with cover options and for selflessly agreeing to be the 'shadow images' on the back cover. The third shadow, of course, is mine!

Last but not least, I'm indebted to my readers who've stood by me throughout.

I hope *Of Love and Politics* is an enchanting journey for you!

Autumn

Aditya

Manhattan, New York

THE WAIT FOR FRIDAY EVENING IS ALWAYS LOADED WITH eager anticipation and with the reassurance that the weekend holds the promise of small pleasures – lying idle, sleeping in, dining out, or watching a film with Sarah – things I am ruthlessly denied on weekdays. The pattern of life at the Kingston Bank office in Manhattan is chaotic. As an investment banker, a major part of my job involves evaluating firms that our client companies might want to acquire. Operating out of Wall Street with a salary that some would consider very generous compared to what my peers get, an opulent apartment just a couple of kilometres away from my workplace, and a girlfriend who is more than caring, life hasn't really given me much to crib about.

As I wind up work for the day, I scan the website of *The Times of India* – a practice I perform as and when I find the time. Besides, the day's online edition goes up at 5am IST, which is about when I am normally winding up the day's work in the US.

The headlines focus on news of the Indian Opposition parties' disquiet over the proposed Indo–US Nuclear Deal. The debate over India signing the deal with the

US to honour the latter's assistance to India's civilian nuclear energy program seems to be getting increasingly contentious. Just two days ago, the Indian ambassador to the US Ronen Sen had stirred up a controversy by likening Indian politicians opposing the deal to 'headless chickens'.

I scroll down further and chance on a piece by someone called Chaitali Sen who slams the deal as 'unequal' and a 'complete sell out of national interests'. It's a fiery piece. She goes to the extent of calling the pro-deal politicians 'bone-seeking canines'. I am amused. I wonder for a while whether Indian politicians are 'headless chickens' or 'bone-seeking canines'. Both descriptions are extreme. From what I know of Indian politicians – and I've known at least one of them closely enough – they are far too layered and astute for everyday adjectives to size them up. And no, I am not interested in politics – in fact it's the desire for un-intruded-upon personal space that keeps me away from my country more than the pursuit of any professional accomplishment.

I scroll to the bottom of the article. A brief write-up about Chaitali Sen says she is a young columnist and member of the CPI-M Politburo. That explains it. I take a print-out of Ms Sen's article, not so much for its content, but because I am amused by the sheer passion she has expended on a stand that deserves little backing. I for one am all for the deal and have an equally strong point of view for the way I think. I realize there is an email address of Chaitali provided and think I might want to write to her.

◆

After work I head towards Roxy café. I can see Sarah sitting at the corner table at the far end – the same spot we've occupied in all but one of our visits to the café. Her pout is visible to me even from a distance. It is natural for her to feel upset as I'm late by almost three quarters of an hour. What is unnatural though is the frigid reception I get from her. She looks through me completely. She fiddles inanely with her cell-phone instead.

In politics they say that the best solution to a vexed problem is to deliberately leave it unattended (read ignored). I'm not too sure whether the same logic applies in personal life. I guess I've been over-optimistic in hoping that the problem would settle on its own. Today, I feel pretty certain that some blunt speaking is in order.

'What would you like to have, Sarah?' I try playing the gracious host.

She ignores me at first. A minute later, she calls out to the waiter and orders her meal – a Mexican dish with noodles, a combination I feel is indicative of her incoherence. I just order a soup as I'm pretty stuffed – more from the chaos in my mind than with the pizza I had at the office cafeteria two hours ago.

Even half way into the dinner, we're largely devoid of conversation. I try to make light of the situation. Seeing her diligently consume her noodles with her fork, I'm reminded of something from the past. I tell her how, as kids, my sister and I would slurp down Maggi Noodles – which had then been newly introduced into the market – and how Dad made many unsuccessful attempts to train us to use a fork, till he finally gave up. But my efforts at conversation prove futile.

As we're finishing off our food, Sarah finally breaks her silence. She does it with a veil of composure which does not take time to collapse. 'Did you speak to your Dad about our marriage?'

I retaliate as calmly as I can: 'Hmm… well, I don't need his permission… I'll get married when I have to.'

'What?'

'I mean, you know it's a crucial year for me. Just wait till the end of the financial year… after that for sure…'

'Another seven months? Two weeks ago you said we'll be married by Christmas.'

'Well, seven months isn't that much. It only gives us time…'

She cuts me short. 'Come on, Aditya you know my state of mind.'

'Of course, and that's what I'm worried about.'

She takes a moment's pause before laying bare her worst fears – something I am not unaware of: 'Aditya… baby, I'm a loser… I've lost every good thing that has come my way. I don't want to lose you. I'm bloody insecure.'

'But why? Have I given you any reason to be that way?'

The composure she's been trying to cobble together is gone. 'Dammit, Aditya. You don't understand. I want to have your baby.'

Now when a woman says something like that to a man even the most insensitive of our breed is likely to be struck silent for a moment. Besides, an emotionally charged declaration of this nature also masks a subtle form of arm-twisting.

After dinner, we go to my apartment for a bit. As my reasoning has been of little use lately, I have actually bought two help books for Sarah which I want her to take home. Once we enter the house Sarah's disposition changes for the better. I guess this swift jugglery of moods that she's been indulging in of late is her way of maintaining a status quo. For me the status quo has been impaired.

Within moments, Sarah has put on a melancholic Bryan Adams number and dimmed the lights. She places her cheek against mine, our lips dangerously close. It is the sort of distance from which two sets of lips would naturally gravitate to each other if the circumstances were more felicitous. They aren't so today and hence one set of lips has to make the extra effort; which it does.

We eventually make love. We hadn't done so in almost a month and I guess it is more a hormonal need for me than anything else for the act is mechanical and devoid of passion. I am also encumbered with a sense of guilt. After we make love, as is her habit, she rests her head on my chest, seeking a reassurance I find hard to provide. Her demeanor in the last couple of hours has braced me to tackle the inevitable.

'Sarah, I think we need to call it off.'

'Sorry. Call off what? Our holiday?'

'You know what.'

A deafening silence descends on the room as I see the anguish cast itself upon the contours of her face. And then comes the outburst:

'I knew it all along. You men are bastards. You just used me, damn you. Now you want to go back and get married to a girl of your parents' choice.'

'Stop it, Sarah. You know how much I've tried to make it work.'

'Bullshit. What's stopping you now? Do I suddenly look like a whore?'

'Your attitude. Your negativity. It's pulling me down. And I want to be free of it.'

Sarah shifts to a lower gear. 'Adi, I swear I'll change my attitude. I'll be the woman you want me to be. But I want to marry you. I want kids from you.'

Now it is my turn to increase the decibel levels. 'Sarah, I'm not worth changing yourself for me. I can give nothing to you, except disappointment.'

'I'll take that because you've already given me my share of joy.'

Her cajoling forces me to mellow down. 'Listen, Sarah, we've had some very good times together. Can't we be good friends?'

Sarah is outraged. 'What the hell? Is this a game? Must we flip flop from friends to being in a relationship and then back to friends? Look, Adi, you got to respect my feelings. It's either you as my lover – or nothing.'

I know this is another attempt at emotional exactation. And in as much as I feel sorry for Sarah, I'm not in the mood to play ball. 'Fair enough. Let's be neither... Let's not be in touch at all for sometime...'

She breaks down and goes out into the balcony... I take a smoke and look for the TV remote. I know the inevitable has happened. Yet I would be lying if I say I am not anguished. I would be lying if I say I had not earnestly tried to make it work. Yes, our relationship has been ailing for sometime, but death, however inevitable, engulfs you in a sense of mourning. And I know I had been a loser as much as Sarah; maybe even a bigger loser because unlike Sarah I came in to the relationship with the advantage of carrying less baggage.

I switch on the TV, and as I normally do, flip through a few channels. I can't move beyond the third channel, though. So disturbing indeed, is what I see – a picture that shakes me like nothing has ever done.

CNN is reporting Breaking News about an Indian minister having been killed in an ambush by Naxalites in a rural district of central India. The minister in question is Nakul Singh Deo, popularly known as Rajasaab. Even as the nation is shaken by the untimely death of a leader who had for long been touted as 'PM material' in the press, I battle with a loss of a very personal kind.

Rajasaab is my father.

Sarah stands behind me. I weep. We hug. Next morning, when it is still dark, she's there to see me off at the airport. We share a parting kiss before I step into the airport. When I turn back to look at Sarah, as I ride up the escalator, my heart weeps as much for her as for me. I board the flight and look out onto the American landscape. I feel lonelier than I ever have with my twin losses. The flight takes off... it's my flight into another world.

◆

Rajnandgaon, Chattisgarh, Central India

It's 7:30 am. I'm up and ready, having breakfast with Ajay Yadav, at the Circuit House bungalow. We're done with the main dish – aloo parathas with saag. Given a choice, I'd have preferred sandwiches of brown bread with egg whites but the cook Rameshwar hasn't heard of brown bread; besides throwing away the yolk seems weird to him. Most people here seem weird to me, for that matter. Or shall I say primitive. I don't have much of a choice, though. I am the Congress candidate for the Rajnandgaon Lok Sabha by-elections, which are to take place exactly twelve days from now.

We chat over tea. Ajay, whom I respectfully call Yadavji has my schedule for the day ready.

'Shall we start?' he asks.

I nod.

'Okay, first things first. Let me tell you that you're starting off with an advantage and a disadvantage.'

'Tell me about the disadvantage first.' I pretend an aplomb I don't feel.

'The disadvantage is that there is a huge anti-incumbency factor working against the Congress. This seat after all has been with the party for the last eighteen years barring two years in between.'

'And the advantage?'

'The same that you get in such situations – sympathy votes, maybe even a wave.' Yadav takes out his file and puts on his glasses. 'You need to understand the composition of the electorate you're reaching out to.' He flips through a couple of pages and then takes out a page which he reads, 'Okay, here it is. Scheduled Caste(SC) 10%, Scheduled Tribe (ST) 27%, Muslims 13%, Other Backward Castes(OBC) 26.5%, Brahmins 10%, Rajputs 8%, Bhumihar 2%, Kayasthas 1.5%, Christians 1%.'

I try and fathom what this means. I am more used to someone reading out the stock values of my investments in this manner.

'Now listen to the strategy for each of these. First the ST: the BJP has been rather shrewd in fielding an ST candidate – Jagdamba Potai. But there is one way you can fight him head on. The Navratras are starting today and a huge number of tribals will be visiting the Maa Bambleshwari temple in the adjoining town of Dongargarh. Jagdamba is known to be a devotee of the Devi. You can get a headstart on him by starting your campaign from the temple.'

'You mean, I'll have to visit the temple right away?' I ask in surprise.

'Yes. Jagdamba is a bit complacent. Besides, the move will be auspicious too.'

I'm not sure about this. The last time I visited a temple was nearly ten years ago, on the insistence of my then girlfriend. I'm worried on another account too. 'But when the villagers suddenly see me there, they might just go into a frenzy. It could cause a stampede.'

'Don't worry about that. I've informed the police. The SP will most probably be there. Besides, if you make an impromptu trip, it would seem you are a genuine devotee. A planned or pre-announced trip would make it appear like an election gimmick.'

I can see the kind of astute planning that precedes the actions of this puny Chanakya. No wonder Yadav commanded such trust from my father, Rajasaab, in the fifteen odd years that he had served as his PA.

Yadav gets a call on his cell. 'Yes, Madhuji…yes… yes. Aditya will be there by 9:30. Make sure your crew is there before that.' He turns to me: 'Madhu is with Star News. In fact, Aaj Tak and India TV will also be there. I can't promise the English channels, though. They tend to be snobbish about vernaculars like me.'

I am not sure how to react. The occasion seems to be getting grander by the moment – the proverbial 'son of the soil' seems all set for the 'mother of all homecomings', so to speak.

I remember visiting the temple eighteen years ago. My father had just won his first election from the constituency. And the visit was meant to express his gratitude to the Devi, whose disciples were supposed to have been instrumental in making the victory happen. This visit would be to seek the Devi's blessings for my win – time does come full circle! I chuckle at the thought of the extreme turnarounds that fate sometimes leads you through.

Yadav continues, 'As for the Muslims, they play a crucial role in Indian elections. Theoretically, 13% may not seem much, but they tend to vote en bloc either for or against a party. And that can make a crucial difference.'

'Hmm…'

'But don't worry about them. They will never go with the BJP. And unlike in UP, where the Samajwadi Party and the Bahujan Samaj Party are strong, here the Muslims don't have much of an option. But, yes, there is something you will need to do over the next couple of days.' Yadav looks up his diary: 'A delegation led by Mohammad Younus, principal of the local Urdu school will be coming to meet you. The state government is planning to make it mandatory for *Vande Mataram* to be sung in all institutions and these people are terribly unhappy about it.'

'But what will I tell him?' I ask, making no attempt to hide my naiveté.

'Just hear him out and empathize with him. Make promises of what you will do after you win. We can't really do much about it.'

I just look on blankly, trying hard to understand the 'desi' concept of social engineering, as Yadav continues: 'As for the OBCs, 50% of them will vote for us because of my surname. Besides, Rajasaab had a lot of clout among the SCs. The Christians are with us after the attacks on churches in Orissa and Karnataka. The problem lies with the upper caste. They have been moving away from the Congress. But, luckily, since the BJP has fielded a ST candidate this time, they might come back to us. That's where you will have to work your charisma.'

I take a deep breath, bemused. My curiosity, or shall I say my lack of comprehension about the Indian hustings, makes me ask a question. 'What about the development, Yadavji? Hadn't Rajasaab brought electricity to most villages and got almost 200 bore-wells built?'

Yadav laughs derisively. 'That's the problem with our people. Till such time as they don't have something, they don't expect it either. Caste and religion contain enough fodder to carry a candidate through. It's when you start giving amenities to people that you spoil them. Their expectations go higher and higher and instead of being grateful, they blame you for what they *don't* have.' Yadav quickly takes another call on his cell-phone before he continues, 'Even Rajasaab had realized lately that nothing works in Indian elections apart from emotive issues. And the BJP is the master of that game.'

I kind of get what Yadav is trying to say and yet I don't want to believe him. 'But aren't we not supposed to do what the BJP does? Haven't we always prided ourselves on being secular and equal to all?'

Yadav's answer is another prolonged laugh. 'You will soon learn what Indian politics is all about. There is a difference of heaven and earth between theory and practice, perception and reality, solution and hogwash. Let's get started. It will take us an hour to reach the temple.'

◆

We drive down to the temple which is an hour away from the bungalow. As we move out of the town and as the countryside unfolds in front of my eyes, I'm reminded of a long drive to Niagara Falls with Sarah. Somehow I have been missing her a lot today. I have barely spoken to her after returning to India.

Sarah and I had first met nearly a year ago on a social networking site. I had just shifted to my new assignment in the US from the previous one in Hong Kong and was battling an acute sense of forlornness. Dad had been pressurizing me to join him, back in India. I was very fond of Dad. I liked meeting and talking to him – but somehow not staying with him. I'm not sure whether he intimidated me. There was an un-bridged zone between us, which, despite mutual effort, we had been unable to cover.

I guess I was just happy being myself while Dad would have been happier if I had been him.

Anyway, on my arrival in the US I'd figured the best way to ward off parental pressure was to be selfish and immerse myself in the pursuit of the mundane; that way I would be left with no time to bother about other people's mundane expectations of me.

Sarah's profile picture on the site was very pretty. She taught chemistry in a local school in Albany, New York. Something in me made me click the button that sent a friend request to her; to my surprise she accepted my request with alacrity. Within a week of that, we'd met.

I was soon to discover that Sarah was fighting her own demons. She was battling a rather unusual syndrome. It wasn't exactly a commitment phobia – quite the opposite, really. It was a quest to trace a person most similar to the person whom she had once deeply loved. Mathew and she had been childhood pals who had known each other from the age of five. Mathew had gone on to join the US army. Sarah went on to be a teacher. The couple was contemplating marriage when Mathew had to leave with the US troops for the Gulf in 2003.

His body was sent home a few months later.

For Sarah, it was death of another kind – the death of the desire to live. After all, Mathew had been a part of her for nearly eighteen years. For almost two years after his death, Sarah had gone into complete depression, in which phase she had two anxiety attacks. Now Sarah was consumed with hatred for George Bush, whom she held responsible for a 'whimsical' warfare that had taken Mathew away from her.

I gathered that Sarah had been under tremendous pressure from her parents to get on with her life. In a desperate attempt to move on, three years after Mathew's death, Sarah first attempted to make love to a man. He was a close buddy of Mathew's and someone who deeply cared for Sarah. They got into a relationship. But three months later, Sarah walked out. She confessed to me that she realized she was only substituting him for Mathew and that on doing a reality check discovered she did not feel for the man at all.

A year later, she got into another relationship with the sports instructor in the school in which she taught. This time the affair was even shorter – exactly five weeks. As on the previous occasion, Sarah found it difficult to involve herself mentally – I doubt there were any emotions left in her. Apparently, the relationship had ended in a rather violent way with the man roughing her up. In her state of being virtually mentally dead, getting into two hasty relationships perhaps marked her desperation to convince herself that she could move on. But she failed.

It had almost been a year since she had gone out. For a woman as pretty as Sarah there should have been lots of suitors. And yet she had resisted them all like the plague. When we met, I think she was looking for a dumping ground, if I may be permitted to use a term that acerbic – a dumping ground for her pent-up emotions. She needed a confidant, maybe even a shrink in disguise, whom she could tell her tales of woe.

I was struck by her honesty and the fact that I could see in her a sincere effort to try and get herself out of the mess she was in. Besides, it does flatter the male ego to protect a woman.

The first time Sarah and I met was on a Sunday. It was summer, but an unexpected breeze had made the evening pleasant enough to entertain romantic notions about my unseen date. When we met, I wasn't disappointed. She had a slightly husky voice that complemented her mellow mental state. We chatted for hours without either being aware of how the time flew. It started off over coffee. Two hours after that, we had wine and a light dinner at a nearby Italian restaurant. Sarah insisted that the bills were paid by her. Perhaps she felt guilty for holding me for so long and thought I was doing her a favour by being a good listener. For my part, I didn't mind the experience at all. Her descriptions of the way Mathew and she had first met in school, their first kiss when they were eleven, the first time they made out when they were thirteen-and-a-half, her shock when she was informed of Mathew's death – were all so vivid, it was almost as if I was listening to an audio novel.

If I had not met Sarah that evening, I'd probably have done my usual thing – hung out with my two best pals, Kelly, and Khalid, a Pakistani, at a pub. But I enjoyed the experience of hearing out Sarah more because it took me to another world, acquainted me with another perspective. In my heart of hearts, I had always wished I could love someone as much as Sarah and Mathew loved each other.

But each time, I suspected my own commitment.

Over the next two days, we exchanged a few sms's. On Wednesday, Sarah called me in the evening and asked me if we could meet. I was loaded with work yet somehow I couldn't say no. I asked her to come over to my apartment as I'd be late getting home. She surprised me again by readily agreeing to this.

We met around 11:30. I ordered in dinner. Her body language exuded ease – as though she trusted me fully. I was surprised by this since all I'd done in our first meeting was to listen to her speak. The power of empathy, I realized, is grossly underestimated. After dinner, we watched a movie on my home theatre. Half way through, I could sense Sarah's interest dwindling. Sarah confessed she enjoyed only boisterous comedies or action flicks. She did not like movies that would make her think. I was dead tired and dozed off on the couch. When I woke up I realized Sarah was waiting for me to get up so she could tell me she was leaving. And she left in no time.

Our first night together, if I may call it that, left me with unusual impressions. I was certain about two things: one, I couldn't possibly be the best of friends with her – our temperaments were different, and two, we would most definitely not be 'boyfriend–girlfriend' because our worlds were poles apart. Still, I somehow felt very comfortable in her company. She inspired a trust not many women can. I knew I'd like to meet her again.

We started meeting regularly. We shared one thing in common – a love for travel. She wanted to travel to India and South East Asia. I wanted to do Brazil and the West Indies. Also we quite liked treks. We decided therefore that every second weekend we'd try and take off on a tour of the countryside. Niagara Falls was to become the first destination of our plans.

The Niagara Falls is simply magical; to watch the sun set there accords you a serenity that is simply out of this world. Something unusual happened that evening, though. From a relatively clear sky, the weather suddenly changed. While most other people present rushed to more sheltered confines, we stayed, exuding an impertinent fearlessness.

As the clouds loomed overhead, it grew dark. The showers, though, were soothing and mild. We were wet. The physical comfort of a hug lent us both some warmth. As Sarah looked up into my eyes, I could see an unprecedented glint in them. It was like she was taking me into confidence over this new experience. After all, this was our first trip outside the city, and our first embrace.

I have realized over the years that certain occurrences are pre-ordained. Yet they are marked by a classic pretence of mutual denial which sometimes takes just a solitary, special moment to be dispelled. Our friendship had been treading up a path where now a physical aspect seemed imminent.

I am not sure whether the transition from a clear night to a stormy one carried some form of metaphor for us. But yes, the transition in our relationship was very pronounced. When the sun rose the next morning, we were a couple, even though we would formulate our own thoughts on it as the days went by.

We returned to Manhattan the next day. Our meetings became a lot more frequent. Sarah would stay over as much as she could. I could sense how much my presence meant to her.

I did not see the point in not going public with our relationship. For one, I realized that I had no clear agenda for my personal life. So when things came to me on a platter, it made sense to trust the ways of destiny.

She took me to meet her parents. Her parents did not seem too comfortable with their daughter's choice; yet they were not in a position to disapprove of me, simply because of the importance I had assumed in their daughter's life

◆

I try to rid myself of thoughts of Sarah lest they should distract me. I remember instead a trip to the temple with my father. We're driving the same route now, yet it seems so different. All the undeveloped area that had huts then, is now concrete, bustling with townships and small scale industries. Dad sure had made a difference to the area and to the lives of people here.

Life for me in the last two months has taken a 360 degree turn. The irrefutable demands of carrying Dad's legacy forward made me quit my job in the US once I landed in India. Luckily, I was allowed to sort out my remaining official work via emails and phone calls.

We reach the temple, which is located on a hilltop at 1600 feet. I have the option of either taking the steps or the ropeway. Two months ago, I'd have most definitely opted for the latter. Today, the situation demands otherwise and I'm not cribbing.

I am greeted by two old priests who recite some Sanskrit hymns. I offer my obeisance. I'm told that the Devi fulfils whatever you earnestly wish for with a pure mind. I know what Dad would have asked for had he been alive. I instantly put in a request for victory. I'm blessed by the priests. The incredibly huge crowds gathered outside and the massive faith almost everybody in town has for the deity, makes me inquisitive. I ask one of the priests about the Devi. I'm told a fascinating tale:

Apparently, when lord Shiva' s wife died, lord Shiva was incensed and he put the dead body of Parvati on his shoulder and started the 'Tandav Nritya'; as he danced, pieces of Parvati's body fell at different places on the earth. These places, where the parts fell, were known as 'Shakti-Pith'... Bambleshwari Devi is also a part of Devi Parvati.

I step out of the temple to a mammoth crowd. 10,000 would be a modest estimate of their number. I can't possibly interact with all of them. As I greet them with folded hands and hand waves from behind a cordon of bamboo sticks, I can see expectation writ large in their eyes – the sort that can intimidate mortals. They want to shake my hand and touch me. They speak in chaste Hindi. I respond monosyllabically with 'namastes' and 'dhanyavaads'. I wonder if the transition from 'hi' to 'namaste' aptly depicts the exponential change that my life has undergone these last few weeks.

I decide to talk to a few of the people to understand their problems One elderly soul complains about the government not having given him the promised compensation for land taken away for setting up an industry. Another talks about the spread of jaundice in certain pockets of the district and how the administration is least bothered. Prompted by Yadav, I dole out assurances. And then something unexpected happens – something Yadav had no reason to anticipate, something that I will never be able to expunge from my memory.

A tribal woman, her clothes torn and tattered, her face streaked with tears, lunges at me. I'm not sure what is happening. I then see a couple of middle-aged men rush in behind her. I realize they are chasing her. One has a steel rod in his hand. They hurl choice invectives at her before they notice me.

'What the hell is happening?' I demand to know.

'She's a bloody witch. She has killed her husband! Today we will give her the punishment she deserves.'

'Killed her husband? How?'

What I'm told horrifies me. It reinstates my worst fears: that this is the real face of India that lies hidden in the superficial veneer of prosperity that our metros project. And this India can't be wished away.

The woman is called Mayawati. Her husband, who used to be a construction worker, worked in Mumbai from where he contracted the HIV virus. The husband had died about a month ago. Her daughter, born some months ago, had tested positive too. And Mayawati's in-laws held her responsible for the suffering of the family. They wanted to punish her. The punishment entailed being stripped naked, paraded through the village, and beaten with chappals.

In a strange way, what I see reinforces in me the vast diversity that so symbolizes my country. I'm compelled to wonder about the destinies of two Mayawatis – separated just by a few 100 kms.

To my shock, I can already hear murmurs from the crowd that suggest they're siding with the in-laws. The woman, on the other hand, continues to plead with me for her safety; every shriek of hers assails my conscience.

I tell the men to back off. 'Nobody will be allowed to take the law in his hands. Besides, nobody has the right to punish her for an irresponsible act of her husband,' I bark.

One of the in-laws is defiant. 'Saheb, it's better you don't meddle in our affairs. Or else none of the tribals will vote for you.'

I simply turn to the police inspector present there. 'Does the law of the land exist here?'

He nods.

'Then take this woman in my car and make sure you file a police complaint against her in-laws.'

To be doubly certain that the woman is not harassed, I ask Yadav to call for my driver, Shahdeo. I tell Shahdeo that it would be his personal responsibility to ensure that he takes her to the police station and gets the police to file the report.

The woman fears for her safety. I ask her if she has relatives other than her in-laws. She tells me that her mother and brother live in a village not very far away. I tell the police inspector to ensure that she is sent to her mother's place under police protection, once the FIR has been filed.

The woman falls at my feet. I raise her and tell her I have merely insisted that the law of the land prevail. I can sense the entire crowd observing me in shock – it is as if I have done something extraordinary. Yadav tells me that politicians in these areas normally look the other way in situations like this. The woman leaves in my car, which follows the police jeep. I turn to mingle with the villagers. Barely have I started interacting with them, that I'm shaken by a loud bang – so loud that the earth shakes. I turn to see my car exploding in flames.

◆

In the evening, as I sit by Mayawati's pyre beside the river, I'm flooded with thoughts. I'm again compelled to wonder at the enigmatic designs that destiny draws on us. Perhaps Mayawati had lived the number of days allotted to her. She was destined to die on this day – either at the hands of her in-laws or by the bomb that was planted for me. Destiny had willed her to be my saviour by putting her in my car instead of me.

Investigations later revealed that my driver had left the car unattended while I was at the temple for over fifteen minutes. That is when a couple of Naxalites, disguised as ordinary villagers, were said to have been seen lurking near the car. It is believed that they planted the bomb underneath, right next to the petrol tank. I feel guilty for Mayawati's death. I offer her family compensation worth 5 lakhs. I wonder for a moment if that is the price of my life.

I'm up the whole night. Sleep eludes me. I may not have known Mayawati, yet the fact that I'm alive because she died, haunts me. I wonder if I belong to this world; or whether I was better off being an investment banker. One part of me is pulling me back to Manhattan. The other part, though, the underdog, is beginning to get the dominant voice. As dawn breaks, I know I will not go back. Nor will my dead body.

◆

A week has passed. I'm woken up early morning by a dream. I don't recollect it properly except that in it Sarah and I are in some exotic locale and all is not well between us. The dream takes me back to what was our last holiday together – in the Caribbean.

Our first couple of days there had been brilliant. We'd stayed in a small cottage off a beach in Antigua. One evening when we realized that the others guests in the resort were out, we had ended up making love inside the swimming pool. Sarah confessed soon after that this was a fantasy that she and Mathew had once talked about but could not get around to executing. She was glad she had done it now with the man she loved. I appreciated the sentiment even though the continued mention of Mathew had begun to bug me.

The outward semblance of everything being fine notwithstanding, I knew it wasn't so. Just a few months into our relationship, I had sensed the first signs of monotony creeping into me. I guess it had to do with Sarah's over-dependence upon me, which at times left me with very little space. I didn't have time for reading any more. Moreover there was a set pattern that her conversations invariably followed – moping about her childhood lover and going on about the need to escape somewhere faraway. Even if I had to sort out a couple of mails on our trips together, she'd come and peep into my laptop from behind. The impression that she'd try to project was that she was interested in knowing more about my work.

That myth had by now been dispelled from my mind. I had gathered it had more to do with her insecurity. She was worried I was secretly interacting with another girlfriend. On the third day of our holiday, when I came out of the shower, I found her holding my cell-phone in her hand. She looked at me accusingly: 'Who's Divya? And why is she waiting for you in New York?'

I was not prepared for her probing tone. 'Good you asked. I was about to tell you. Divya is an old college friend. She's come to New York on a vacation and didn't know I was here.'

'Is she single, committed or married?'

'Divorced.'

'I see.'

Sarah's next query was weird and unprovoked. 'Were you ever involved with her?'

Well, I'm an honest man. 'Yes. Some eight years back,' I said.

She asked me a host of other questions that carried the tenor of an interrogation. And finally I pronounced what I had to. 'Okay, listen, we're leaving a day early. Divya has to leave for India the day after and I really want to catch up with her for a few hours.'

Sarah didn't contradict me then. Perhaps she was playing safe. She didn't know how I would take to her opposition. But I could immediately see an insecure, sulking kid in her.

Just an hour later, over dinner, Sarah sprung upon me the biggest of all surprises. 'Listen, Adi, my parents are contemplating shifting to Canada early next year. They'd really like to see us married before that.'

For want of a confident reaction, I looked down at the food.

Undeterred, Sarah had gone on: 'Well, how about the end of next month?' When she realized the absurdity of her deadline, she added as an afterthought, 'It's okay if you need another month to sort out your official deadlines. But let's definitely do it by August. Besides, we can then travel to India and your father can throw a lavish party for us.'

I was left with little option but to tell her that the marriage wasn't possible before Christmas. Stretching it by those few months, too, was a futile effort on my part to buy time. That trip was the beginning of the end of our relationship.

◆

I shrug thoughts of Sarah aside. In another half an hour I will be starting off the campaign. The mood, though, is still sombre and I guess that is how it will be for the rest of the campaign. Nonetheless, I can't be thinking about it. I have a responsibility to live up to.

I flip through the couple of Hindi newspapers that are brought to me. There are two articles that catch my attention. One that says the BJP has decided to oppose the Nuclear Deal. The other is an amateurish comment by this young BJP leader, Brajesh Ranjan. It says that the Congress has always been soft on terror and that during elections we've even secretly colluded with the Naxalites. These comments manifest in my mind what my father had always said of the BJP – that it is a party of desperate hypocrites.

Yadav joins me and tells me there is some tension in the district. Some hardcore Hindu groups had decided to stage a protest against the decision of a prominent Urdu school to not have the *Vande Mataram* sung in it. I am disappointed. I wonder if the ideal of composite nationhood is just wishful thinking. I'm reminded of Yadav's comment just two days back – on the indispensability of emotive issues. I wonder why religion should be held hostage by our vicious political agendas.

A thought plays in my mind. I take out an old picture of Dad and Mom as newlyweds. A fact that nobody, including me, seems to remember about me is that I'm perhaps the best example of national integration. Mom was a Muslim. I thus am a full Indian – half Hindu and half Muslim. Dad had fallen in love with Mom when they met at Cambridge University, where both studied. Mom belonged to the royal family of the Nawabs of Cambay in Gujarat. Much against the wishes of my grandfather, Dad had married Mom because he believed in his love. My grandfather, just in case you'd like to know, was a prominent lawyer and a well-known leader of the Jan Sangha. My great grandfather was the king of

Bundelkhand. And that is from where my Dad's reference as 'Rajasaab' originates.

I'm not sure whether it was my Dad's decision to marry Mom that triggered Dad's estrangement from my grandfather, but yes, Dad and Granddad disagreed on almost everything from that point onward. Dad, thereon, embarked upon a course in life that made the differences irreconcilable. He embraced the rival party, Congress, and snapped all ties with his father.

Mom died when I was three. Dad never married again and immersed himself in work. Dad was consumed with just one ferocious passion – to work all the time and to bring in change in the country. But Dad's life had a loneliness that scared me. In an unsuspecting way, his pattern of life had made him impersonal. He'd talk about issues, ideas and policies all the time. I adored him for his selflessness towards the country, yet I could always feel the emptiness in his personal life. Also I felt that for all the effort that he put in, he was not rewarded enough. I can say this much – had Dad belonged to any another political party, he would have been considered a potential PM; not so in the Congress. And this, if I'm allowed to admit it within the four walls of this Circuit House, is the failing of my party.

I don't remember much about my mother. She went away when I barely knew the world. Yet I know what a wonderful being she must have been simply from the fact that she remained irreplaceable for Dad. Much of the way a person behaves has to do with what he goes through in his personal life. And it was not difficult for me to deduce that Dad's phlegmatic propensities were largely borne out of the fact that destiny had abruptly ended his sojourn with his soul-mate. Dad was brave not to let the world know, but I knew he was unhappy. My tragedy was that in his projection of a brave, self-motivated man he never acknowledged his grief, leaving our distance un-bridged.

It is from Dad and Mom's diverse ethnicities that I derive my rather pluralistic name – Aditya Samar Singh. Samar is an Urdu name given to me by my mother. It means a positive outcome. Interestingly enough, Samar is also a Hindu name. That's how close I find the two cultures to be. By constantly fanning communal passions, these fundamentalist Hindu groups are only doing a Jinnah – whom they now consider secular!

◆

It's 12:30pm. The scorching sun doesn't dent my spirits; nor that of the nearly 5000 people attending my rally. I'm addressing a gathering at the Ramlila Grounds. I follow Yadav's advice and try to focus on local issues that have emotive appeal. I talk of how Rajasaab, on his personal initiative had supported the Bambleshwari temple trust with personal contributions that had provided for the construction of wells, which have made water easily accessible for devotees. In keeping with the expectations of the crowd, I dole out promises. I talk of drumming up national interest for the tribal festivals – Goncha and Madai – which could draw in tourists from across the country and benefit locals. I talk of organizing a tribal crafts exhibition at Rajnandgaon every year that would improve the economy of the place. I talk, in a veiled manner, of the ruckus created by Hindu right-wing groups. 'Nobody will be allowed to divide the people in the name of religion,' is all I say. Yadav has specially cautioned me to go soft on the issue. His reasoning – it's a lot easier to sway the illiterate tribal people with religious rhetoric; therefore by criticizing the Hindu right-wing groups I might be bringing them closer to the BJP, which patronizes these groups. And I trust Yadav completely on such judgments.

I'm in the middle of my speech when I see a police convoy appear. I have an intuition that something is amiss. And so it is: a group of Hindu hardliners have clashed with Muslims over their refusal to chant the *Vande Mataram*. In the ensuing clash, two people are said to be critically injured, while seven others have sustained injuries. Disturbance has been reported from at least two other places in the district, following which Section 144 has been clamped upon the district. The order prohibits any public gathering. As such, I have no option but to end my speech abruptly.

As I leave the venue with Yadav, I feel helpless.

'It's all pre-planned. They know they can't defeat you any other way. Hence, they whip up communal sentiments elsewhere. Bloody hell.'

I feel a rare fury – something I experience once in a few years. And I explode: 'What else do you expect from a party of small-time baniyas? You think they know a shit about international affairs to oppose the Nuclear Deal? This is all they can do – make people clash. Hypocrites, that's what they are…'

Yadav just looks at me in surprise. My suave, cool image does not allow for this. I am livid and depressed.

◆

Much later in the night, I ruminate. I wonder once again about the stark thought that has crossed my mind so often in the last few days – do I belong here? With every new instance however, my resolve to stay is getting stronger. I know they think I'm a 'gentleman' who can't hit back. This time I will; I promise.

My disappointments for the day are not over. I switch on my laptop and open my mail – almost after a week. I find a mail from Sarah.

She's invited me to her wedding with one Francis Aemilio Otieno. I don't know whether I should feel happy or upset, but I wonder from where Sarah would have found someone with such a grotesque name. The previous losses were inflicted by nature; they had the hand of god in them. This loss, I feel, is one that I have I brought upon myself.

I feel terribly, terribly lonely.

I switch on the TV to distract my mind. Watching a BJP MP holding forth on TV does little to make me feel better.

Brajesh

KARAN GUPTA: MR RANJAN, JUST WHY IS YOUR party so adamant about having the *Vande Mataram* sung in all schools? If Muslims feel uncomfortable, why force them? Aren't there bigger issues to deal with? Why make another trivial emotive issue take centrestage?

Brajesh Ranjan: Well, that's where we differ from other parties. It is the dearth of knowledge of our national history that makes people say it's a trivial matter. *Vande Mataram* was the national cry for freedom from British oppression during the freedom movement. Rabindranath Tagore sang *Vande Mataram* in 1896 at the Calcutta Congress Session held at Beadon Square. Agreed, that the latter stanzas of the poem sound like a hymn sung to Goddess Durga. So be it. Let us not discard the historical significance of the song and the role played by it in motivating scores of freedom fighters. Giving it a communal tinge and allowing institutions to discard it is another instance of the Congress' pseudo-secularism.

Karan Gupta: Coming back to one of the BJP's favourite issues – Terrorism and National Security. You have been insisting on getting back stricter anti-terror laws like the POTA. But tell me, Mr Ranjan, terrorism continued unabated even during the six years of NDA rule. Isn't then your demand just rhetoric?

Brajesh Ranjan: Karan, what one needs to understand here is that to avoid the misuse of the law one cannot do away with laws altogether. Going by that logic, we don't need a Constitution either. In any case, so far as the misuse of the POTA is concerned, this is baseless propaganda that certain parties have been relentlessly spreading to increase their vote-bank.

Our bigger concern today is that in the last three years, the UPA, with its inaction, has turned India into a soft state. For the first time perhaps in the country's history someone convicted of an attack on Parliament and sentenced to death is not being hanged. What message does this send: that, we are helpless and can do nothing to fight terrorism?

Also, the nature of terrorism that we see today is different from what we saw during the NDA rule. Then, terrorism was sponsored from across the border. It is no longer so. The growth of home-grown terror modules has made it far more challenging for authorities to fight them. And the least that political parties can do is not make matters worse by indirectly shielding terrorists.

Karan Gupta: Mr Ranjan, the problem with your fight against terrorism is that you communalize even terrorism. The Gujarat Control of Organized Crime Act (GUJCOCA), for instance, proposes to be far more draconian than POTA. And critics believe its misuse will be imperative under Mr Modi.

Brajesh Ranjan: Trust me, it's not us but the Congress and other parties who communalize terrorism. By constantly demanding judicial enquiries into police and army actions they have negated the credibility of these institutions, besides demoralizing these forces. Why do you have to cry foul every time there is a terrorist encounter? Why can't you just trust the competence of our country's law-enforcing authorities? And where do Human Rights Activists vanish every time terrorists kill innocents? And yes, the BJP stands unequivocally committed to its policy of zero tolerance towards terrorism.

Karan Gupta: Okay, let us come to the situation in Orissa. There are substantiated reports that the Bajrang Dal has been consistently terrorizing Christian tribals. While several cases of churches being ransacked and houses being torched have been reported, in extreme cases, villagers have also been murdered or burnt alive. Would the BJP support a ban on the Bajrang Dal in the same way that it did on SIMI?

Brajesh Ranjan: The BJP condemns violence in all forms But the context here is completely different. Over the past several years, Christian missionaries have been working on a concerted plan to convert poor tribals by offering them incentives. We have consistently opposed that. This practice unfortunately has existed unabated for decades and I have on record Mahatma Gandhi's opposition to the practice. Gandhiji had called proselytization, under the cloak of humanitarian work, 'unhealthy' and 'the greatest impediment to the world's progress towards peace'. Having said that, we condemn violence and anybody indulging in violence should be booked.

Karan Gupta: Well, Mr Ranjan, you really make it sound so simplistic... Why did you then need to ban SIMI? Those SIMI members indulging in terrorist acts could simply have been booked too?

Brajesh Ranjan: The ban on SIMI was instigated by several incriminating intelligence inputs that we had been getting, about its links with certain external groups and over its dubious sources of funding.

Karan Gupta: Okay, the BJP likes to position itself as the sole custodian of national interests. Why then are you opposed to the Nuclear Deal? Critics believe the BJP is simply frustrated about the fact that the credit for the deal would go the UPA.

Brajesh Ranjan: That's a load of rubbish. The BJP is opposed to the clause contained in the Hyde Act which prohibits us from carrying out any tests in future and makes it an unequal deal. We feel that it impinges on our sovereignty.

Karan Gupta: But aren't you wary of being seen on the same side as Left parties? I mean, both of you seem united in your opposition to the deal?

Brajesh Ranjan: Please don't compare our stand with that of the Left parties'. Unlike the Left, we have always advocated closer ties with the US, both of us being the world's largest democracies. Our opposition to the deal, like I said, is over a specific clause. We would still favour re-negotiating the deal, whereby our national interests are protected. The Left, on the other hand, is opposing the deal for completely different reasons. For all you know, if the same deal were with China, the Left might blindly support it.

Karan Gupta (*laughs*): Okay, last question… The BJP is going through a crucial phase. Where does the party head after Mr Advani? Will it break into smaller groups?

Brajesh Ranjan: I'll tell you what – the best thing about BJP is that, unlike the Congress, it is not centred around an individual or a clan, but on a clear ideology. We do have a good base of second rung leaders, all competent enough to take the party forward. So trust me, we won't face any problem on that score.

Karan Gupta: But you can't deny that Narendra Modi seems like a clear front-runner as of now to take over the party leadership? And strange as it may seem, your top leader has thrice been refused a US visa?

Brajesh Ranjan: I wouldn't like to comment on this.

Karan Gupta: And do you see yourself leading the party one day?

Brajesh Ranjan: (*laughs*) Well, let me just say I won't shy away from any responsibility that the party confers upon me.

◆

It's 11:05pm. I'm done reading my files, checking the important news channels, and soaking in my share of relevant information. Time to make my customary daily call to my parents.

The first thing that Amma asks is if I've had my food; the second, if the domestic helps have done their work, and third, if all was alright. Pitaji is on the parallel line. He's a good listener, or so I'd like to believe. He is taciturn and barely says anything unless I ask him about his health. He's been a diabetic for the last decade but after his retirement, three years ago, he has been taking good care of his health. For my part, I ask them if all is well in Allahabad. After these routine queries there's barely any conversation left but my parents' loneliness and my concern for them makes me stretch the conversation.

They try and chip in with their opinion on national issues. I respond only monosyllabically. And then they nag me, like they do every time we speak, about what I do not want to be told – to get married. Their reasoning follows a set pattern: they are worried for me and it is about time I settled down. I am getting old. They are getting older. I should have someone to take care of me.

I wonder how many others have been in this peculiar dilemma vis-à-vis their parents – of loving and caring for them and yet not being able to relate with their way of thinking. Or is the problem more pronounced in the case of loners like me, who beyond a point, find it difficult to relate with anybody?

I'm not too sure about that, but yes, I'm a restless soul. I get bored when I'm at a party for more than half an hour; I get bored talking on the phone for more than five minutes; there are at least fifty books that I've left half way – not so much because I didn't like them, as for my impatience in sitting through them. I sense in me a constant urge to move on to something new – so irrepressible that it scares me. I'm not sure what breeds this restlessness. I guess I suffer from some form of perpetual internal dissatisfaction. This has to do in part with the state of affairs in the country and in part with my own self. At times, I feel as alienated from my parents as with the new world I entered three-and-a-half years ago, ever since I became an MP.

I was born at a peculiar point in time in our country's history – a time when democracy was marauded by the very authority meant to protect it and the country was in a state of internal Emergency. 1975 it was. My father, a professor of physics at the Allahabad University, was in jail then. His crime – he opposed the dictatorial traits of the same party that he had always supported – the Congress. Pitaji, in fact, still is a Gandhian to the core. He stood by Nehru in his college days even when the country blamed Nehru for the Chinese aggression of 1962. He was all for Indira Gandhi when she became PM in 1966. When Indira Gandhi got Bangladesh freedom from Pakistan, Pitaji likened her to Goddess Durga.

Pitaji's disenchantment with the Congress party started only in Ms Gandhi's third term as prime minister. It was when Ms Gandhi's election to her Lok Sabha seat was quashed by the Allahabad High Court over an issue involving electoral malpractice that she retaliated to the growing opposition with a series of hostile actions that culminated in the clamping of Emergency upon the country. That was the point at which Pitaji's alienation with the Congress was complete. Pitaji openly supported Jai Prakash Narain and joined his movement thereon.

At a time, when professional journalists were forced to toe the government line or else face arrest, Pitaji wrote two fiery articles in a local daily on how the Congress was no longer the nationalist force it used to be. In one of the pieces he wrote, 'Any leader or government who usurps the democratic rights of its people is anti-national in character. It is the ill-fortune of our people that the Government which has so far condemned and crushed the Naxal Movement due to its allegiance to the revolutionary Maoist philosophy has today adopted identical means to stick to power. Power corrupts and absolute power corrupts absolutely and irredeemably.'

The result: Pitaji was soon behind bars. And this at a time when Amma was pregnant. I'm told that that was the darkest time for our nation. There was a sense of acute despondency among the people. Since independent India was still young and inexperienced, huge uncertainty prevailed throughout. Many of the almost one million people arrested doubted they would ever come out of jail alive. And worse, there were very few working women in those days. Hence, the wives of those arrested had to lead a particularly tough existence, often depending on the generosity (read mercy) of well-meaning relatives. Luckily, Amma taught in a local school. Pitaji came out of jail in January 1977, after eighteen months of being behind bars. I was already more than a year old by then. I'm told that for a week after his return, he wouldn't let go of me, and would just sit there with me in his lap.

I'm not sure if my aversion for the Congress started while I was still in my mother's womb; or whether it had something to do with the excruciating tales about the Emergency that I heard from relatives through my childhood. What's ironical is that the Janata Party, that formed the government with such high hopes, eventually disappointed Pitaji to such an extent that he became averse to political discussion of any kind. He is said to have ended his tryst with politics by writing an article. In it he wrote, *'The Janata Party government has given us another classic example of the abuse of power. It is surprising how all those seemingly principled leaders who liked to believe they were crusaders of democracy, when exposed to the responsibilities of governance, become no more than disgruntled, power-hungry hawks willing to go to any lengths to outdo each other. India, today, unfortunately needs another Mahatma. But then even the Mahatma couldn't prevent Partition. How can a present-day Mahatma then rein in the naked avarice of our pretentious leaders?'*

Pitaji's words gave an apt indication of his dejection. From then on he concentrated on his teaching career and even went back to do his PhD.

I'm not sure what initiated my interest in politics. But the first seeds of my political awareness were sown seventeen years ago. The year was 1990 – another terribly dark patch in the nation's history. The country had been pitched into a virtual civil war over the Anti-Mandal agitation; and even as the country burnt, the government fiddled. I was fourteen then. V.P. Singh's capacity for destroying social harmony and creating caste-wars in the short span of his premiership remains unprecedented in history. It was in a grim situation like this that the educated Indian voter, having given ample opportunities to the Congress, started pinning hopes upon the BJP.

Mr L.K. Advani, who was then the president of the BJP, embarked upon a peculiar nationwide tour on a van that was transformed to look like Lord Ram's chariot. The tour, called the 'rath yatra', was meant to mobilize public opinion in favour of the construction of a Ram temple, at a disputed site, believed to be the birthplace of Lord Ram. Unlike what critics of my party would have everyone believe, I for one followed Mr Advani's speeches in those days very closely and I can vouchsafe that they were not communal. He did dwell upon the Congress' appeasement of minorities for the sake of votes. He talked about the need for a national identity that Lord Ram, known for his rectitude and fairness, would symbolize. He, in fact, drew a parallel with the reconstruction of the Somnath Temple undertaken immediately after our independence, of which I doubt the so-called intellectuals of our generation have much knowledge.

That age, when you're fourteen or fifteen, is a very crucial stage so far as the shaping of your ideological moorings is concerned. And I must confess that the plain-speak of Mr Advani did have a big influence upon me. Having said that, I must add that I condemned and still do condemn a few of the irresponsible right-wing local leaders who have antagonized the minorities. The BJP is not about Muslim bashing. It is about an undaunted upholding of national interests.

◆

2001. Having passed my UPSC, I had joined the Assam cadre of the IAS . I was posted as the District Commisioner of the Dhubri district of Assam. Dhubri, as a district, is peculiar both for its geographical location as well as the nature of its population. The district is bound both by inter-state and international borders i.e. West Bengal and Bangladesh in the west, Goalpara and Bogaigoan district of Assam and the Garo Hills district of Meghalaya in the east, Kokrajhar district in the north, Bangladesh and the state of Meghalaya in the south. So far as its population is concerned, an alarmingly high percentage is what I call 'transient population'. Labourers who crossed the border during the day to work returned to their homes in Bangladesh at night. Given intelligence inputs that Bangladesh was becoming the breeding ground for anti-India terrorist activities, such a situation was bound to throw up unusual challenges for the administration. The fact that Dhubri is the most densely populated district in the country today didn't make the problem any simpler.

In the zest of youth, I went that extra bit in discharging my responsibilities. I mingled a lot with the locals, especially in areas closest to the border. I participated in cricket matches played between two blocks of the district – all just to understand the people better. Even if I was invited for a wedding in the family of a person I barely knew, I would make it a point to attend. I was also on very good terms with some of the local police inspectors, whom I would occasionally call over for a drink. The end objective of all of these was to dig out and obtain relevant information first-hand.

Over a period of time, I discovered something intriguing. The local workers who came in daily from Bangladesh were given work permits that they were supposed to show while crossing the border, on their way in or out, if asked to do so. This however, did not make it mandatory for workers to return every evening. And given that a lot of these workers had relatives on the Indian side of the border, there was a high likelihood that some of them stayed back. What appalled me though was an unofficial intimation from my counterpart in the Garo Hills district of Meghalaya that his administration had noted a systematic pattern in some Bangladeshi workers crossing over to Meghalaya every week. What was worrisome was that these workers would then proceed to the North Cachar district in a similar pattern.

This information alarmed me. Thereafter I kept an extra vigil on Dhubri's border with Meghalaya and to my shock my vigilance only corroborated the report of the DC of Garo Hills. This movement pattern was ominous. One possibility that we could deduce was that these people would spread across to the other parts of the country and possibly join the Indian sleeper cells of terrorists. What was even more incriminating was my finding out the dubious role played by a rather influential local politician in patronizing these people. I immediately shot off a letter to the Cabinet Secretary expressing my concern. I was assured that the matter would be looked into. When that didn't happen over the next two months, I spoke to the press. This was sufficient for the local politician to start a tirade against me, accusing me of dividing people by unnecessarily sowing the seeds of discord. I was transferred to the Kokrajhar district in what was called 'a routine transfer'. Another 'routine transfer' followed five months later to Jorhat.

These routine transfers proved de-motivators of a vicious kind. I mean, they took place at a time when I had already put in a lot of effort in the two districts and wanted to see my labour come to fruition. In Kokrajhar, for instance, I had initiated a massive education drive for tribal children, which in two years' time would have made statisticians re-work their data significantly. My stint at these places was cut short by negative vested interests. What hurt me even more was that my problems stemmed out of the noblest intentions; I mean, if my inference about the motives of the transient Bangladeshi group was proved true it meant a war against the state was being hatched and I could do nothing about it.

I was beginning to realize that my job no longer excited me as it had when I had started off.

Moreover, with the experience of my three-year stint as an IAS officer, I had an interesting observation to make: real power, in a democracy, in as much as one would like to believe it is so, isn't vested in the people or the bureaucrats, but in our politicians. Therein lies the need for good souls to enter politics, instead of just sitting on the sidelines and cribbing. After all, it was the Mahatma who had once exhorted us to be the change that we want to see around us.

Coming back to Kokrajhar, I was so passionate about the project that I sent in a special application to the Cabinet Secretary urging him to allow me to stay on till the project was complete. When this was rejected, I quit.

I quit on 27th Jan, a day after Republic Day. My quitting was impulsive. After I had unfurled the national tricolour at the Civic Grounds, and while the function was still on, reports came in that two low-intensity blasts had occurred in the neighbouring districts, killing about six people. It was at the function itself that I lost my cool and had an emotional outburst: 'You ought to be happy that only two blasts occurred and just six people were killed,' I shouted. 'The way extremists have been given a free run in Assam, I won't be surprised if the entire state burns very soon!'

My outburst was reported in the state papers the next day. That day itself, I got a show-cause notice from the Government. I decided to quit and faxed my letter to the Government. The Government responded by not taking cognizance of it. Instead I was 'sacked' and a press statement issued to that effect.

I had reasons to feel betrayed, maybe slighted too. After all, I knew how hard I had worked in the last three years. To be sacked on disciplinary grounds was a travesty of justice. Moreover, it left a blot on my credibility.

I issued a press statement in Guwahati a day later in which I sounded a historic caveat. I wrote,

'The north east is a region that is dear to me. Given a choice between my home state U.P. and Assam, I chose Assam as I felt it needed a lot more attention. My experience today suggests that apart from attention, it needs the right attitude and integrity. What I'm able to infer today and I sincerely hope I'm wrong, is something scary – the north east might soon become a lost battle for the country. It is a volcano that is waiting to erupt. How can a region as vast as this, which has seven states and where infiltration is rampant, have no real laws to identify and curb the menace of an international proxy war? How long will we hide the tribal unrest that is rampant in many parts of the state and the frequent clashes between Bodos and Bangladeshi Muslims? How many more compromises will our politicians make for the sake of petty votes? I refuse to be a part of a flawed system where I'm supposed to aid a selfish political agenda rather than the principles of good governance. I'm glad to be relieved of my job. And to put it on record, I quit the same. Attached is a copy of my fax to the Government, which shall bear testimony to this.'

I'm not sure whether my quitting was an act of idealism, impatience or rebellion, but I could feel an inner voice in me urging me to brace up for bigger responsibilities.

One month later, I met Mr Advani. What I had not realized was that my controversial exit from the IAS and the issues raised by me in the press conference had brought me a popularity whose power I wasn't entirely aware of. I guess the real point that marks one's transition from relative obscurity to a position of reasonable consequence, is tricky to decipher. For one, you are the last person to be aware of your worth. It's normally the verdict or perception of other people that makes all the difference. And this is where the importance of meeting people who appreciate you for what you stand for, gets underlined.

In a meeting that lasted nearly an hour, I shared Mr Advani's concerns about terrorism and infiltration. I ended the meeting offering my services to the party. A week later, I was asked if I wanted to contest the Allahabad Lok Sabha seat. For a moment I was taken aback. I had always secretly nursed a desire to represent the seat which has been graced by the likes of Lal Bahadur Shastri, Hemvati Nandan Bahuguna and Amitabh Bachchan. And here, I was being handed a chance that would mark my tryst with history! I grabbed the opportunity with both hands.

However, the seat was no cakewalk. Even before I hit the campaign trail, I faced opposition from the most unexpected source – my father. His pessimism when it came to politics was such that he likened me to an avaricious man whose over-ambition made him lose all that he had. Pitaji felt it was a cardinal blunder on my part to have quit the IAS. Fortunately, Amma took up my cause this time round.

Two days later, the entire family offered prayers at the Sangam for my victory. I took the holy dip and prayed for my wish to come true. While it was to be obviously expected that I'd pray that I become an MP, I also prayed that I may one day become the PM! The swapping of initials was not a faux pas, just a manifestation of the more ambitious side of me. Since I had already realized that political power is what can bring in the change we want, it took me little time to decide that absolute change can be brought about by absolute power – which in our land is commanded by the Prime Minister's Office.

My innings in politics thus started in 2004. I was twenty-eight-and-a-half. I am told that that is an age when most of urban India is still trying to sort out its woes – both of the professional and the personal kind. I was quite happy on the professional front. I knew that politics really was my final calling. Problems pertaining to my personal life remained unsorted however, and if at all, the last three years have made them far more complex.

◆

It's 2:30am. My Talkatora road residence is unusually silent – the sort of silence that I experience when I struggle for sleep at this hour. And I've been doing that a bit more frequently in recent months. I'm not sure whether this propensity should be a cause for concern – I certainly don't consider myself an insomniac. I'm stressed out, though.

I think about the day ahead. I have to go for an early jog, come back, meet some visitors from my constituency, attend a meeting of my party's parliamentary board, take leave from it at mid-day and fly down to Rajnandgaon for an election rally. And then I might have to visit a TV channel studio later in the evening for a panel discussion. It promises to be a long day. Yet slumber eludes me. I'm consumed by a stark desolation that only those in public life can feel and comprehend. I have sadly realized that the more your life gets shared with people, the more deprived it gets of personal bonds.

I look at my watch. It's too late to call Shweta. Maybe, she's still working on her thesis. I don't really want to expose my vulnerability to her. Instead I seek escape in intoxication.

I pour a whisky for myself and wonder why paradox symbolizes my existence today. I have caring parents, yet I can't be happy talking to them. I have umpteen women falling for me, yet I can't fall in love with any one of them. I wonder why the power I've acquired in the last few years has led to a disproportionate rise in insecurity.

I do realize that if you're a celebrity, it becomes much more difficult to find a match. And there are several factors – some conscious and some which you're not entirely aware of – that contribute to this deadlock. In my case, I just feel I've evolved a lot quicker than most others my age. Till I was in college, my existence was rather nondescript – neither was I noticed for my brilliant grades nor was I so bad as to be considered a jerk.

However, once I had a job my workaholic side came to the fore. There are jobs that are target-oriented and then there are those where the targets are infinite. To be in a position where I could usher in positive change in people's lives filled me with a sense of responsibility I had never known before. And I guess that is where a different side of me was born. After finishing off all pending official responsibilities, I'd remain awake till two in the morning, reading up stuff about our history, our administrative system, local literature, et al.

This transition bound me to a more internal existence. In my free time, I'd simply immerse myself in books or on the computer, rather than socialize or make friends. While the few friends that I had did point out the detriments of my new found passion, I for one did not mind it or worry about it. Accumulating knowledge imbued in me a sense of informed authority which I was not prepared to relinquish. Initially, I would not even feel lonely. I guess I enjoyed the company of the characters – real and fictitious about whom I'd read and researched and into whose world I'd transport myself.

This habit of mine continued much after I'd quit the job and shifted base to Delhi after becoming MP. The result – I'd confine myself to the house almost every evening. When old friends, at times, would drag me to a pub or party, I wasn't able to stay there for long.

It goes without saying that this habit of mine was bound to jeopardize any possibilities of meeting young and interesting women. Those with whom I had the most absorbing discussions over work were not inspiring enough otherwise. The thing about an achiever that distinguishes him or her from lesser mortals is the sheer drive for perfection. Therefore, apart from being diligent in my work, I'd hate myself if I put on flab or if I under-performed in a game of squash or for that matter if I wasn't aware of the latest innovations in internet technology. This constant need to upgrade myself, I guess, imbued a certain perfection, which I was understandably prone to expect in my potential partner. Women who did not maintain themselves – with bulky thighs or un-waxed arms and legs – were an instant put-off for me. So were women who smoked – I couldn't stand a woman smoking. You are within your rights to dub me a chauvinist for this. Neither for that matter could I stand an overly loquacious woman, blabbering about stuff I considered insignificant.

No, I am not arrogant. Others are mediocre.

Over time, the issue of my marriage became a major bone of contention between my parents and me. Every now and then, my father would dig up some five or six marriage proposals that appeared in the Sunday TOI and would send them across to me for my perusal. It would take me a few seconds to reject them all. I'd call them all 'losers'. Pitaji would lose his temper and call *me* 'the biggest loser'. He once reminded me of the duties enshrined in Hindu beliefs – to pay back our debt towards our ancestors. And one of the ways of doing this was to father a child, which could not be done without being married.

Pitaji's reasoning would amuse me no end. For my part, I'd tell my parents that my intentions were noble; that I too wanted to get married but would not do so for the heck of it; that it was important for me to really fall in love with the girl I chose to marry. I'd be blasted yet again on this and my idea of 'falling in love' and 'the right girl' would be mocked at. Parents are adept at indulging in subtle blackmail. For instance, how would you react to a line like – 'It's your life, do what you want… All we'd like is to see you settled in our lifetime.' A sentence like that can make you feel really miserable – so much so that you immediately look at corrective action.

The friction that this topic generated had led me to tell my parents not to bother. I told them, I'd find my bride on my own. I'd specified to them that there were no time-lines attached to the task, though. It had to do with providence – as and when I fell in love.

However, on lonely nights like this, I'm constrained to wonder if I've ever fallen in love. Can I ever do so in the future? In my present state, I have serious doubts about it. After all, I still remember clearly the words of my last girlfriend, at the time of our separation:

'You are just too full of yourself to ever fall in love with anybody apart from yourself.'

Her words invariably come back to haunt me. I cannot vouch for or against the statement. I know it is an assortment of various traits that constitute a being as complex as me. I am an achiever. The biggest mistake that people sometimes commit is to try and change themselves, much against their nature.

I do not wish to do that and undo whatever I have accumulated through my conviction.

There is another peculiar human trait that adds to problems for souls like me. Thanks to our hyperactive minds, we often have an image of ourselves which sometimes is in stark contrast to who we really are. And we sometimes get so obsessed by that image that our everday living sees a constant battle between the perceived image and our real self. It is not difficult to predict which of the two wins more often.

That perhaps also explains why I've not been successful in relationships. I guess I expect a lot because my perceived image of myself is one of upholding propriety. I like to believe I stand for a certain idealism. This propensity often leads to me being condescending of others without my realizing it.

For example, in the last three-and-a-half years I've been in one serious and two non-serious relationships. At present too I'm in a confused relationship. I am within my rights to term the non-serious ones a fling but I shall not do that. I shall not disown any facts of my life. Thus, serious and non-serious here are distinctions based purely on the longevity of the relationships as also my sincerity in trying to make them work. As far as the confused relationship is concerned, a less evolved soul is likely to call the relationship an 'open relationship'. I beg to differ. For me it is a relationship where there are sufficient factors to draw the partners into a bond, yet insufficient to bind them into a commitment.

Okay, I'm not going to tell you about my serious relationship now. It's already 3:20am and I'm too tired; besides if I tell you all about it now, you might form your own perceptions of me. I'm not sure if I can trust you with so much so early. But let me just tell you the grounds on which I broke off one of my two non-serious relationships. I would call it a form of temperamental incompatibility.

I realized I could not spend my life with a girl who smoked like a chimney and thrived on liquor. She wanted me to live life like ordinary people – have a blast every weekend with her group, who to my perception comprised junkies and wannabes. I realized her lifestyle would invariably clash with the discipline that I'd been trying to cultivate in my life. Ultimately, I gave her an ultimatum: to give up smoking or to let our relationship go up in smoke. She chose the latter. In hindsight, I am sure I did not love her. I was looking for a valid reason to escape her.

What do you say to that? I'm not sure if the incident is going to lead to accusations of vanity or high-handedness against me. To be honest, I think I want a girlfriend on my terms, just as I've had almost everything else in life. At this point, you might call me a male chauvinist pig. I'm prepared to risk that. If I can come to terms with being called 'communal' day in and day out, 'chauvinist' is mild in comparison.

After hearing me out, you still think I'm vain? I am sorry. I have a point. My viewpoint here may also have me called 'Capitalist' – something you've accused my party of. I don't care. I am proud of my party and of myself.

Apologies if my analogies may not amuse you. It has partly to do with lack of sleep and partly with the intoxication that I'm seeking escape in. But I'm an honorable man and I speak the truth.

I look at my watch again. I'm tempted to call Shweta. I dial her number, but cut it before it rings.

Shweta is the one with whom I'm into that slightly ambivalent bond. She teaches anthropology at Delhi University and is working towards a doctorate in 'Gender divisions in the Indian context'. I wonder what the study really entails, but for me, as a layman, her subject is fascinating. Fascinating, because it involves the study of Indian tribes. And since my party has entrusted me with the responsibility of examining and preparing a report on the voting propensities among different Indian castes and tribes, somewhere we have a common area of interest. Also, in the melee of people that I come across, I tend to look out for the ones who can teach me something. Shweta is among these.

What started off with my fascination for her subject was to lead to a fascination for her. As a research fellow, she is brilliant at her work. As a human being she is equally superb. The problem I think is in her overly unassuming demeanor which clashes with my ambitious self. To be more specific, no tenacious go-getter would want to be constantly told, 'God how do you survive in this dirty world of politics!' Or, 'How can you think work all the time?' Or, 'If I were in your place, I'd have done this...' Or, 'I would never do all this.'

The thing about making it on your own steam is that it breeds a certain egotism in you, no matter how humble you project yourself as. And the last thing that you want to be constantly told is to do or be something that is the antithesis of what you stand for.

Shweta and I are very comfortable with each other. Since I am free only late at night, she often drops in then. We chat over dinner, exchange notes, listen to some music and then my chauffeur drops her home. We do not feel the need to stay connected during the day or for that matter for a week if my work calls me away; and yet when we meet the next time round, the comfort level remains. I've realized there has to be something special to her – after all, she's made her way into this position in my life over umpteen other women.

Yet, I am also aware of something just as important – I am not attracted to her in the sense of a lover. I find her too sedate, too predictable, or shall I say, bourgeois, to be the lover that I crave; as in my professional life, I guess I look for challenge and a sense of achievement on the personal front too. No, I'm not in love with her. I still want to believe in love; I still want to believe I can fall in love.

◆

Don't recall when I dozed off but it's 7am and I'm woken up by the alarm. I feel just that wee bit hungover. I can't let it upset my schedule though. I gulp down a glass of lemon water. At 7:40, I leave for my jog with two SPG commandos for company. I jog on the roads in the vicinity of India Gate. I'm back in an hour. I take a quick shower, pray, grab a bite, and then come out to meet a few people from my constituency who've come to see me. I quickly take note of their problems and in no time I'm off for the Parliamentary board meeting which is supposed to start at ten at the party office on Ashoka Road.

We begin by singing the *Vande Mataram* before getting down to work. On expected lines, we pass a resolution that censures the government for increasing prices and its inability to combat terrorism. I can sense some amount of ambiguity on the issue of the Nuclear Deal. A section of the party members feels that in opposing the deal we might upset middle-class voters who seem to be in its favour. Another section feels that in acquiescing to give up on future nuclear tests, which the deal in its present form entails, we will be allowing our sovereignty to be impinged; and that shall go against our nationalist credentials. We decide eventually that we will oppose it.

I leave at eleven as I have to fly down to Rajnandgaon to address a rally. I'm supposed to take a flight to Raipur and to drive down to Rajnandgaon from there. As one of the younger and more charismatic leaders of the party, I get invitations from state units to address election rallies. And I'm only too keen to oblige. One, because it gives me an opportunity to travel across the country and meet people first-hand; two it always motivates me when I am given additional responsibility. I decide to read up some stuff about the rival candidate; homework always helps. The moment I land at Raipur Airport and switch on my cell, I'm intimated via an sms from my service provider of at least a dozen calls from Amma. It worries the shit out of me. Even as I call her back, I pray all is well. She takes the call.

'What happened, Amma? You were calling?' I ask her.

'Everything is fine with you, na?' Amma sounds tense.

'Of course I'm fine.'

'Thank God. Since your phone was unreachable, we were worried. We keep hearing about the Naxal nuisance every now and then. Beta, please take care and be safe.'

I'm irritated, annoyed, and amused all at once. Some traits are really so bourgeois.

'Amma, relax, I'm no longer an ordinary citizen. I've come here to represent my party and I'm being given due protection.'

'Beta, what does protection in this country mean? It's useless. Please avoid going to such places.'

'Amma, don't worry. I'll talk to you later.'

I realize parents will be parents. Their care and concerns are valid; but so is my call of duty which demands that I don't allow anything to distract me from the task at hand.

◆

At a well-attended rally, I slam the Congress for its duplicity on key issues of national interest:

'The Congress, either for want of courage or integrity or both has always played into the hands of terrorists and secessionists. History will tell you how the Congress had once nurtured Bhindranwale in Punjab, till he became a menace for the Congress itself. Similarly, had the Congress ever being sincere in curbing the Naxalite menace, it would never come to this level, resulting in one of its senior ministers being killed. On the contrary, we have reports that local Congress leaders even tacitly collude with Naxals at the time of elections, with the promise that they would not curb these activities. The Naxalite movement is the

biggest threat to our internal security today. We have evidence of the existence of a Maoist Corridor, right from Nepal to Andhra Pradesh. We also have reports of jihadi terrorist groups building contact with them…

'We stand committed to eradicating Naxal terrorism. Our state government's initiatives against the movement needs your support. Besides the Congress candidate – what's his name – Aditya, is a novice, who knows nothing about the place and who probably won't be seen in the constituency after the elections. You must vote for the BJP which has the courage to walk its talk.'

I refrain as much as possible from making personal references to the Congress candidate. Besides, I have been following recent Indian elections closely. And I know for sure that Indian voters are maturing. Soon enough, propaganda might cease to be an important influencing factor. What will matter is deliverance.

The party-workers are buoyant after my speech. We realize the contest is tough. Yet our candidate, Jagdamba Potai, is confident my speech will boost the morale of the local cadre. With elections just three days away, we're gearing up for a close contest.

It's dusk and I'm driving back to Raipur, from where I have to take the return flight. On the highway, on a roadside dhaba, I see a cavalcade of nearly half-a-dozen cars. The local MLA, who is accompanying me, tells me that it's Aditya Samar Singh and his men. It seems they have halted at the dhaba on their way back from campaigning in the rural areas. My car has crossed the dhaba. But I tell my driver to make a U turn. I walk up to Aditya. He looks just as surprised as everybody else there. He wears a confident smile, though, which I appreciate.

'I've heard a lot about you. I thought I'd stop and say hello,' I say.

He's taken by my gesture I'm sure, but he is astute not to show it. 'Hey. Thanks a ton. I appreciate the gesture.'

'So all set for D-Day?'

'Absolutely. Your candidate might have to forfeit his deposit.'

'Well, well. Pedigree has its benefits.'

'And vilification its detriments.'

'Sure. I wish you luck.'

As I am about to leave, Aditya says, 'Anyway, good we met. I wanted to clarify a couple of things.'

I wait for him to speak.

'One, a party that has lost some of its biggest leaders to terrorism can't be accused of being soft on terror. And two, I don't think you can call me a novice. True, you are my senior in politics, but politics has been in my blood… you can bet I won't disappear after the elections. I'm here to stay.'

Aditya's people, I'm sure, have informed him of my speech.

'I wish your party had figured this out after the first assassination at the hands of terrorists. Anyway, I like your spunk. How I wish to see the same in your party.'

I leave. Even though our interaction has been laced in good measure with sarcasm, it is clear to me that Aditya's intentions are noble. I see a spark in him; a determination, which I hope is not just a façade. The BJP does not believe in political unsociability. To be honest, I think I'd like to see this dude in Parliament.

◆

My flight lands in Delhi at a quarter past eight. I'm supposed to drive straight to the studios of CNN-IBN. I switch on my cell. I try calling a party-worker who co-ordinates media appearances. I can't get through. I realize there's no signal. To my surprise, none of my co-passengers are receiving a signal on their phones either. Even as I set foot in the airport, I can sense something ominous. To my relief, my cell finally rings. It's a call from the party headquarters. A party-worker, who had been trying to call me for the past half-hour has finally got through. What he says leaves me numb: Serial blasts in Delhi have killed at least 50 and injured above 100.

Through the course of my journey to the TV channel studio, I'm briefed on the latest developments in town. Every minute adds to my woes. I'm told of newer casualties and of more unexploded bombs being discovered. Rage fills my insides. Seldom have I felt as helpless as on occasions like these, when innocents are murdered so effortlessly. I get another call. This time I'm told that a TV channel has received an email from an organization called 'Lashkar-e-Hindustan', who have claimed responsibility for the attacks. I'm told that the attacks are an act of revenge for the killing of Muslims in the Gujarat riots. I feel violent. For a moment, I feel like telling these perverts that if this is how you seek revenge, then I don't regret what happened in Gujarat at all.

Within moments I realize the thought was just a momentary reaction. No, I can't play into the provocation that these terrorists want us to fall. They want to divide us and instigate many more riots of the Gujarat kind so that they can justify their terrorist strikes for the next several decades. I'm glad our own Muslim brethren don't think that way. Nor do the Muslim leaders of my own party.

The increased police checks have led to a traffic slow-down. It's still going to take about twenty minutes before I reach the studio. In my agitated state my thoughts veer back to the collateral damage that the last spate of bomb blasts in the city had wreaked on my life: it had caused bereavement of a different kind, of a relationship that though shaky may well have survived had it not been inflicted that final, fatal blow.

◆

Ten months ago, Delhi had been rocked by a similar series of blasts. It happened on an unsuspecting Saturday evening, just when it seemed to me that I could be falling in love. I had been dating this lady for the past several months. We'd had some fabulous thought-provoking conversations and some great sex. Even though our opinions would invariably clash, I guess it was the ability to take on each other's notions that had drawn us close. I was attracted to her in a way that I'd felt for no other woman.

On that fateful Saturday, I drove my lady out of the city for dinner to a resort on the Jaipur Highway. We reached the place by 7:30. I had planned to surprise her by proposing to her that day. Barely had we entered the resort that we were greeted by the morbid news. Delhi had been rocked by a series of blasts. Some 30 were already reported killed. More casualties were feared.

Needless to say, the blasts robbed me of my romanticism. For that matter, the entire resort wore a sombre look. We decided to just have a cup of tea and leave. I had no idea of the kind of contamination that this seemingly innocuous stretch of ten minutes had in store for our relationship.

It goes without saying that I felt devastated. I lashed out: 'Bloody hell! How many more terrorist strikes are we going to have? It's become a monthly affair now. And the worst part – the enemy is faceless – for all you know, he could be a person living next door or working in your office.'

My lady's reaction was rather cold: 'Well, communal riots and persecutions do have long-drawn-out repercussions.'

'What do you mean by that?' I asked her, livid.

'Wasn't that what happened in the Gujarat genocide? Even today, the way minorities are being killed in Orissa and churches ransacked – doesn't that amount to terrorism as well?'

'Are you trying to justify these terrorist strikes?'

'No, I'm not. I'm trying to make you understand why people take to terrorism.'

'Great! But my understanding it won't make the act less criminal, will it?'

'But that's where the problem lies, Brajesh. We attack the symptoms without getting into the diagnosis.'

The debate got more contentious. 'Look, what happened in Gujarat was shameful. But does that mean we will have to bear these terrorist strikes for the next hundred years? Isn't there a criminal justice system to book the culprits responsible for communal killings?

'Hah,' she snorted derisively. 'What law of the land do you talk of, Brajesh? Can you tell me just how many culprits have been convicted for the 1984 Delhi, 1992 Bombay or the 2002 Gujarat riots? They all go scot-free.'

'Well, so do a lot of terrorists who are behind these recent blasts. Don't they?'

'But then we've had biased laws which were simply meant to trap scapegoats.'

I got miffed. 'Listen, don't mix issues, all right? I know one thing – everytime a terrorist strike occurs, it rattles me. It makes me fear that tomorrow someone from my family could be the next victim. Do you realize that some 30 innocents have lost their lives today? Some 56 did a month back, 75 odd died in Hyderabad before that? We need far, far stricter laws to end this menace.'

'And shouldn't there be laws to stop killings by the state?'

I wanted to slap her at that point. How could my girlfriend talk like this? Wasn't she at all affected by the gory deaths these terrorist strikes resulted in?

'Brajesh, trust me, it hurts me as well… My point is just that communalism and terrorism are interlinked and for me *both* are terrorist acts.'

'The problem with people like you is that you are defensive and incapable. You can't fight terrorism hands-on. So you put the blame on us.'

When I think of the episode in hindsight, I think I kept hoping through the altercation that my lady might share my anguish and blast the terrorists in as many words. Since that didn't seem like happening, my tone got progressively more belligerent: 'Dammit, you're simply justifying these terrorist strikes by putting the onus on communalism. If I go by your logic, tell me, why is Pakistan today at the receiving end of terrorism? Tell me something, do you have faith in our judiciary, in our legal process? Isn't a legal trial on for all communal riots cases?'

'You must be kidding, Brajesh. The judiciary of this country sucks as much as some of the politicians do. We've talked about this before. I have no faith in the judiciary.' She was unfazed.

By this time, my indignation had surmounted manifold. I felt more defeated by the attitude of the lady I thought I had been all set to marry, than with the terror strikes. Not that I was unaware of my partner's moorings but perhaps it took a calamity like this to manifest how differently we could think. A brief moment of quiet preceded my terse final retort. 'You must leave this country,' I said.

The lady was stunned to hear this. And as soon as I said it, so was I. I mean, from wanting to propose to her that evening, to telling her to leave the country – the damage couldn't have been more decimating! But I stuck to my guns. So unrepentant did I feel at the moment. I repeated my last sentence, this time adding my rationale to it. 'Yes, you must leave this country if you have no faith in it.'

The death toll from the blasts, thus, was one above what was officially reported; it was the death of a relationship that was mortally wounded in the terrorist attack and succumbed to injuries soon after.

◆

I've reached the studio. I have a fair idea of the kind of debate that lies in store tonight. So I'm not too bothered on that score. However, deep inside, I am feeling utterly incapacitated. As a representative of the people, there is no bigger failure than the inability to protect your people; the inability to assuage the fear that was writ large on everybody's face outside. As I wait for the recording to start, I mull over the vexed issue. I end up feeling increasingly vindicated about what I have felt on calamitous evenings like these.

For all that we deify the Mahatma, I doubt if Gandhism can help us in solving contemporary perils that plague world politics. At least, so far as terrorism is concerned, it is high time India drew its inspiration from Israel's Mossad.

Chaitali

IT IS AS HUMID AS SEPTEMBER AFTERNOONS IN Delhi can get. Who's bothered about the atmospheric temperature though when there's all the heat that sloganeering generates?

I'm in the heart of central Delhi – at a place called the Jantar Mantar voicing our party's disapproval of what we consider was a 'fake encounter'. Five days ago, the police had stormed into a flat in north Delhi where four students were staying. In the shootout that ensued, two of them were killed, one injured and apprehended, while the fourth managed to escape. These students were all undergraduates at Delhi University.

What intrigued us was that at least four different versions emerged of the shoot-out – one from the police, the other from the home ministry, a third from local people and a fourth from the journalist of a Hindi daily, who strangely enough knew of the operation beforehand and was present in the vicinity when it happened. This led us to suspect that the shoot-out was pre-planned. It was perhaps a desperate step undertaken by the Congress government at the centre to thwart the BJP's relentless campaign of it being soft on terror. We've already demanded a CBI enquiry into the shoot-out and today's protest march is meant to mobilize public opinion towards our stand.

As one of the youngest and more aggressive members of the Politburo, the party is the perfect pedestal for staging protests of the kind that we've planned today. I'm supposed to address a gathering of about a thousand people, after which I shall lead a protest march to Parliament, where I will be joined by two senior party members who will address the media.

I'm a bit nervous as this is the first important rally that I have to address singly. And even though I am more or less clear about what to say, I am anxious. Plus, I know that the momentum of the speaker depends entirely on the enthusiasm and involvement shown by the listeners. Time for me to do my talking:

'Brothers, and sisters, we condemn terrorism. If anybody is found guilty of indulging in a terrorist activity, then he or she needs to booked under the law. But if the police itself indulges in acts that are no less heinous in nature, then the police are terrorists too. And this protest is against what we consider a staged, fake encounter...

'When we discuss the issue of Muslim youth taking to terrorism, we cannot discuss it in isolation from the chain of unsavoury incidents that have taken place in the country in the last two decades... The fact is that extremist right-wing Hindu groups have killed minorities at will, first in the riots in Mumbai and other places, following the Babri Masjid demolition and then in Gujarat in 2002. When you see your family members or relatives butchered in the manner that they were and the law itself standing by helpless, it is not entirely unthinkable to see some of the more impressionable members of the community hit back with terrorist strikes.

'No, I am not justifying these terror strikes. What I'm trying to say is that these right-wing communal groups are equal terrorists.

The law of the land should be amended to treat them at par with terrorists. Till communal murders stop, I doubt that a conclusive solution to the problem of terrorism will ever emerge.

'What is even more worrying is the bias shown by government institutions such as the police against the minority community in carrying out investigations. I'd like to especially caution these institutions and sound a warning bell for them. I wish to tell them in no uncertain terms to be fair in their investigations. Having a long beard or hoisting the Islamic flag in your locality does not mean you're a terrorist. If these institutions allow their judgment to get coloured with prejudice or malice, it will only add to the persecution of certain sections and render a solution impossible...'

◆

I think I'm happy with my speech. It was short – about twenty minutes – and it struck the right chord with the listeners. I touched on all the topics that I'd meant to, without dragging them too far. The turnout was pretty good – considering that I'm pretty raw in politics and just finding my way.

We're all quite upbeat as we start our march towards Parliament. The media turn-out is impressive too. However on our way we're confronted by something we'd have been better off without. We see another protest gathering. These protestors are led by a local BJP state leader. They are demanding stricter laws to combat terrorism. They're shrill and venomous – attributes which so characterize them.

I ask my people to steer clear of them. For, if I know the psyche of the BJP, they would want their activists to clash with ours and ruin our march. That is the last thing I need.

Unfortunately, even the presence of the police can't prevent an episode. Some of our members retaliate to provocation by BJP activists. The result is a clash between a few members of the two groups that results in injuries to at least six people. Our march is stopped and we're asked to disperse. I protest against the decision and offer myself up for arrest. In the ensuing drama, along with some hundred members, I'm taken to the Parliament Street Police Station. The other members are asked to disperse or just stay put where they are. Chaos prevails for a good 45 minutes before we are finally released on instructions from the police headquarters.

Thus it is only around 4:30pm that we finally reach outside Parliament, almost an hour-and-a-half behind schedule. I am joined by two other leaders of the Politburo – Kallol Basu and Rajashekhar Yohanan. The three of us address the media. We talk about the same things that I dwelt upon in my speech. After the arrest drama, I am even more indignant.

The country cannot be held to ransom by the hawkish attitude of right-wing parties. By disrupting our peaceful march with violence, they've provided another instance of their intolerance towards anyone who does not toe their vindictive communal line.

◆

It's 11:30pm. The day has been gruelling, but I'm not tired; nor am I complaining. I'm working on a speech of another kind. I have to address what is perhaps going to be the country's largest gathering of queers. Though the dictionary meaning of the word would be 'strange', the term today has largely come to be used in reference to LGTB (lesbian, gay, trans-gender, bisexual) communities as well as those perceived to be members of these communities.

In the very first place, let me say that I am opposed to this usage. If you ask me, they are not strange. They are who they are. And in the continued usage of this term, they are in an indirect way, playing into the hands of those drubbing them. But since they don't seem to be in any great hurry to do away with the term, and I'm too preoccupied with other stuff to make the effort myself, I shall concentrate on other issues for now.

And, just in case you want me to specify whom we are fighting, it is our government. By refusing to repeal Article 377 – an archaic law enacted by the British in 1860 in India – homosexuality amounts to being a punishable offence. We must thank the Indian politicians, though, for their inefficiency in enforcing laws: as in everything else, India is a soft state on this account as well. I can't think of any documented incidence of a gay couple being convicted and being put behind bars for indulging in the act. The drive behind this movement has been to get this act repealed and to decriminalize homosexuality in the country. And lest there be further ambiguity, let me clarify – no, it's not the CPI(M)'s stand that I am espousing.

The stand is my very own.

A political activist by day and a gay rights activist by night!

Is it that complicated?

Well, every interesting mix of causes carries a long tale of omissions and commissions and mine is no less replete with them, in what I consider has been a life less ordinary.

◆

As a five-year-old kid, I led a quotidian life in Kolkata lived entirely under parental supervision. Life was as blissfully ignorant as it can only be at that age. I'd joined kindergarten at the La Martinere for girls and drove down there everyday in a car that had something which other kids would fancy very much – an orange light on the top. I would always wonder why other cars did not have this. Baba told me this was a reward given to good and honest people by the government. I did not have the mind to wonder if my friends' parents were dishonest and bad people; their cars, after all, did not have the orange light. .

It took a national catastrophe – the assassination of our PM, Indira Gandhi, and the ensuing nationwide riots – to acquaint me with the significance of the orange light. When the whole country remained glued to a newly befriended toy called television and tearfully watched Mrs Gandhi's funeral, Baba did not come home for two days. As the Deputy Commissioner of South Calcutta district, he was busy ensuring that the minor incidents of rioting that had taken place were curbed. The fact that sporadic violence against the Sikhs had been reported from almost all parts of the country had made the administration more vigilant. That day, Ma explained a lot of things to me ie, that Baba was an IAS officer, whose job was to help the government in ensuring smooth administration; that Mom was a professor of Nuclear Physics in the Jadavpur University; that Baba was a Bengali Brahman and Ma a Tamil Iyer

Brahman; that they had met at Delhi University where both studied at the famous St. Stephens college; that both grew close and fell in love when they were preparing for the Civil Services; that while Baba went ahead and cleared the exam, Ma instead opted for higher studies.

It is generally supposed that children of inter-caste parents mature faster. In my case, the combination was the highest pedigree, being a half Bengali Brahman and a half Tamil Iyer Brahman – both communities known for their high intellect and learning; the only difference between the communities being that the Bengali was said to be more rebellious and the Tamil more idiosyncratic.

I guess that makes me an idiosyncratic rebel!

I did find myself becoming socially aware sooner than my peers. And as a bureaucrat, my father was dealing with politicians, which made me politically aware as well.

Baba went on to become Secretary in the state's Education Ministry and a year later, was transferred to an assignment at the UN in Geneva. I realized later that this assignment caused a rift between my parents. Baba had wanted Ma to shift with him; Ma wouldn't oblige. The reason – Ma was pursuing her second doctorate and did not want to impede it.

Baba soon shifted to Geneva and I stayed back with Ma. I was just nine then but I could sense that Ma would often be miffed – I didn't know what about, though. Whenever Baba and Ma spoke on the phone, they'd end up fighting. Once I tried to eavesdrop into their conversation via a parallel phone line; but the conversation ended abruptly.

Soon after I thought Baba and Ma had resolved their problem. Baba would call her late at night and Ma seemed quite happy and relaxed talking to him. One night, when the pressure of a weekly school test kept me awake till later than usual, I heard Ma on the phone. As I hadn't spoken to Baba for almost a week, I rushed to the parallel line and just called out for him. To my surprise it wasn't Baba. Ma later told me she had been talking to a colleague of hers.

Six months later, Baba and Ma filed for divorce. And this man, whom I'd intercepted on the phone, came to the fore. He was ten years younger than Ma and her student. Ma made a rather concerted effort to make me understand her position or to justify herself or maybe both. I was told that she and Baba had probably been hasty in deciding to get married that early; that a college romance did not mean they'd be happy as man and wife; that Baba had, over the years, got sucked into work and had no time for anything else; that Ma had been wanting Baba to take a few weeks off for a road trip of the north east; that she had been so kicked about it but Baba just didn't have the time or the interest; that Ma had been trying to tell Baba that they had been drifting apart, to which Baba had just one solution – come and stay with me in Geneva.

On his part, Baba was stoic. He hardly said anything to me except that he and Ma were not meant to be married any longer.

I was ten years old when Ma one day took me out for lunch. Her new partner was to join us. I knew this would be my first meeting with the villain. Adarsh was his name. We met at a Chinese restaurant in Park Street. He looked barely out of college. He tried to charm me by indulging in sweet talk about my food tastes and offering me chocolates that he'd got for me. He probably had no idea that there were far bigger issues going on in my mind to forget them all with this bribe. I didn't say a word. My silence must have seemed terribly odd, for Ma chided me:

'Chaitali, now will you please smile a bit before you have your food?'

I ignored her.

'Look, Chaitali, you're being rude to our guest and this is just not done, okay?'

'And what you both have done is done?' I shot back, agitated.

Adarsh must have felt guilty, for he promptly intervened. 'Listen Jayanthi, you both carry on... I will catch up with you later.'

'Wait,' I retorted. 'You guys carry on.'

I went up close to Adarsh. I still remember the anticipation on his countenance at that moment. Probably he had hoped that I'd embrace him. Instead I spat on his face; the act surprising me more that it would have done Ma or Adarsh. Having done this, I ran off to Ma's car which was parked outside and shared a pack of biscuits with the chauffeur. This car didn't have the orange light anymore and I was left wondering if all goodness and honesty had gone away with Baba.

I'm not sure whether it would be called 'punitive action', but two months later, I was packed off to a boarding school in Darjeeling, known by the name of Loreto Convent.

Before I come to my exploits at the Loreto Convent, let me tell you more about my defiance. Six months after having being sent to the school, I returned home for a week. And this time again, I repeated the unthinkable. Yes, I spat on the devil's face once more. I was enraged at his audacity, he had come home, that too when Ma was away. It's another thing that this time round I was meted out corporal punishment. For the first time ever, Ma raised her hand on me and beat me black and blue.

◆

In my hostel, I was perhaps the most fearless of my class: it was like I had seen so much so early that the fear of spotting ghosts or going to the washroom through the empty corridor in the dark gloom of a chilly winter night – which so scared the other girls – seemed no big deal to me.

One night I opted for some perilous fun. I woke up my friend Monica in the middle of the night and convinced her to come with me to the banyan tree – which, all the girls insisted, was haunted by the ghost of a dead villager. To my surprise, Monica had the courage enough to agree. However, from about 100 metres away from the tree, our confidence went for a toss and every step that we took was laden with fear. Monica did think of fleeing once, but I held her back. And when we finally reached the tree, we were jubilant that nothing happened to us. We laughed and mocked the ghost because there was none. By next morning, we had been accorded a prized position among the students – we had become famous as the two brave-hearts who had shooed the ghost away! And we basked in the glory.

Monica and I grew closer as years went by. We had a few things in common – notably, impaired parenting. Unlike in my case though, her parents were separated by the will of nature – her dad had passed away when she was three. Her mom, a pediatrician in Delhi, earned well enough to afford her boarding school education. Like me Monica was brave. The rigours of real, irreversible tragedy had made Monica immune to lesser fears. We were both good athletes and would do well on the annual sports day. Like me, she had a rebel streak in her and we sometimes did incredibly crazy things. We'd be almost vying with each other to outdo each other's crazy streak. Our individual madness was mutually contagious.

In high school, in our final year, we were to have this annual dance event between us and the boys of St. Paul's – popularly known as the 'socials'. Officially, the idea behind this do is to encourage interaction between the opposite sexes in non-co-ed institutions. Obviously, there was nothing official about the official idea. What 'socials' unofficially meant for us was the initiation of a legitimate 'dating' contact, should both concerned parties be game.

I had developed a pretty strong crush on this cute Assamese guy, whom I had spotted in the market a couple of times. His soft features and straight hair made him look damn hot. From my sources, I had learnt his name was Partho. Now the night before the party, I developed another craving. I wanted to kiss this dude. I'm not sure whether my desire was propelled by the passionate smooch between Anil Kapoor and Manisha Koirala which I'd seen in a recent movie. But I had been wondering what I'd feel if I were Manisha.

There were two other nagging worries too. One, I wasn't sure whether I'd manage to get the right situation at the social to be able to kiss him; two, I wasn't sure I would know *how* to kiss. My first concern was allayed by my optimism – I knew if I wanted something intensely enough, I'd do it, come what may. The second concern bothered me a bit more. So I went up to Monica, who lay on her bed, reading a book. I asked her to stand. I held her face, tried looking into her eyes amorously, then shut my eyes and kissed her.

I must confess today that I shut my eyes, not out of involvement in the act, but to hide the disbelief of my action from my own eyes. Monica's eyes though were wide open and till date we laugh incessantly when we recall the incident. That was Monica's first kiss as well. And since she too had been meaning to kiss her crush at the social, she subsequently employed some experiments upon me – which went on well past midnight.

A few months later, Baba, who was by now back in India on an assignment with the Central Government, remarried. It was then that I finally accepted the presence of Adarsh in my life. Adarsh and Ma had a small baby. I went up to Adarsh, who feared the worst again. This time though, I rendered an apology. Baba, in his cryptic way, had been right. He and Ma had indeed not meant to be married beyond a point. That Baba and Ma were happy with their new partners, only proved this. Somewhere, though, I started feeling alienated in their new set-up. I started feeling a strange un-belonging. Though subtle, it would disturb me. I felt a need to run away to another world. However, it took the ways of destiny nearly five years to make this happen.

◆

London was a breath of fresh air, as pleasant as a place can be. Far from the incessant rains I had been bracing myself for in London, the weather was mild and pleasant; their summer was like Delhi in February.

I had just got myself enrolled for a postgraduate program in Economics at the London School of Economics. And for company, I had none other than my bosom buddy from my boarding school days. Monica had opted for a program in Political Science. As we couldn't get hostel accommodation we lived together in a small studio apartment on the mezzanine floor of a building barely 500 metres away from our college on Houghton Street.

Our batch had a good assortment of non-British students. Half of these students were Indians, most of them guys – none exciting enough for me to bother befriending. It was almost a week later that my impressions were to change. In walked Siddharth, an Indian student who had been on the wait-list.

Sid brought with him a wave of energy and style and an ultra-cool attitude. He never cared about the way he looked. His sex appeal lay in his aloofness. Sid was a big draw among the girls from the day that he came in. They'd hover around him like bees and I must confess I envied him for the impartial manner in which he handled them all – arousing hopes in all of them yet meeting the expectations of none. I guess to be 'single, eligible, and yet unavailable' is the most seductive thing a man can do. I was smitten by him, much before we became friends

When I think of it now, I feel there are certain people whose faces just draw your attention all the time. Not faces you consider breathtakingly handsome or anything. To me the most attractive man is one who has a touch of vulnerability in him – which the world may not notice, but a girl like me would. I was discerning and intuitive. There was something about this guy that was telling me there was a lot to be explored and unraveled. I felt the sort of intense attraction towards him that I'd waited to feel for a man for a long time now.

Sid soon became good friends with two of our classmates – Keith and Raghav, and the three would hang out in a group. He was closer to Keith and they'd often be seen having long discussions. We'd tease them by suggesting a gay motive to their friendship. Raghav, by the way, was a damn good looker – tall, dark and handsome. Of course those of us who had a silly fixation for fair skin would not go his way. Raghav did show a distinct fondness for me though, which I quite appreciated. The fact that I had a huge soft corner for Sid, however, ensured that Raghav kept a distance from me – even if in his heart of hearts he may have nursed some pretty strong feelings for me.

Soon enough, Sid, Keith and Raghav moved into a shared accommodation pretty close to where we stayed.

Since my attraction for Sid was no secret, I never let go an opportunity to be with him. I'd try to sit next to him in class, even if that meant engaging him in forced conversation the moment he entered, and asking him out for coffee on the pretext that I needed to discuss some notes with him. I'm told that a gleam would surface on my face every time I saw him, leaving little to the imagination. Sid, on his part was extremely nice. He'd be as soothing as a best pal can be. Yet, he never really showed much interest in anything beyond that – a relationship, or at best an affair to begin with.

I worried about the reasons: maybe, I came across as a bit too overbearing. Maybe, I had overestimated my attractiveness. Maybe, he had someone in his life, in some other part of the world. Or maybe, he just wanted to concentrate on his career and not get distracted by women.

The last of these options seemed the most probable in his case.

But then, how was I to contain my feelings which to my own surprise were only getting more uncontainable by the day? The strange thing about falling in love is that the more unresponsive the object of your desire is, the more you feel attracted to them.

When my feelers to him didn't work for nearly two months, I shot the bullet from close range. It was a Friday and we sat next to each other, attending a lecture on Marxist economy. Though I had by then become a great fan of Karl Marx, that day I just couldn't follow what the professor taught. My attention was elsewhere. From the corner of my eyes, I kept a close watch on Sid, who looked at the professor with a diligent expression that couldn't hide the fact that he wasn't following either.

'What are you doing this Saturday night?' I mumbled.

'Sorry?'

I brought my leg close to his, touching his thigh with mine.

'Dude, I said what you doing this Saturday night?'

'N... nothing...'

'Coming on a date with me...?'

He took a good thirty seconds to respond. He finally took his pen and scribbled something on my notebook. 'Of course...'

◆

That Saturday night, we watched a play at the famous West End Theatre. The play had an unusual take on the nebulous line that sometimes separates love and friendship. While I enjoyed every moment of the hilarious act, Sid was more restrained. I figured he probably preferred action movies to mushy plays. For a moment I wondered if he could be romantic at all.

My doubts were allayed that night itself. After getting thoroughly sloshed – we were both more than half-a-dozen pegs and two tequila shots down – he came in to drop me to my apartment. Monica was not home that night. She'd left a note saying she was going to meet her local guardian.

I don't remember another occasion in life when I've been that drunk. Add to that the bonus of being with the man I'd secretly been lusting for. We stumbled up the stairs, Sid and I holding on to each other as we laughed. Outside my door I rested against the wall; Sid held on to me from the front. I unbuttoned his shirt and gently caressed the hair on his chest. They were short like he'd recently shaved. My weird imagination had me trying to guess how hirsute his other prized part would be. And since I'm given to going for what I make up my mind about, I undid the top button of his jeans and inserted my hand in. I was pleasantly jolted though by his lips grabbing mine. What a violent kiss that was.

I shed my modesty and stripped to my bare essentials. It was not entirely a coincidence that I happened to be wearing the only thong I possessed that night. Sid took a wild fancy to it. They say that body odour is a pivotal component in precipitating carnal attraction. It must be true because there was something about Sid's bare body that inflamed my desire.

The next morning I woke up to find a naked Sid standing in front of me, holding out a coffee cup. I realized I was just as naked as he was. We didn't seem to be in any sort of hurry to cover up as we made morning coffee conversation. Strangely, Sid spoke about a myriad things – the play, the dinner, the tequila that had done us in and his friend Keith– but he didn't broach what had happened between us. I wanted to talk and share my feelings with him, but held back.

Monica, who had with her by then the expertise of at least one steady relationship, told me later, with a fair degree of conviction, that having sex with the guy, in the situation that I was in, was bound to be a catalyst of sorts and would bring a huge change in our relationship. She was pretty sure that we'd both behave and react differently the next time we met.

How I wish Monica had better knowledge. That was not meant to be. Sid behaved as though nothing had happened between us. His selective amnesia led me to wonder if our lovemaking had been something too normal for him and whether he'd done it with other woman on the sly. My anxieties grew by the day. I knew he had conquered my narcissistic, invincible self. I knew

I wanted to be with him all the time. His indifference only added to my desperation.

Two weeks later, when things didn't seem to improve, I confessed my feelings to Sid. And I did it in class, as both of us waited for the professor to arrive.

'Listen, Sid, I have to tell you something. I love you, okay?'

I'm not sure whether a proposal can sound more abrupt than that, but I meant it.

Later that day, Sid did his part of the talking. 'Look, Chaitali, I really like you. You're a damn good girl. But I'm not sure you're what I'm looking for.'

'You can't be sure till you take this further, right?' I reasoned.

'And what if things don't work? I have a feeling our temperaments may not match. Wouldn't that shatter you?'

I was damn impressed by his sensitivity. I mean, every other guy whom I'd come across in college would have grabbed an opportunity to lay me more often. Sid was different. And every action of his only further vindicated my choice.

'You know what, Sid – sometimes, the person in question is so special that you're prepared to risk the heartbreak. I won't mind being in a relationship with you and not getting you, but I'd regret not giving it a try at all.'

Appreciating Sid's caution, we got into a consistent dating arrangement, without really expecting too much from each other. I've never been too clear about the fine distinction between dating and seeing someone. But I must say I was impressed with Sid's focus. Once we started dating, he distanced himself from other women and we'd end up spending most of our time together. Interestingly, Sid came across as someone a lot more mature than what his age would have him be. I guess this is why we hit it off. Besides, there was something else that set him apart – and that had to do with his beliefs about the way our relationship ought to evolve. He believed that we ought to be activity partners in the right sense – watch and talk about plays, literature and maybe discuss politics and the economy and see if we appreciated each other's views.

I must confess here that the first three months that we spent together were quite fascinating for me. It was like I was getting acquainted with a new and unknown thought process that I'd wholly subscribe to. And it was damn fascinating to experience it unfold in front of me bit by bit. I didn't mind the absence of sex at all.

Every relationship has a honeymoon period. In our case the longevity of it was about three months. After that, I was confronted with a dilemma – it would have been unnatural for me to not feel horny. But Sid's insistence on keeping the relationship asexual became a dampener of sorts. He would insist on going back to his apartment every night.

One night, when we did get an opportunity to be together and I coaxed him for sex, he sounded rather stand-offish. 'Listen, Chaitali, please don't force me into something I don't feel up to. There will be a time for it. Right now, I'm still not confident of our future. And I want to avoid a sexual relationship at this stage.'

A guy speaking to you like that is bound to send mixed signals to you. You're sure to admire him, yet hate him or doubt him as well. I let it be the way he wanted it. In hindsight, I think I was insecure of losing the guy I loved. After all, the fact that our togetherness had made me the object of envy of many of my female friends was a fact I knew too well. I knew that quite a few of them were hoping we'd break off, so that they could get their hands on Sid.

Two weeks later, Monica wanted me to come along with her to her local guardian's place. As they were to bring in Monica's niece's birthday and it was a Saturday, we were open to the idea of staying back for the night. Sid stayed back at our apartment when we were away, so that he could study in privacy. I got my periods that night and since I wasn't feeling too well, I decided to return home. Sid had perhaps forgotten that I had a set of spare keys with me or perhaps he was just too engrossed to bother. But what I saw that night is an image I cannot forget all my life.

Sid was fucking Keith with the passion that I'd relentlessly hoped to see in him. Some sights are so tellingly obvious that they don't need any explanations. I'd got all my answers there and then – why Sid compulsively avoided having a girlfriend, why Keith and he would discuss things in private all the time, why he seemed more enamoured of my butt and why he was so keen on an asexual relationship. What remained a conundrum though was that first night when he made love to me like he really loved me.

◆

A week went by – one in which shock and disbelief made me retreat into a virtual cocoon. I went to college just twice after the episode, that too when being at home made me feel too depressed and helpless. Sid had been desperately trying to talk to me. I'd been avoiding him for I knew what it would be – an apology, an explanation, a reasoning out – I had expected a lot more from him.

Finally, on Monica's insistence, I agreed to meet Sid at a relatively desolate café, far away from where our college mates normally hung out.

'Chaitali, I'm sorry. I'm sorry for hiding the truth from you. I'm sorry for leading you on...'

'Sid, what are you? A gay or a bi...?'

By now I'd given up all hopes of a third option.

'Gay.'

'Then why didn't you tell this to me at the start?'

'Because I kept trying to convince myself I was straight. I kept trying to tell myself that my attraction for men was a passing phase, or at best that it was natural and that in the end, I'd still fall for a woman.'

I was zapped into silence and he continued.

'But now my experiment has failed. Despite my best efforts and the fact that I had someone as attractive as you falling for me, I got back to what I found natural for me.'

I gathered that I was thus Sid's guinea pig – an experiment that was supposed to help him overcome his misconceptions. It made my blood boil. Sid for his part was by now pleading for forgiveness.

'Please, Chaitali, for god's sake, don't misunderstand me. I may belong to an affluent family but my Gujju folks in Surat would commit suicide if they know that I'm a homosexual. It's still treated as some kind of unmentionable disorder in my town. My behaviour and reasoning may sound weird, but trust me, my relationship with you was my last and most desperate effort to be counted among the normal in my society. I have failed and I'm really, really sorry for making you suffer.'

I just did not have the words for a reply. I felt a hatred for him that was hard to combat. Just as I turned to walk away, he grabbed my hand. The most bizarre twist was yet to happen.

'Chaitali, I want to give you something,' said Sid, his speech laden with self-doubt. 'I want you to go out with Raghav. He likes you a lot and you won't find a better guy....'

To my utter surprise, Raghav was sitting on the adjoining table. Perhaps Sid had planned this meeting after taking Raghav into confidence.

The human mind sometimes acts as perverse as it can get. It is strange that people often want redemption, but on their own terms. Sure, Sid must have been feeling very guilty for what he did to me, but what on earth made him think he'd wash off his guilt with this gallant gesture? For that matter, I'm not sure whether it was gallant or mean. Perversion has various modes and maybe he just wanted some vicarious fun – watching Raghav do things with me that he couldn't. I had every reason to ridicule Sid for this puerility, yet I did just the opposite.

'Sure, I had been waiting for this date with Raghav,' I responded perkily.

Sid and Raghav were stumped by this response of mine. So was I. But I guess the sadist in me wanted to outdo Sid in the hurt he had given me. In no time, Raghav and I were off together. I still remember Sid's expression at that point. He tried to look brave and happy but his face had crumpled in defeat.

I hung out with Raghav the whole evening, watching a movie. All the while that Raghav thought I enjoyed his company, I cried within. Cried for what had happened to me, cried even more for how I was avenging the happening. That evening with every moment that I spent with Raghav, my indignation grew. I realized that my capacity for drink had suddenly increased. I must have gulped down some eight or nine pegs that evening. And when even that failed to soothe things, I did the unthinkable. I landed up with Raghav at Sid's place. Sid and Keith were naturally astounded to see us entwined in each other's arms, sloshed out of our minds. I was not to stop at that. I took Raghav in, locked the inside room and asked Raghav for an unusual favour.

'Come on, dude, do me…Come on! What are you thinking? Do me I say!' I roared, ensuring that Sid would hear me and realize what he must have done to make me feel this way.

Raghav, like any guy in such a situation of easy availability and drunken stupor, brought himself close and was about to grab me when there was a loud sound. Yes, I'd slapped him hard.

'Keep off, you swine,' I shouted and ran out of the door.

As I came out, I saw Sid weeping profusely in one corner. Keith tried his best to stop him, just as a spouse would, but Sid was inconsolable. When Sid saw me, he begged me for forgiveness. The abject sight of a weeping Sid begging me brought about a significant change in my mental state.

Sympathy replaced fury. And I started wondering if my supposed act of avenging myself had actually transformed me from a victim into a culprit.

A week later, I apologized to Sid and told him I'd like to be friends with him again. That Sid knew my friendship offer was borne out of sympathy, made real friendship difficult. In the remaining months of our course, Sid and I couldn't drive away the awkwardness that had crept into our relationship. I couldn't help feeling that my hasty quest for a lover had lost me a great friend

Now I had neither.

I returned to India in the early January of 2002 and joined Pepisco in Gurgaon. I walked into my new office without any woollen protection on what was the coldest day in Delhi in the past twenty-five years.

This small act of defiance was just a prelude to the many more defiant acts that I was to put up through the year.

◆

On the 27th of February of that year a catastrophe occurred; one that triggered off a chain of the most demonic behaviour that mankind can indulge in. A train compartment carrying Hindu pilgrims burnt down, killing 58 people. In the subsequent rioting that followed in the next three months, more than a thousand people were butchered.

Some reports did suggest that the train was attacked by a 500-strong weapon-carrying Muslim mob. However I shall stick to using the term 'burnt'. I use the safer term as two enquiry commissions constituted to probe the fire have come up with two very contradictory findings.

While the Nanavati Commission states that the burning was 'pre-planned', the Justice Banerjee Commission states that it was accidental. It goes without saying that all the right-wing leaders and Narendra Modi have unequivocally maintained that the fire was pre-planned and conspired.

While the burning of the train compartment may be mired in confusion, there is no dout about the pogrom that followed.

The first incidents of attacks on the minority Muslim community started in Ahmedabad, where Hindus began throwing stones at and later burned down a Muslim housing complex known as Gulberg Society. The initial violence was believed to have been instigated by unsubstantiated rumours, endorsed by a senior VHP leader, of Muslims having kidnapped three Hindu girls during the Godhra train attack. In Naroda, according to Human Rights Watch (HRW), at least 65 Muslims were killed, many of them women who were sexually assaulted by violent mobs. According to HRW in its widely-quoted report, the barbaric mobs were guided by voter lists and print-outs of addresses of Muslim-owned properties – information obtained from the local municipal administration. They were aided in many cases by the police who allowed them a free run.

Violence was reported from almost all across the state and in varied execution patterns. A high profile case involved an ex-Congress MP Ehsan Jafri who was surrounded by Hindu mobs while many other Muslim residents in the area took shelter in his compound. Jafri was believed to have contacted the local police stations and the administration to save the people from the ever-increasing throng but no police reinforcements reached his place and the few policemen present were ineffective and unwilling to control the mob. Eventually, he was burnt to death, along with fifty others.

Fourteen people, including women and children, were killed by a mob at the Best Bakery in the town of Vadodara on the night of 1st March. On March 3, fourteen members of Bilkis Bano's family including her two-month old daughter were killed in a mob attack near Chapparwad village in Dahod district. Seven women, including Bilkis Bano, then five months pregnant, were reportedly raped.

Such violence was bound to have a retaliatory effect and attacks on and killing of Hindus too were reported from certain areas. According to an official estimate, 1044 people were killed in the violence – 790 Muslims and 254 Hindus (including those killed in the Godhra train fire). Another 223 people were reported missing, 2,548 injured, 919 women widowed and 606 children orphaned.

There are times when the magnitude of a calamity is so overwhelming that it doesn't matter whether you are safe or not. The Gujarat violence left a similar impact on me. It brought in me a gloominess of unusual proportions. The pain of the macabre images that played on TV channels and in the print media just wouldn't go out of my mind. I'd wake up in the middle of the night, experiencing nightmares.

In all this, there was one particular image whose impact was overwhelming. It was a picture of this man called Qutubuddin Ansari, crying and begging for his life with folded hands. The way the picture appeared in the papers, it almost seemed like he was personally begging me. I don't know why but the image revived another disturbing memory that I'd been trying hard to erase – of Sid, pleading with me for forgiveness.

What was more baffling was the sheer apathy of the government towards the killings. This was the same BJP government that never ceased to blow its trumpet when it came to fighting terrorism. And here it was, itself giving a new definition to terrorism – state sponsored and made foolproof by the backing of the Central government.

In May, when my anguish got the better of me, I quit my job and went to help the victims. I stayed in Ahmedabad for almost a month trying to help displaced victims staying in camps, resettle. Later I travelled to Baroda. At every juncture, the first-hand account of the incident was many times more earth-shattering than the stuff that I had read. I mean, what sort of a cannibal would kill someone, chop their body into parts, burn them and then dispose them off in unknown places? That was the kind of barbarism that I got to hear of. There were times I'd almost puke just hearing these horror stories and wanted to flee. And then I'd tell myself that fleeing was what I'd been doing all my life.

Soon enough, I'd donned the role of crusader – fighting against government terrorism. I knew it would require a humongous struggle to bring the countless butchers to book, most of whom enjoyed political patronage; and that booking their political bosses might never happen. The Delhi Riots cases after all, had gone on for a good twenty years. These too might go on for that long. I might be an aunty by then. My personal life might take a massive beating. I was prepared to risk all of that; so intense and unrelenting was my anger and pain and the resolve to overcome them both. Yes, this would be the ultimate test of my courage.

For the first year, I, along with a couple of other activists focused on getting the riot cases shifted out of Gujarat. There was a huge risk of the witnesses being threatened, harmed or bribed within the state. It was quite a task to ensure they did not turn hostile at the last moment. As was expected, the cases proceeded at a tardy pace.

Along the way, a stark realization dawned on me: that to be heard in India, you needed to be in politics. I understood that I would have to do so to succeed in my mission. I would need to align myself with a political outfit. And this is where a new set of options emerged. My fascination with Karl Marx was no secret. Neither was my aversion for both of India's frontline political parties. If I despised the BJP for its communal agenda, I abhorred the Congress for letting the BJP succeed in its machinations. Had it not been for Congress' duplicity on the issue of secularism in the last several decades, the BJP would never have come this far. That left me with little option but to look Left-ward. Besides, I did remember an important dictum in politics that said: your enemy's enemy is your friend. That the BJP and the Left were worse than sworn enemies, does not even need reiteration.

There may have been another reason why I opted for the Left. Baba's younger brother, who was nearly ten years younger to him had quit his studies at the Presidency College, Kolkata to join the Naxal Movement – an extremist right-wing offshoot of the Indian Marxists. This was in the early seventies, before I was born, and after the Left parties had been voted out of power in West Bengal. For weeks, my uncle had been untraceable.

And then, one morning, his dead body was found in an open ground near Esplanade, along with those of three other students'. They were purportedly nabbed from a village in Midnapore, killed, and their bodies deliberately abandoned in the city to warn people of the consequences that supporting the Naxal Movement would draw.

This was before I was born, but then they say that certain traits are in your blood. When I called up Baba to tell him of my decision to join the CPI(M), his first response was of a long pause. I couldn't help feeling that it might have revived memories of the unsavoury chapter involving his kid brother.

Communism in the Indian context is as interesting, as it is confusing. What started off at the time of Independence as a 'democratic struggle' against the imperialist state was to soon turn into a revolutionary struggle. It is worthwhile to note here the impressive inroads made by Communists in the early years after Independence.

In the general elections in 1957, the CPI emerged as the largest Opposition party. The CPI also won the state elections in Kerala, thus forming the first non-Congress government in the country. In subsequent years, internal warring among the different party factions was to lead to the party breaking into various splinter groups, at times the splinter group turning out to be more powerful than the original party. Thus in 1964, CPI (Marxist) was born; this was followed by the birth of CPI (M-L) in 1969. It is interesting to note here, that what triggered off a series of conflicts that eventually led to the formation of the CPI(M), was the issue of loyalty towards the Indian state in the Indo-Chinese war of 1962… It would shock many of our generation to be told that a significant chunk of the Communist leaders of the time perceived the war as a conflict between a Socialist and a Capitalist state, and thus took a pro-Chinese position. It is equally startling to note that this chunk included the likes of the legendary Jyoti Basu and Harkishan Singh Surjeet.

May 25, 1967 was to mark another watershed development in Indian Communist history. On this fateful day in a hitherto unknown village called Naxallbari in north Bengal, a section of the CPI(M), led by Charu Majumdar and Kanu Sanyal, legitimized armed revolutionary peasant struggle against oppressive landlords. The next few years saw a different level of uprising altogether, which was to assume varied forms at different stages. Ironically, the Naxal Movement, coincided with a growing unrest that students in urban centres such as Calcutta were feeling due to growing unemployment. It is noteworthy that a good number of college students were to soon support the Naxal Movement, and this was to include my ill-fated uncle. The faction of CPI(M) leaders who supported the Naxalite Movement, subsequently broke away from the party and formed the Communist Party of India (Marxist-Leninist) in 1969.

Today, the various Left parties exist under a vast umbrella called Left Front. It is amusing to think that almost all of these parties, some of which revolve around the whims of a single leader, invariably think themselves to be the rightful inheritors and torch-bearers of Communism.

Like any other movement would, modern day Indian Communism has acquired a form that is significantly different from what its founder leaders of yesteryears would have envisaged. To my understanding, the most interesting thing about Communism in the present Indian scenario is that we've actually likened ourselves to the Socialists of the past. I feel we have replaced the Socialism of the seventies, which would be the domain of Socialists like Ram Manohar Lohia and Jai Prakash Narayan. Thus, any disinvestment proposal of the government is bound to come under our scanner. Much on expected lines, we've retained our original anti-US and pro-China bias. For that matter, we still like to think of ourselves as pro-poor and are the only party that has consistently opposed irrational economic liberalization in the last fifteen years. We have always thought of it as a flawed policy that widened and magnified the economic divide. We still advocate austerity as a principle and policy.

It is ironical that the rightful inheritors of Socialism – Laloo Yadav, Ram Bilas Paswan, Mulayam Singh Yadav, Nitish Kumar and the like, have either joined hands with the Congress or with the BJP or oscillate between the two. On the other hand, the Left parties, irrespective of remaining stagnant and confined to two states – Kerala and West Bengal – have stuck relentlessly to their anti-Congress and anti-BJP stance, considering the BJP the bigger evil. It is also noteworthy here, that the original Communist propaganda that advocated the transfer of power to the peasantry has somewhere gone for a toss.

The WB chief minister, Buddhadeb Bhattacharya, for that matter, is as pro-industry as any votary of Capitalism might be. And the fact that Communists have more or less come to terms with him manifests the erosion of Communism's basic plank.

The two most potent driving issues for us, today, are our fight against Communalism and our fight against American Imperialism. In a strange way, we find stark similarities between Bush and Modi. And we'd like to see the back of both of them.

However, as a young Communist leader, I am hopeful of re-instating some of the concepts of Karl Marx into the working of Indian Communist parties. I am still keen on a classless society, regardless of how far-fetched that may seem. What is most paradoxical is that I see this happening in some of the more capital perceived centres, without it even getting due cognizance.

◆

It's 3am and I'm still wide awake. In exactly seven hours from now, I will be addressing the queer community. Ever since life took a cardinal turn, after Sid and after Godhra, I'd promised myself not to waste time on idle thoughts. On rare occasions though, like today, I've failed to keep the pledge. The reason why I tend to give in of late, is because I'm recuperating from another turmoil, which I haven't yet mentioned to you. I'm not sure if I ought to talk about it now.

It's something I hold very dear to me – my second interlocution with that beatific feeling called love.

As on the first occasion, I wasn't lucky this time round either.

The smallest memory of it sends me into a tizzy. I know if I succumb to my memories now I'll lie awake all night and then arrive for the lecture feeling completely zonked.

Instead I think about one of the more pleasant conversations that I once had with the object of my love…

We sat at a restaurant past midnight and into the wee hours of a Sunday morning. Both of us were sufficiently drunk to disregard the propriety that we were meant to uphold in public. A weird idea struck me and I wondered aloud, how, by virtue of personal habits, one could tell apart a Congressman, a BJP guy and a Communist.

He attempted an answer: 'Okay, at a coffee shop, a Congressman is most likely to go for Irish Coffee, a BJP guy for lemon tea and the Communist for black tea,' he said.

'And how do you deduce that?' I asked, amused.

'Well, the Congress reflects exoticism – whether in terms of its leader or policies. The BJP prides itself in being seen as more earthy and homespun. And the Communist would just go for the cheapest beverage.'

I couldn't help laughing at his fuzzy logic. The fact that he sometimes took his craziness so seriously was probably what endeared him to me.

'And which actress would these people go for?' I goaded him on.

'Well, the Congressman would probably go for Kareena Kapoor, the BJP guy for Bipasha Basu and the Communist for Konkana Sen Sharma.'

'And why so?' I giggled.

'Well, for the Congress, the pedigree of the contender is most important. BJP likes local sensations – those who are self-made – and the Communist would be content with someone who fulfils the very basic acting utility with no add-ons of glamour etc., – basically someone as bland as him.'

'And how would their views on, let's say, homosexuality differ?'

'Well, the Congress guy would be largely non-committal. The BJP guy is likely to denounce it and call it an affront to our age-old traditions. And the Communist is most likely to stand up for homosexuals.'

'And what would their stand imply?'

'Well, it can have many interpretations' – the glint in his eyes, foretold the barb that was to follow – 'but the most obvious interpretation is perhaps that the Congress guy is bisexual, the BJP guy straight and the Communist gay.'

Both of us broke into a delirious laugh. That both of us were high, made it difficult to control our laughter.

To be frank, such moments of levity were few between us; you see the object of my love belonged to the BJP.

Winter

Aditya

AS EXPECTED, I WON THE RAJNANDGAON SEAT BY a margin of well over 90,000 votes. Today is my fifth day in Parliament. The winter session is on. The day is unusually cold and foggy outside, but not so inside. In here, a contentious debate over the Nuclear Deal is about to begin. I am supposed to make my first speech today. And I've chosen to advocate India's nuclear cause. Protocol would ideally demand that the External Affairs minister or his deputy or some senior minister speak on the issue. However as both the minister and his deputy are out of the country, and the issue has been of keen interest to me, the high command has acceded to my request. Needless to say, I am feeling damn nervous and wondering what on earth made me put myself in this situation.

I remember a speech that Dad gave in 1999 when the NDA government had to prove its majority on the floor of the house. I would rate that as Dad's best speech – so high was its impact. The NDA government lost that trust vote by a record solitary vote and I feel sure Dad's speech that day had the power to make at least one member change his/her voting preference.

What made Dad stand apart was his sincerity. I am privy to the kind of research that he undertook before making a speech in Parliament or answering a query as minister. I've tried to emulate him today. I've spoken to a nuclear scientist, a defense expert, our foreign minister and foreign secretary to ensure my facts are right. In addition to facts, an orator needs deft articulation and a sharp presence of mind, more so when he has to respond to a motion. Incidentally, the speaker from the Opposition benches, moving the motion against the deal is none other than Brajesh Ranjan. He speaks first:

'Respected Sir, for all the stories floated by the architects of the proposed Nuclear Deal that this would liberate India from "nuclear apartheid", Article 5.2 of the 123 Agreement rules out transfer of any sensitive nuclear technology. This will have to be amended before any such transfer can take place…

'….Article 6 (iii) does talk of "consent to reprocess". However, it becomes operative only after India has set up a dedicated reprocessing facility and the two sides have agreed on arrangements and procedures… There is no mention of what would happen if the two sides do not reach agreement on these arrangements and procedures.

'Article 14.2 implicitly looks at the issue of India undertaking a nuclear test. But India won't be able to take such a decision independently. It is obliged, together with the US, "to consider carefully the circumstances that may lead to termination or cessation of cooperation". It mentions discussions will "take into account whether the circumstances that may lead to termination or cessation resulted from a Party's (read: India's) serious concern about a changed security environment, or as a response to similar actions by other States which could affect national security."

'Sir, this obviously is an escape clause for India to carry out a test, should it decide to do so in response to testing by China, Pakistan or by any other country. However, a one-year notice for testing means that India cannot immediately decide to test *in response to external stimuli. The clause imposes obvious and deliberate impediments to India's security concerns.*

'Sir, these are just some of the clauses which leave no doubt about the deal being an assault on India's sovereign credentials. This deal is like a golden cage for us in that it binds our independent powers to safeguard our national security interests, yet gives us a false reassurance of supremacy which is nothing more than window dressing. I repeat, Sir, the deal in its present form goes against our national interests and hence, the BJP and the NDA have decided to oppose it.'

◆

I hear Brajesh out. I feel that somewhere the conviction is missing from his speech. I have heard him on TV before and have known him to be far more articulate and persuasive than he sounded today. I think this happens when you're not entirely convinced about what you're speaking. I have reasons to believe that traditionally the BJP ought to have been the biggest supporter of the deal. After all, we go by perceptions and any move that is pro-US is bound to be seen as being anti-Muslim. The BJP is one party whose politics wouldn't mind it being in that position. Why then is it adamant about opposing the deal? I guess they're taking their role as the Opposition party far too seriously.

It's my turn to speak. I'm trembling within even as I start. And no, I'm not as upbeat as I ought to be, because the thought of Sarah's marriage today is eating me on the inside:

'Respected Sir, I have heard my esteemed colleague Brajesh Ranjan with great amount of interest. Yet, in the end, I can't find his apprehensions over the specific clauses of 123 Agreement

*to be anything beyond another vain attempt to project his party
as the sole protector of national interests.*

'Sir, international affairs between countries today are guided
to a significant extent by well intended interpretations. It's like
deciding whether you want to see the glass half full or half empty.
There are, after all, no absolute-win situations anymore. And such
interpretations involve analysis in relative terms. I can, without
an iota of doubt, vouchsafe that this is the best deal that India
could have got in the prevailing circumstances.

'To begin with, I would like it to be noted that the preamble
to the agreement itself is significant for it accords the same status
to both parties and adds that their respective nuclear programs
will be respected. Furthermore, respect for national sovereignty is
reiterated, as also non-interference in internal matters. By virtue
of these alone, it may be safely inferred that the agreement does
not prevent us outright from carrying out nuclear tests.

'The assurances of fuel supply are contained in Sections
5.6, 2.2b and 5.4. They dispel the claim made by critics that
any amendment by the US Congress would by default prevent
the US from making these assurances. On reprocessing, the
fear that the US will tie us down has been dispelled by the
specific commitment that negotiations will begin within six
months of an Indian request, and they be completed within a
year thereafter.'

So far, so good. I'm aware that my last paragraph
does not allay the concerns expressed by Brajesh. I've
merely tweaked what he said and done so with a degree
of assertion that helps me sail through. To be frank, most
MPs have little knowledge of the nuances of the deal.
That helps those with a better understanding of it to get
away with some unintended glitches. I progress, thus,
from pitching facts to articulation:

'Sir, it is important to note here the attendant circumstances under which we have carried out our nuclear tests in the past. Nuclear tests are not a daily need. They ought to be undertaken only in extraordinary circumstances. And in the present global scenario, our scientists are fairly convinced that we do not need more tests, unless necessitated by unforeseen, extraordinary, extraneous developments. By "unforeseen, extraordinary, extraneous developments" I refer to any eventuality involving Pakistan or China. Under such emergent circumstances, it becomes the prerogative of the government to take all steps to protect our national interests. In those circumstances, we shall have the right to test, in as much as the world will have the right to react.

'Assuming that such a presumptuous situation does arise, we still have full confidence on the deft execution of our diplomatic initiatives and the wisdom of our political leadership. We will always strive to get the best for the country, in the same way as we have striven here.

'Without taking more time, sir, I would like to equate the debate over the Nuclear Deal with the debate in the pre-Independence period over the adoption of the English Language and Education. While those who opposed the language feared that it would corrupt our age-old educational brilliance, those who advocated its learning had realized its indispensability and saw it as an empowerment. In hindsight, we would agree that the latter approach was correct.

'This Nuclear Deal, sir, is our empowerment. It is our passport into the privileged league of powerful nations that we've wanted to be counted in, for decades. Let us not forget that since 1974 various governments of ours have striven to achieve this. Yet none could make it happen without us having to relinquish our nuclear weapons. This, however, marks our tryst with history. It enables us to engage in nuclear trade with the world, while *retaining our nuclear weapons. Isn't this historic? Isn't this a dream come true?*

'*Sir, the Nuclear Deal makes us enter a privileged league that is bound to bestow greater bargaining powers to us. This is an unprecedented opportunity to be grabbed and not squandered. It can lead us to the position of strength in world politics that we've always wanted to be in; at the same time, wasting this opportunity will take us back 33 years.*

'*Sir, I would end my speech with an apt quotation from Shakespeare's* Julius Caesar: *"There is a tide in the affairs of men. Which taken at the flood, leads on to fortune; Omitted, all the voyage of their life is bound in shallows and in miseries."*'

As I end my speech, most of the 110 odd members respond with boisterous applause. And just in case you're surprised by the number – 110 – don't be. That's how many members participate or attend serious debates. What I learn from my first speech is that while facts are important, it is equally important to lace your speech with nationalist sentiment. Indians like a good display of patriotism, even if it doesn't go beyond tokenism.

My speech by my own modest assessment has been impressive for a debut speech. Yet I feel a lump in my throat as I conclude. And no, I'm pretty sure it has no co-relation with what is happening in the confines of this august House. Instead, it has to do with what will take place tonight in another part of the world.

As the House disburses for lunch, I bump into Brajesh.

'Good work, dude. You spoke well,' he says.

'Unlike other Congressmen, who don't quite have the spunk?' I grin.

Brajesh just pats my shoulder and turns to leave. He looks subdued.

'Brajesh, tell me, personally do you really oppose the deal?'

He wants to say something, but holds himself back. He shrugs. 'We'll talk about this at length some other time. Right now I've got to rush. And yeah, congrats on a good debut speech.'

I'm not sure whether I should feel a triumph in his evasiveness. Politicians are after all not expected to be explicit.

◆

I'm at the India International Centre, speaking to a scribe. I'm elaborating on my speech in Parliament earlier in the day. My logic is sound, but my articulation isn't. My mind is with Sarah. The scribe asks me if all is well and I tell her it's fatigue. I complete the interview and decide to move out. Just then a dusky attractive woman walks up to me. She's got long hair, a bit curly at the edges, and a warm smile. She must be reasonably tall too – 5 feet 6. She seems to recognize me. I don't know her.

'Hi, I'm Chaitali…Chaitali Sen,' she says offering her hand.

'Oh. The columnist and CPI(M) member? Good to meet you,' say I.

'Same here…' she smiles. 'I followed your speech in Parliament today and must say you defended your government quite well. I was here for a meeting and just leaving when I spotted you. I thought I should say hello.'

'I'm sure you'd not have appreciated my speech. By your logic, I'd have become a "bone-seeking canine" today,' I said, quoting from her article.

She smiled. 'In politics we sometimes make acerbic remarks to drive home our point. But that shouldn't diminish our respect for a diverse perspective, if well espoused…I mean, I'm sure neither am I so opposed to the deal as to consider its supporters "bone seeking canines". Nor is the deal as friendly to India's concerns as your speech made it sound today.'

'Hmm… you're intelligent.'

'You bet I am. You tweaked the apprehensions expressed by Brajesh around to sound like they were incentives in our favour. That's something only an intelligent conman can do.'

Her pro-Brajesh stance leaves me bit surprised.

'You called me a conman? Why, is Brajesh your boyfriend?' I ask her out of the blue.

My query apparently upsets her.

'Nah…'

I am done with my share of the talking over the Nuclear Deal for the day and feel quite drained. I'm most certainly in no mood to talk about it anymore. I have been thinking of going for a drink to a fabulous place that I happened to discover only last week. Don't know why, but I find myself proposing to Chaitali that she join me. She surprises me by accepting with alacrity. I'm surprised by the fact that she doesn't once ask me where we're headed.

We're at Aqua at The Park, New Delhi – it offers the best al fresco escape from the clutter of the capital's politics. It's 8pm and the temperature must be 4 degrees but I don't mind it in the least. A landscaped garden terrace opens directly from the 24-hour restaurant. It has been designed as a cool, classical white outdoor space with an iridescent blue pool. A raised seating area cantilevers over the pool and from below this a cascade of water plunges into the pool.

We occupy a space adjacent to the pool. The smell and feel of water accords me the sense of equanimity that I've thirsted for all day. I order an Italian wine for both of us. I sense Chaitali's surprise. She doesn't voice her reactions, though. All she does is wear a bemused smile, which I must confess is damn attractive.

'So what makes you do what you're doing?' she finally queries when both of us have taken our first couple of sips.

I look at my watch. 'Isn't it obvious? I'm either celebrating or mourning.'

'Well, there's a world of difference between the two. What is it – celebration or mourning?'

'I'm doing both – celebrating *and* mourning.'

'Celebrating your speech in Parliament and mourning that your father is not alive to have witnessed it?'

I've gulped down the first glass as though it were fruit juice. It gives me the confidence to blurt my heart out. 'Have you ever felt a sinking sort of feeling... the sort that you feel when you know you're losing someone you dearly loved?'

'Yes, twice.'

'Hmm... well, then you'd understand my state of mind.'

She pauses; my words seem to have re-kindled some old hurt of her own. 'In fact, I've still not overcome the sense of loss I felt the second time it happened...'

'Really? Then we have a lot in common.' The desperation in my voice draws a stare from her. I look at my watch again. I'm overwhelmed with sadness. 'This very moment, the girl I love is getting married to someone else. I'm sad we could not be together. In fact, till a week ago, I kept thinking I would go back and tell her I'll marry her. She'd have consented.'

'So why didn't you?'

'I loved her. But I realized I was not *in* love with her.'

Chaitali listens to me intently as though she relates with all that I say. 'Well, there's a decisive difference between the two,' she assures me.

'Somewhere I realized I loved her more out of my sympathy for her. I realized that it would not be fair to her later on.'

A chilly breeze blows across the place. Silence descends between us. It's like my words have transported Chaitali into a similar memory of her own. She's a caring soul.

'Hey, you should have got a muffler. You need to cover your ears.'

Ahem. She cares for me too. God bless her.

'It's okay. For someone who's lived through the American winter, this temperature is nothing.'

I can sense something going on in her mind. 'You know what, a lot of times you realize how much you love the person after you lose the person,' she says.

'That's what happened with you?'

'Yes.'

'And why does that happen?'

'Mostly it's because of your baggage which sometimes de-sensitizes you without your realizing it. You tend to be in denial, you don't realize the worth of what you have. You're kind of emotionally absent.'

'You talk so much sense.'

Our conversation is interspersed with reasonably long stretches of silence, brought about by rumination. I think this evening is providential. I'd never have imagined I'd be talking to a Communist and a fierce opponent of the Nuclear Deal in a milieu as apolitical as this, and that I'd be discussing matters of the heart.

I'm half way through my second glass of wine. She's just completed her first. The inebriation level is just about right to propel the interaction further. 'Did you ever get a chance to go back to your lost love?' I query.

She laughs.

'In one instance it was not possible. It would... well... it would just require a lot. Just forget it...'

I can sense her struggling to find the right words. 'A lot? As in?' I probe.

'He'd have had to change his gender preference.'

'What?'

'Yeah... he was a homosexual.'

I choke on my drink. To think that this gorgeous lady had fallen for a gay man. 'Why, couldn't you find a straight guy?'

'Stupid, if I knew he was gay why would I have been in the relationship?'

'I see.'

'And the second guy... Well, I realized how much I loved him only after he was gone from my life.'

'Well, then go and tell him now...'

'You think it's that easy?'

'Is it that difficult?'

'To be honest, I did that just before I met you...' she tells me.

'What?'

'Reiterated to him how much I loved him... pleaded with him to get back with me.'

'And?'

'Well it's only when both partners haven't moved on that it makes sense to talk to an ex.'

I get up and walk right to the edge of the pool. In the state that I'm in, Chaitali perhaps fears that I might fall, or maybe jump in. She walks behind me, worried.

I kneel by the poolside, dip my hands in and splash my face with water. It takes the life out of me – it's that cold.

'Are you crazy?' she almost shouts at me

I laugh looking at her.

'It feels damn good. Try it...' I hold her hand, surprising her even more.

'I'm feeling a lot better in these last couple of hours, a lot lighter. Thanks for the company.'

I sense she likes the press of my hand gently holding hers. It comforts me as well. I can see her big deep eyes grow bigger and deeper as we hold hands. Bong girls by the way, I realize, have the best eyes. They're just so alluring; their attractiveness grows in moments like the one I'm in, right now.

'Have you ever fallen in love on the rebound?' she asks me.

'Nah... Don't think it's a good idea.'

Another half hour goes by. The staff has set up a bonfire a few feet away from the pool. It feels a lot better now. Not sure whether it's the company or the warmth generated by the fire, or both. I can sense a certain chemistry with the lady. Moroccan lamb cutlets and prawn kebabs are now brought to the table. Rum has replaced wine as we're both convinced about the beverage's superior capabilities to help battle the cold.

A thought suddenly strikes me: 'Hey, I'm sorry I forgot this altogether... is it okay for us to be seen in public like this?'

She looks around. 'Well, I can't see the crew of India TV lurking anywhere. Of the two couples here, one seems American, the other is just too absorbed in each other to bother with us.'

I relax again and the conversation veers to something that has been brewing in my mind.

'Tell me, Chaitali, how often is it that you fall in love because you really love the person? And how often is it that you do so because you had prepared yourself to fall in love and the other person just happened to be the first viable contender to come into your life at that point?'

My query has her thinking. 'Hmm... I agree... For a very long time after I first broke off, I shut myself to everybody, and when I decided to fall in love again, I went for it whole hog.'

I hold her hand again. I guess it is to communicate to her that the sense of loss that I was feeling has been salvaged considerably. I look at my watch. Sarah's wedding ceremony must be over. I have lost someone I loved, but in Chaitali I think I've acquired a friend for keeps.

By the time, I drop her to her home on Shahjahan Road and return to mine on Mother Teresa Crescent, it is a half past twelve. It's been a long day and I'm terribly exhausted. Just as I'm about to hit the sack, I get a message on my cell. It reads: *Thanks for the lovely evening... feeling a lot more positive after talking to you. Take care and sleep tight. Goodnight.*

Care for another evening like the one we shared today? I sms back.

Pat comes her reply: *Day after evening?*

◆

Over the next month Chaitali and I meet twice and sometimes thrice a week. The venues are diverse, but there's one thing they have in common – they're well away from the reaches of Lutyens' Delhi and hence reasonably safe from the prying eyes of politicos and the media. Mostly though, we meet in the lawns of my house, where I arrange for a bonfire on the evenings when Chaitali comes.

I get acquainted with her espousal of the 'queer' cause. I think that's a brilliant initiative. I mean, it takes a lot for someone who is straight to tread the extra mile and stand up for queers. On one occasion, she wants me to come with her for a seminar on gay rights. I acquiesce initially, only to develop cold feet later and bow out. I guess I want to be politically correct. And conventional Indian political thinking demands that such 'lesser issues' be ignored. Chaitali, that way, is gutsy enough not to be bothered about her party's stand on the issue. I admire her for this.

When Chaitali returns from the seminar, we enjoy some interesting banter. She tells me that each one of us has a latent ability to be attracted towards the same sex and that in one out of every five beings such proclivities are more pronounced – the ones we regard as 'queer'. I scoff at her statistics. Nonetheless, I wonder that if it were true, then it is amazing that none of our political parties has ever tried to reach out to this crucial pie. For a moment I think I should speak to my party bosses of this important vote share. By the next morning however I'm sure such topics won't be considered serious enough in the Indian scenario.

I used to be quite passionate at one point about playing the guitar. That's something I'd do almost regularly till three years ago. Now that I tend to have a little more time in the evenings, and the paradigm shift in my life makes me feel forlorn, I want to get back to it. To my surprise, Chaitali is quite good at humming songs – both English and old Hindi ones. We spend some good evenings together where I play the guitar and she sings. My staff probably finds our chemistry strange and funny. I don't really care. Chaitali's presence fills the vacuum that I'd have otherwise grappled with had I been spending the evenings alone in my study or meeting vacuous people. Yadav, for his part assures me that my unusual bonding with Chaitali will be kept under wraps.

The growth of friendship into courtship and love – if at all it takes place in that manner – has always fascinated me. I'm wondering how I would define my relationship with Chaitali at this point. I'm sure such thoughts would occasionally cross her mind too. And yet, I guess we both realize it's best to sometimes avoid the analysis and experience the togetherness.

I'm sure there's an intense mutual dependence that we have on each other. We enjoy each other's company, either by choice or for want of an option. We're both loners. And two loners coming together, makes each more sociable towards the other. Come to think of it, the arrangement couldn't have been better in the circumstances. And yet the underlying questions that hover over the relationship's future cannot be wished away.

For instance, how long can we continue to meet in this covert fashion? Agreed, we are just friends, but can we arrive, say at the Republic Day parade together and expect that all will be calm and normal in our party circles? On second thoughts I feel maybe I'm more emotional than the lady or just that I'm more attracted to her.

People who think a lot and who are in the sort of relationship that Chaitali and I share, sooner than later, feel the need to attempt defining the bond. According it a definition becomes important on account of another reason: the private space that we give ourselves, away from the intrusion of the world, is bound to lead to underlying sentiments of possessiveness. And these sentiments can, at times, manifest suddenly, out of the blue.

One evening we were in the middle of yet another stimulating discussion. As always, Chaitali had come up with an absorbing topic. She told me that that the chain of unsuspecting events that leads to two unknown people to meet and to be drawn into meeting again has an interesting term to it: synchronicity. Synchronicity, she told me, is the experience of two or more events that are causally unrelated occurring together in a meaningful manner. In order to count as synchronicity, the events should be unlikely to occur together by chance.

I mull over what she said. If I had met Chaitali on any another day or in any other place, would I have opened up to her the way I did? Yes, I agreed this thing called synchronicity did have a defining role in bringing us close.

In the middle of our conversation, Chaitali got a call. I gathered it was from a close friend. She excused herself and ended up talking for a good twenty minutes, before she returned.

'I'm so sorry...that was Sid. He's in India for something very important and we just needed to talk...'

Our bond is not in any sense evolved enough for me to feel possessive or even envious; Sid in any case, I know, is gay; and Chaitali in this modern age is within her rights to keep in touch with an ex; yet all these things notwithstanding, I can't help feeling a little disconcerted by this untimely disturbance. This unwarranted possessiveness I feel is reason enough for me to deduce that Chaitali indeed means a lot to me.

I've been meaning to have a discussion with Chaitali. I'm not sure whether she's fast filling up the space that Sarah has left vacant. I mean, my relationship with Sarah had begun on a similar note of restraint and guardedness. The intensity of it dawned on me only when she was no more a part of my life.

Is my life now treading a similar path, with a new partner?

I wonder why cynicism has become such a common phenomenon in our lives today and in all our relationships. Why can we no longer be suckers for that ultimate romance, immortalized in the cinema of yesteryears? As I dig deeper, I realize that it is unassailability that makes love all the more intense.

I don't know whether this again can be termed synchronicity but destiny sometimes shows you the way out of complex situations like these.

My way out is an official trip to the US. As part of a five-member group of Parliamentarians led by senior MP Ghulam Mohammad, we are to participate in a UN summit on the Control of Organized International Crime in Washington. Around the same time that I am to be out of the country, Chaitali has planned a trip to the interiors of Karnataka where a group of 10,000 eunuchs are meeting for an annual festival of theirs. She wants to go there for academic purposes. I feel protective of her and want to tell her not to go. But I decide to stay quiet – she's not my girlfriend, after all.

◆

In the wee hours of the night, Chaitali drives me to the IGI airport. An unanticipated technical snag results in a couple of hours' delay. We decide to kill time in the coffee shop at the Centaur. Over a cappuccino, which is unusually strong, I begin to feel queasy. There is something about this US trip that gives me the jitters.

I guess it's my state of mind – the turbulent last evening that I had spent in the US seems to have eclipsed my brighter memories of the land.

'Chaitali, You know something…?' I start.

Chaitali looks at me.

I take an unusually long pause.

'What?' she says. 'Tell me…'

'Forget it.'

'Oh, come on, why are you suddenly acting like a shy bride?'

'You know… I was just thinking…' I pause again.

'Thinking what?'

'That, we'd be good as a couple.'

My words are met with a hoot of laughter. It puts me in a spot of embarrassment, as I quickly attempt damage control.

'Chill, Chaitz, I was just sharing a passing thought.'

I've always thought Chaitali is more perceptive than other women I've met. What she tells me, while still trying to control her laughter, only corroborates this.

'No, you weren't, darling,' she says and adds, 'Beware of the perils of a rebound attraction, Mr Aditya Samar Singh. That's not the best thing to get into.'

◆

Ghulam Mohammad Khan is a 68-year-old senior politician who has represented the Ramnagar constituency in UP for a record seven terms since 1984. In the first three terms he was elected on a Congress ticket. Subsequently, after the Babri Masjid demolition in December 1992, he quit the party. As such, he had to relinquish his LS seat as well. He fought the same seat independently after that and has continued to represent the LS seat as an Independent since. I find his achievement damn impressive. I mean, to win as an Independent candidate in the Indian system, five consecutive times, requires sterling credentials.

There are many factors that make Ghulamsaab an object of envy in political circles. A descendent of the nawabs of Lucknow, Ghulamsaab is a highly qualified person – schooling from Lucknow's La Martiniere, college from the Aligarh Muslim University, after which he went to Harvard to acquire a degree in law. He returned to become a lawyer in the Supreme Court before he quit that to take his father's legacy forward. His father and before that his grandfather, were senior Congress leaders.

Even after quitting the Congress, Ghulamsaab has enjoyed a lot of respect in the party. Or else he would not have been leading this delegation. Ghulamsaab, too, is said to still have a soft corner for the Congress. However when quizzed about this, his response is a heartily dismissive laugh.

We start an interesting conversation on the flight. I am particularly impressed by some of Ghulamsaab's views, which are radical to say the least. He is of the opinion that the International Court of Justice (ICJ) should be increasingly involved with countries that are victims of terrorism abetted by their neighbours, in order to seek financial compensation from the perpetrator countries. This becomes more pertinent in cases where there is evidence of countries employing terrorism as an instrument of state policy.

'Physical aggression only leads to the loss of innocent lives; financial punishment, on the other hand, breaks the backbone of the country. No country can allow its financial structure to collapse,' he says, his words laden with conviction.

I mull over what Ghulamsaab says. 'Ghulamsaab, the idea is brilliant, except for one hindrance. I'm sure India's rise in the global arena intimidates a lot of countries. Are you sure that if we move the International Court of Justice against Pakistan, the important world powers will refrain from linking Pakistan abetted terrorism to the *root cause* as they call it – the settlement of the Kashmir problem? And when that happens, we'll hopelessly continue to move around in circles…'

'Exactly. That's the biggest impediment to the problem – the dual role played by the world, especially the US, in tacitly allowing Pakistan to get away with all it does.'

'Hmm… well, but territorial disputes are endemic to so many countries. That does not mean that all of them resort to waging proxy war. I think an ideal situation will be where we isolate terrorism entirely from its blamed stimuli. I mean, a consensus should be forged among leading countries that while terror attacks are settled by the ICJ, the territorial disputes, in so far as possible, should be settled by mutual dialogue.'

Ghulamsaab's response is another hearty laugh. 'That is quite a wishful scenario, keeping in mind the selfish stakes that the powerful nations of the world would have in the nations locked in dispute. Or else, this is precisely the position that India would want the world to adopt.'

'And what would these selfish stakes be?'

'They're varied in nature. For instance, what if an important world power is the chief supplier of defense equipment to one of the countries locked in dispute? The world power would find it difficult to take a tough stand against its client. And that is how they complicate issues by going back to the "root cause".'

'Hmm…'

'On the other hand, the Indian government's compulsions have, in the past, forced it to act selfishly as well.'

'Like, where?'

'Well, post 9/11, India had the option of joining the US war against the Al Qaeda. But then the fear of a domestic backlash always puts us in a defensive position.'

'Would you have supported that?' I ask, surprised.

'Why not? Right now, we're nowhere – we aren't really involved in the war against Al Qaeda; yet, at the same time, India is on their hit-list. I think a tough zero-tolerance approach towards terrorism is the only solution.'

Ever since I took oath as an MP, I've been virtually given to believe that any move against a Muslim country will offend the Muslims within our country. I find Ghulamsaab's reasoning damn objective.

'I don't think any sensible, patriotic Muslim in this country would have a problem if the US decides to finish off the Al Qaeda. Our issue was with their mindless misadventure in Iraq.'

I can't help feeling that Ghulamsaab is different from any politician that I've met in these last three months. I remember Dad had always spoken very highly of him. But listening to him now, I know why he would have found it difficult belonging to a mainstream political party.

He is the honest and outspoken Indian Muslim that a political party would be wary of. He dares to speak the truth like few can. 'Ghulamsaab, I just feel you should join the Congress again. As an Independent your voice has a limited reach. I think Indian Muslims need a leader like you.'

Ghulamsaab takes a deep breath. 'When I was in Congress, my voice was subdued. I could not speak this clearly. And you want me to go back there?' He laughs.

There is something about his laughter that gives me the impression that it's covering up many unpleasant experiences. I think it induces me to have a more prolonged interaction with him.

Another interesting vision he has is that all member countries of the UN should have a mandatory extradition clause between them, which actually implies doing away with the necessity of having bilateral extradition arrangements. I feel that again is a wonderful idea. I want to talk more, but have to end this interaction here. Ghulamsaab has to join another member of our team, seated in another row for a discussion.

As he stands up to change seats he says something very interesting. 'You know, we have some brilliant leaders in our generation but they couldn't achieve much for the nation because they couldn't rise above their own selfishness.'

He adds, a tad more thoughtfully, 'Your generation is slightly more sensible and enterprising. But there needs to be a way by which the best young leaders from across parties speak in one voice on issues of national importance. That is where you need to work more closely with the younger leaders of the BJP like Brajesh Ranjan, and he with you. The same applies to leaders of different countries as well.'

◆

It has been five days since I landed in the US. The convention is over. Thoughts have been exchanged, ideas mooted but I am left mulling over what Ghulamsaab called the *'complex selfish stakes that powerful nations of the world would have in the nations locked in dispute'*. I am left to wonder if these conventions would serve their purpose till all the powerful nations were rid of their complex selfish stakes. But if they did they wouldn't be super-powers. I'm left wondering if the last few months have already imbued a certain cynicism towards the US in me. I wonder why dealing with the US requires exemplary astuteness – on the face of it we have to make all the right noises about friendship, while inside we are insecure and watchful.

This transition of mine from being uninhibitedly pro-US just six months ago, to having a more realistic, neutral disposition now, underlines the rapid evolution that is underway in my worldview. Why then am I stuck in one position on the personal front? Was it because of the abruptness with which the relationship ended? Given that I respect propriety, is it that I want to meet Sarah once and give it proper closure?

The truth is, I'm in no hurry to return home. While the official delegation flies back to New Delhi from Washington, I take a day off and go down to New York. I catch up with Khalid and Kelly. We have lunch at 'Ahluwalia's' an Indian restaurant just two streets away from my Kingston office. We chat about a whole lot of things – Kingston, my new life, the developments in Khalid's and Kelly's lives. Then Khalid broaches the subject I have been trying to avoid: 'Yaar, Sarah and you should have made it work.'

I don't have an answer. Instead I pop a query: 'Have any of you spoken to her lately? Are you in touch?'

Both shake their heads. 'We were just too surprised by her sudden decision. There wasn't any motivation to go to her wedding. So we ignored the invitation. I did call her, though, a couple of days after her wedding, and congratulated her.'

Pause.

'Would she be happy? I mean, did she sound happy when you called?' I sound absolutely naïve.

'Are you?' Kelly asks me.

No, I'm not.

'Do you still love her?' she prods me further.

'I still miss her.'

In a place like Manhattan, when you are engaged in work around the clock, you crib about not finding time for yourself. But then, when you find yourself absolutely free, as I am now, the place actually feels hostile and unbearable. Kelly and Khalid have gone back to work after lunch. I have a few free hours at my disposal. I don't feel free, though. I'm constantly haunted by thoughts that don't easily leave me.

I dial a number that I haven't dialled in a long time. The phone is perhaps disconnected. I call the number a dozen times. In the next two hours I land up in Central Albany's Delmar area – a few lanes off Park Street. I've been to the place just once – when Sarah brought me here to introduce me to her parents. Yet I remember the by-lanes vividly. The last 50 metres, though, is an arduous journey for me, every step heavy with doubt and a question mark over my motivations for treading forward or rather backward in my life. I move up to Sarah's door. It's getting dark.

I ring the bell. There's no answer. I ring it again. Still no answer. I wonder if anyone still lives there. Maybe, as Sarah had mentioned, her parents have moved to Canada. Sarah must have moved elsewhere with her husband. I ring the bell one final time and just as I'm retracing my steps, the door opens. 'Sorry I was in the ba...' Sarah stops mid-way, confounded by the realization of who her visitor is.

I feel a whole gamut of emotions when I see Sarah – relief, nostalgia as also the fear of more hurt being in store. She's lost a lot of weight.

'Adi… What a surprise!'

Our eyes are moist as we hug each other hard. She leads me in. From inside I hear the voice of a man talking on the phone – loud enough to be heard outside.

'My husband…' she explains. 'He's talking to an old friend.'

I feel sheepish to have landed up like this. I try to accord an excuse to my visit by telling her that I was in US for some work and would have been happy just talking to her on the phone; but as her phone was not reachable, my concern brought me here.

'Ah, I see… so you still care about me…' she smiles.

'You don't?' I ask her diffidently.

From inside I hear loud laughter. Her husband it seems is deep in animated conversation with a bosom buddy. She gently shuts the door on him. This also accords some privacy to our conversation. I notice that Sarah has dark circles under her eyes. I quiz her about them and she tells me that it's natural for a newly married couple who are very much in love to be sleep deprived. I can sense a certain bitterness in her, as also a veiled attempt to hurt me. I don't blame her. I don't blame myself. But I do realize the futility of landing up here. I realize how bad a judge of people and situations I am. Sarah was probably never as fragile as I thought her to be. Or maybe I sympathized with her more than I should have. In the end, she's found solace, I've got chaos.

I am not in the mood to stay any longer. Nonetheless, Sarah pesters me to have a look at her wedding pictures.

She takes out a large album and shows me her man. What I see baffles me – the man is much older than her. Sensing my surprise, she tells me how it all happened – how Francis, born of a Mexican mother settled in America and a Kenyan father, was actually brought up in Malaysia; work later brought him to the US where a quick growth in his career made him stay back.

'And what does your husband do?'

'Oh he runs a small travel agency of his own. So in case you're looking to book your flight tickets for home, he can do that at a discounted rate.'

'Thanks, I've got my tickets.' I laugh off her offer.

I take note of the fact that Sarah has not bothered to update herself about the changes in my life – an aloofness that has remained consistent from the time I first met her. I want to leave. I am almost relieved I don't have a place in her life anymore. Yet I'd be lying if I say I'm not feeling a deep hurt. Her swift leap from me to Francis makes me curious enough to ask her:

'But how did this happen, all of a sudden?'

'Oh Adi, certain things are just destined… Two weeks after you left, Francis met me at the local bus-stop. He told me he crossed the place everyday and would invariably spot me there. He told me I had a grace he hadn't seen in other women and that he could tell I was always lost in my thoughts and upset about something. He told me he'd fallen in love with me. I found it crazy and told him he was a flirt. Two days later when I returned home, I was shocked to see him talking to my Dad. I heard him tell Dad that he had fallen in love with me when he first saw me and that he'd do everything to keep me happy.'

'And you gave in?' I asked, surprised.

'Was there a reason for me not to? You wanted to wait till eternity, right? Or till you found a saner girlfriend?'

I was in no mood to contradict Sarah. Her actions had once again proven she was crazy.

'How old is Francis?' I ask her.

'Fifteen years older than me. That's the age gap between us, if you're curious to know.'

'Sarah, you could have spoken to me just once before getting married.'

'Would that have altered your decision?'

Our conversation is interrupted by the arrival of her husband. He is loud, garish and unsophisticated. From the physicality of their body language, though, Sarah and Francis indeed seem to be in love.

Sarah introduces me as her good friend from India. Francis doesn't bother to ask anything more about me. He is warm. His 'warm' hand-shake, though, carries savage intensity. Then he turns to Sarah and reminds her that they have plans to go out. Sarah tells him she'll just freshen up with perfume. He tells her to forget it, her body odour is attractive enough and plants a lingering kiss on her lips. I feel terribly out of place, more so with what Sarah tells me, beaming at her spouse: 'You know, Adi... I couldn't have asked God for anything more. In just the last two months Francis has filled my life with all the joy that I was deprived of – all my life.'

Francis gets inspired enough by this declaration to kiss her more brazenly. She protests but gives in. I witness a sight I'd have never imagined to see: a girl whom I've kissed and loved, whose faith in love and relationships I helped revive, kissing a stranger while I stand passively by. I want to shut my eyes, run away or just blind myself, but I have to be brave. I'm glad this moment marks my freedom from guilt and concern about Sarah.

On the flight back, I yearn to be with Chaitali and speak to her.

I want to cry my heart out to her.

I want to tell her how much I miss her.

◆

I arrive at IGI in the wee hours of the morning. Chaitali is waiting for me. We drive to the same coffee shop that we had gone to eight days ago, before I flew out. We occupy a table by the window. As another dawn casts an attractive combination of light and shadow on Chaitali's face, a silence descends on us.

They say absence makes the heart grow fonder. After meeting each other almost every second day, we're meeting after a gap of eight days this time. There's so much to talk about, yet the flow of conversation is stilted.

'So you think we can really get into a relationship?' Chaitali asks abruptly, stumping me with her query.

I chuckle at the course matters of the heart take. We're both extremely fond of each other, we both like spending time and talking to each other. Yet scepticism demands that we probe our attraction for each other.

'Are you sure our bond is not a need but what we really want?' I ask her, playing the Devil's Advocate.

Neither of us has an unambiguous answer. As we drive out together, I feel more confident of solving this conundrum soon.

◆

I arrive at Ghulamsaab's house on Kushak Road at around a quarter to nine. I'm greeted warmly by him and his wife, Noorjahan. His 'begum' as he calls her, looks incredibly gorgeous, even in her sixties. To my surprise I find another, rather unexpected, guest – Brajesh Ranjan.

Ghulamsaab informs me that Brajesh and he form a sort of mutual admiration society. Brajesh would often tell him – 'Ghulamsaab Indian Muslims need representatives like you'; while Ghulamsaab would often tell Brajesh – 'Promising young leaders like you should not be in the BJP.' I'm surprised when Ghulamsaab tells me that one night Brajesh had nearly convinced him to join the BJP! Sensing my surprise Ghulamsaab laughs and clarifies, 'I was a little drunk that night. Brajesh had probably tampered with my drink.'

Within minutes, over an exotic South African wine, we end up discussing what has become the flavour of the season for politicos. Ghulamsaab tells us why he feels Muslims are the biggest victims of jihad.

'What a tiny fraction of the community does, leads to the whole of it getting typecast. This typecasting then leads to a sense of victimization and subsequent retaliation among those who are not at fault. And in certain cases, the perpetrators actually end up winning sympathy. It's a vicious circle, you see,' he avers.

'Hmm…'

'It's really heart-wrenching to see how educated people are coming into the trap of jihadis,' says he and takes out a couple of printed sheets from a file. 'Here, I've got a copy of Iqbal's statement which the Anti Terrorism Squad (ATS) will be releasing to the press tomorrow. Read it.'

Ghulamsaab gives us a copy each. I get the impression that Brajesh knows the guy. What I read is a heart-wrenching, first-person account:

The Denouement of a Muslim Terrorist

I am Sajid Faisal, an Indian Muslim. I was born in 1980 in a liberal Muslim family based in Bangalore. My father worked as a physician in a private hospital and my mother worked as a schoolteacher. We are two brothers and a sister. We were brought up in a reasonably liberal manner – while we celebrated and observed all Muslim festivals with fervour, we were taught to respect other religions equally. One of my best friends, Gopal, would invariably fall sick during our Idd parties. And on his birthday he'd forget to invite me. It was not too long before I realized the reason for this avoidance – his parents did not like him mingling much with a Muslim's kid.

The late eighties and early nineties were a particularly turbulent phase in the country. The issue responsible for all the communal tension was the Ayodhya land dispute, which Hindu groups claimed was the birthplace of Lord Ram. A mosque existed on that land and the fight was to reclaim this land and have a temple re-constructed there. This issue held the law and order situation of this country hostage for several years. In October 1989, one of worst communal riots took place in Bhagalpur, in which more than 1000 people, a majority of them Muslim, were killed. 116 people were brutally murdered in just one place – their bodies were buried in a field, in complete defiance of the curfew. That happened before the advent of satellite TV and hence we don't remember it as strongly as we do the Gujarat riots. I was nine then. I remember my parents would be extremely disturbed in those days and discuss a lot of things privately. On one occasion, when I managed to overhear them, I realized it was about the fear and insecurity that the riots had caused in the Mulsims.

Yet my parents never let any bitterness develop in me or my siblings. In the 1992 World Cup final between Pakistan and England, when I rooted for Imran and his men, I overheard one of my friends, Shikha, say, 'Obviously, he'll support that team... he is a Muslim.' I wondered why I had to be made aware of my Muslim identity so often. I cheered for Imran and Inzamam more vociferously after hearing Shikha's comment.

And then Dec 6, 1992 happened – a day that shamed history and which will never go away from the memory of any Muslim. The collapse of the edifice of Babri Masjid carried a symbolic message – that Hindus in this country had managed to fell Muslims conclusively. Just the next day, in an India–South Africa one day match, Azharuddin, regarded among the best fielders of his time, dropped two simple catches. I'm sure he must have been distracted by the morbid images of the collapse of the Babri Mosque.

Bolstered by the demolition, Hindu groups wreaked havoc among Muslims in Mumbai. Brazen, uncontrolled arson and rioting resulted in the killing of scores of innocent Muslims. What was particularly disturbing was the partisan role played by institutions, such as the police force. The infamous Suleman bakery episode where nine people were killed in police firing and some 78 arrested only manifests this. The foul play of the police is evident in that they came up with several contradictory versions of what really happened. Worse, an eighteen year old distant relative of one of my college friends, Salim, was picked by the police from his residence in the Chunabhatti area right in front of his parents and taken for questioning. For the next five years, he languished behind bars as he was framed under the demonic Terrorist and Disruptive Activities Prevention Act, TADA. Post the 1993 blasts there were several other cases of TADA being cited even on petty criminals and in some cases, on people who had nothing to do with anything other than their work and family.

There was no way these unsavoury incidents would not have led to a feeling of persecution. I remember some of my more vociferous relatives saying, 'We should have migrated to Pakistan at the time of Partition. It's a crime to be a Muslim in this country anymore.' But thanks to my broadminded parents, I was taught to respect the law of the land.

In college, I was in a relationship with a girl called Tamanna. She belonged to the lowly Chambhar community among Hindus. Last I heard of her, three years ago, was that she had to break off with her Brahmin boyfriend of two years because the guy's parents were not prepared to have a low-caste bahu. But in our courtship days, she could never once mention me to her parents – she knew they would outright reject a Muslim.

I moved on in life because that's what the brave are expected to do. After becoming a software engineer, I took up a job in Bangalore. And that's when the Gujarat riots happened. I don't need to even reiterate how barbaric they were. But worse, the government had a weapon called POTA. They again detained scores of innocents for years – their only fault being they were Indian Muslims.

For once Gujarat changed my thinking. I was no longer prepared to put up with the pittance that Muslims were getting in this country. I could no longer live the merciless existence that the Hindus and the government had left us with.

It made me think and research a lot about the state of my community. And my findings were disturbing. The percentage representation of Muslims in any government job of consequence fell abysmally short of their percentage of the total Indian population. Worse, in many cases even nationalized banks tended to show a bias against them, as compared to other minorities, especially when disbursing loans. Muslim-majority villages were deliberately deprived of infrastructure and decent approach roads. The level of literacy among Muslims was abysmally low.

Worse, my own younger sister who works as an assistant director in films in Mumbai had to struggle for a month to find accommodation, as most decent residential societies were wary of renting out their flats to a Muslim.

I had begun to sense a change in the way I felt about things. For instance, the spate of bomb blasts that the country had seen lately did not trigger in me the same condemnation that it would have, say ten years ago. And when it became clearer that some of these culprits were ordinary Indian Muslims – some students, some professionals – who had been compelled to become terrorists, I felt a strange empathy with them. Mom and Dad still ridiculed these terror antics and for once I got into an argument with them. My point was what they did was wrong; but what was it that pushed ordinary people from ordinary families to this level? After all, they were our brothers.

That was when I met Rashid Multani at a mosque in Bangalore. Rashid was a rich businessman from Mangalore and must have been in his late thirties or early forties. He ran a fleet of some 30 inter-city buses. This ensured he did not have to do anything more in his life to be financially secure. One day after namaz, he broached a conversation with me. The conversation focused on the torture that Muslims were being subjected to in Mumbai after the 2006 train blasts. We soon got down to talking about how Muslims were suffering everywhere.

And soon enough I learnt that Rashid ran a terrorist organization – Lashkar-e-Hindustan. He had accomplices and sleeper cells spread across 16 cities and 12 states of the country. The whole idea was to lead up to a stage where all of these units would prepare for simultaneous assault. A special team had been entrusted to thrash out the ways in which one of our members could be slipped into the security set up of Modi and assassinate him. At first it just shocked me. I was then given a CD to watch. The CD carried first-hand accounts of persecution of some 100 Muslims from across the country. It moved me. Over three meetings, Rashid convinced me that pleas and appeals don't work in this country, might and aggression did. With our incessant attacks, the government would be left with no option but to give Muslims their due.

I thus joined the movement. Immediately, I was sent off for an intensive, month-long indoctrination and training in the dense forests near Mangalore. After that, I attended two 2-day camps – the first near Aligarh and a second near Munnar in Kerala. The purpose of these was to interact with our accomplices from other parts of the country. We were all accorded different names before our mission began. Thus I became Wasim Iqbal. Similarly I wouldn't know the real names of all those whom I met. But there must have been 25-30 of them in either place. Neither did any one of us know the role that we'd be subsequently asked to play – that was entirely Rashid's prerogative. The objective of these meets was to motivate us by making us share our individual angst, and pool it, to accumulate it into a redoubtable whole.

After I returned to Bangalore, Rashid seemed particularly impressed with me. He was aware of the fact that I was a fitness freak. One day, he asked me to prepare for a special mission – to assassinate three BJP leaders in Delhi...'

◆

No sooner have we read the statement that Brajesh lashed out: 'This is all crap, Ghulamsaab. If an illiterate spoke in that manner I could understand. If we go by this logic, every Hindu should become a terrorist. After all, for centuries, we have been invaded, plundered, our temples destroyed, our women raped…'

I look at Ghulamsaab's grim expression. He looks terribly upset. 'What has happened for centuries can't be undone. But yes, after Partition we had a golden opportunity to make a fresh start.' Ghulamsaab sighs, 'But we messed that up too.'

'I guess we ought to have been stricter and banned all communal forces,' I say.

'The problem is much deeper, son,' he says with regret. 'After we achieved Independence, Nehru wrote a letter to the chief ministers of all provinces wherein he pointed out that *'despite the creation of Pakistan as a Muslim homeland, there remained, within India, a Muslim minority who are so large in number that they cannot, even if they want, go anywhere else. That is a basic fact about which there can be no argument. Whatever the provocation from Pakistan and whatever the indignities and horrors inflicted on non-Muslims here, we have got to deal with this minority in a civilized manner. We must give them security and the rights of citizens in a democratic state.'*

Ghulamsaab went on, 'Nehru never liked his party associating with any sectarian force – either Hindu or Muslim. Nehru was sagacious and had the long-term interests of the country in mind. His daughter, unfortunately, thought otherwise. It was under Indira Gandhi that the patronization of retrograde, reactionary sections of the community began. She brought in the fatwa culture wherein clergies were asked to issue fatwas to their followers to vote for the party. In return, grants to madrasas and other religious institutions were increased. The result – the liberal, progressive Muslims started to be ignored and isolated and real development of the community was stalled.'

We hear Ghulamsaab in rapt attention. One of his attendants lays out the biryani and korma that his begum has prepared. Begum Noorjahan is at her hospitable best. Ghulamsaab goes on.

'I would hold the attitude of the Congress party responsible for much of the plight of the Muslim community. Their unwise pampering of the Muslim community made a ready breeding ground for the BJP. And the less said about the BJP's opportunism, the better.'

By the time we have the biryani, I am full – not just with the richness of the food but also with the thought-provoking fare that Ghulamsaab has spoken about. What he said doesn't make me feel proud about my party; it doesn't, I'm sure, make Brajesh feel any better about his. I arrive at the inference that if accountability for the present state of anarchy has to be fixed, a myriad sources will have to bear the brunt of what is a collective national failure.

◆

After dinner Brajesh and I decide to go on a drive – our informal interaction at Ghulamsaab's place has given us the comfort level for some dude bonding. We get into my Honda Civic. I am at the wheel. Our security detail accompanies us in Brajesh's car. After doing a few unplanned rounds of Lutyen's Delhi, we land up near India Gate and decide to have ice-cream from a street vendor. Two policemen recognize us. They greet us with a respectful smile. I decide to have a Choco-bar, Brajesh opts for a Cornetto. The cold of the ice cream fails to keep us cool as we talk.

'I was thinking about Wasim's confessional statement. Dude, you'll have to accept that your party has played a big role in creating terrorists,' I say, deliberately playing him.

'Well, your party is lucky in that case. Even after you guys were responsible for the death of 3000 Sikhs in Delhi, Manmohan Singh, instead of becoming a terrorist, chose to become the PM.'

I must say I wasn't prepared for this sarcastic retort. A few moments later, I say, 'Manmohan Singh apologized on behalf of Congress for the Sikh riots. Shouldn't your party do the same?'

For once I find him uneasy. His struggle for an answer is a defining moment for me. It tells me a lot about him. Yes, he's a nice bloke and my first friend in the new world that I'm still getting to know and comprehend.

◆

I'm in Rajnandgaon on a small visit. Last night I had to attend the marriage ceremony of the daughter of a local MLA. I barely know the MLA but Yadav told me that he had stood by my father through thick and thin and that Dad had regarded him highly. That was sufficient reason for me to attend the wedding. But the more important reason is something else – it marks the beginning of my first development task as a public servant.

I'm supposed to utilize a Constituency Development Fund, amounting to Rs 2 crore each year. I have decided to spend it on setting up three small dispensaries in three of the worst-off blocks of the district. But that isn't sufficient. After all, you need good doctors too. So I convinced two of the more competent doctors – a pediatrician and a physician – working in one of Delhi's most well-equipped private hospitals to quit their jobs and come here. It has taken me the convincing power of a lifetime to make them agree to such a drastic change. But eventually I guess they were convinced by my claim that two years in the heart of real India would give them the sense of fulfilment that an entire lifetime in a private five-star hospital would not. My end objective is clear – I want the deaths caused by curable diseases like jaundice, malaria and other forms of viral infections to come down to zero. If I may be honest here, I've decided that an important chunk of the doctors' salary, over and above what they get from the government, will be borne from my Constituency Development Fund.

I've named the dispensary after my father. As I stand at the inauguration I feel that these are the things that would make Dad prouder of me than my winning an election. After all, his guiding principle in politics was to always serve the most under-privileged. With newer ideas, I shall henceforth be doing that more aggressively.

◆

Once the inauguration is over and I am on my way back, my thoughts slip elsewhere – to Lutyen's Delhi, where my emotional journey has been treading an interesting course. A month has passed since I came back from the US. From about thrice a week, Chaitali and I now meet almost every day – except for the odd couple of days that I am too caught up with party affairs or when I'm out of town. Our two conversations at the Centaur, just before and after my US trip, were turning points for us – it made us both a little more conscious of the growing intensity of our bond. That both of us are weary of our emotional baggage and have no pressing inducement to precipitate those graduations, is also obvious enough.

Irrespective of whether we formalize our relationship, our behaviour towards each other shows the same care and belonging that a committed couple's would. Therefore, we more or less, stay connected through the day. Chaitali knows virtually all my engagements for the day and I know hers.

Chaitali, being a little more caring than me, sends me an sms around lunchtime to ask if I have had my food. If she has had a bad day at the Politburo – brought on by the ranting of some irascible old Communist – she vents her anger by sending me a funny/sarcastic sms about the same. On days when I'm terribly busy, we catch up for a bit at the fag end of the day. As the frequency of our meetings has increased and we aren't in a position to make our relationship official yet, we like to meet more in each others' homes.

By the time I enter my Mother Teresa Crescent home, it's nine. I ask my staff to get a special dish of rice and fish curry prepared for us; fish is Chaitali's favourite. Post dinner, we end up watching a movie.

This is when our relationship is finally allowed to mature. We're seated next to each other watching Keanu Reeves and Sandra Bullock make out on screen. Almost simultaneously our replication of their lovemaking starts. As I pull her closer to me she rests her head on my shoulder; I rub her lips gently with my fingers; she sucks my finger; I like the feel of her wet lips sucking the tip of my finger. Soon enough we stop the movie to cuddle and caress. I can sense Chaitali would like to keep her clothes on for now. I don't mind either. If too much happens in one go, there's little anticipation left.

This intimacy leads us to expand the horizons of our bond. It's 2am and I ask Chaitali to stay back. After having sex with our clothes on, we thus also spend our first night together.

I wake up slightly before her. I don't know whether to call it a metrosexual trait or simply a desire to take care of the lady, but I make tea for Chaitali. I wake her with a cup of green tea with honey.

I can sense her exhilaration, as much as she can sense mine.

I serve the tea, along with a query: 'So how would you rate our first night together?'

She laughs. 'You know, someone once told me – it's not difficult to find people whom you want to sleep with… the challenge lies in finding someone you want to wake up with.'

'Damn interesting! So how *did* you like waking up with me?'

'Well, so far, so good,' she chuckles.

'By the way who was the enlightened soul who said that?'

'Just someone. Forget it.'

I can make out he must have been someone special. From what the guy said, I gather he must be sensible and reasonably well experienced too.

Three days later, on a Saturday night, I lie with my head in Chaitali's lap, on her bed. The dim light of a corner lamp creates just the right milieu for a romantic night. We talk about many things – work, movies, friends and the like. She tells me about her friend Monica, who is a research associate at the Institute for Peace and Conflict Studies. I tell her how I sometimes miss my life in my Manhattan office. She puts the music on. I want to hear Hoobastank; she's in the mood for old Hindi senti. I go with her choice.

She plays a sensuous number from a 70s film – 'Phir wahi raat hai...' As the song plays, I sense it reminds the lady of someone. Its lyrics and feel are sufficiently tantalizing for me to drop my inhibitions. I kiss and cuddle her. I'm tempted to go further and strip her. She reinforces the limits and I respect her for that. We retreat into rumination and into the songs that follow – each as enticing and tormenting as the other.

Some ten minutes later our immobility ends. Chaitali comes close to me and plants a soft kiss on my lips. Her kiss deepens till she is aflame with passion – the sort of passion that has a very good chance of leading to wilder things. In no time, she's on top of me, her long hair falling on my face. Ears and neck can be the most potent arousal points for men, especially when stroked by someone as attractive as the lady operating on me. I tug off her pants as she rips off my shirt and unzips my trousers; At one point, I do sense a momentary hesitation in her; it's like, she pauses to suddenly think about the implications of what's happening. Her quandary, results in me feeling unsure, as well. And then she turns around to being more decisive and brings in the culmination.

For the remainder of the night, even though I sleep at her place, I find Chaitali withdrawn. I don't read much into it. My inference is that such mood swings are not unnatural when one goes through emotional, psychological or hormonal changes. And Chaitali must be going through all of these given that, like me, she's coming out of a turbulent past. I try to talk to her about this, but as she isn't forthcoming enough, I give her the space that is needed in such a situation.

To my surprise, Chaitali's withdrawal continues for the next few days. Barring her solitary message enquiring about whether I've had my lunch, it's me who has to now reach out to her. And I do that because I'm attracted to her. Four days after we make out, I meet her over coffee. She doesn't look too well. I ask her if all was right. She is evasive initially, and then decides to talk.

'You know what, Adi…We must give each other some space because we don't know yet which way it's gonna go…'

'Sure,' is all I tell her, wondering if it's ever possible to decipher what really goes on inside a woman's mind.

'Adi… I have a request… Can we just avoid sex?'

The request and the way it is put forth, surprises me again.

'Sure,' is all that I can manage, yet again.

A week after that, we make out again, almost as hastily as on the first occasion and, ironically, on Chaitali's initiation. This time I am careful to use protection. The end result is no different: she's again lost in a strange form of withdrawal. I once again have to reach out to her. This time I find her unwell. She tells me she's got her periods twice in the last ten days and the bleeding has had its toll on her. On further probing, she tells me that it's probably the effect of popping pills to avoid pregnancy twice in these last few days. 'You know, Adi, I fear that something is wrong with my psyche. I'm plain scared to get close to another man or let another man enter me. And it's causing strange hormonal problems in me.'

I think I understand her state of mind. I don't blame her. I wonder why I'm destined to fall for women who need more of my sympathy than love. Or why I invariably end up substituting empathy with love.

For one month, we go in reverse gear. We meet, talk, hang out, watch movies, discuss stuff, but keep the bond strictly unphysical. And then as the freshness of spring replaces the winter chill, it buoys my expectancy. I'm tempted to confess what I'm feeling to the lady.

One fortuitous night I discover I still have enough romance in me to surprise myself. Post dinner and post midnight, I shun my security cover to personally drive Chaitali to the Aqua, where we had first met. Luckily, it being a week night, there aren't many people and no TV crew either. There, at the poolside over a shared can of Diet Coke, I formally propose to the lady.

'Chaitali, I love you and want to spend my life with you.'

She is not overly surprised.

'Aditya, I'd like that too.'

I'm not celebrating yet, as I can gather she's not sure.

'But...' She doesn't know what to say.

'But what?'

'N...nothing... I don't know. You know, *talking sometimes just spoils it all*. Let's just live it the way we feel...'

◆

That night, we make love – our third time but probably the first when it's not hasty or rushed into. I guess both of us are surer now about what we're getting into and I think Chaitali is so right when she says – *talking sometimes just spoils it all*.

We're consumed in our togetherness – we've been making love for the past hour. I've entered Chaitali once. She doesn't seem encumbered by any guilt/indecision/regret; rather she seems to have enjoyed it. This time round, she's the one taking the initiative. She's atop me, showering me with passionate kisses and bites all over. She wants me to take her with her on top. It promises to be amazing. Sarah never cared to do it that way.

However, at the penultimate moment Chaitali goes numb. She just freezes and looks at me bewildered and lost. My conjecture is that she's reminded of something she holds dear. Or perhaps, in my visage, she's seen the face she's been trying to exorcize. Hit by an attack of the invisible demons in her mind, Chaitali just blacks out. I am left confounded and scared like never before.

Ten minutes later, when her senses are restored, she tells me something that rips apart my soul.

'Adi, I've tried to move on, to living a life together with you. But it just doesn't happen for me. I doubt if I can love a man again. I doubt if I can ever be in a relationship. These emotions are just so dead in me. And every time I've tried to revive them for you, I've failed. I'm sorry, Adi… I'm sorry but we can't go any further.'

She breaks down and I cuddle her as I would my kid and put her to sleep. An hour later, she's found refuge in sleep; my sleep is gone, though. I walk up and down the lawns of my garden, even making my security wonder about my motives.

I'm disappointed. I'm heartbroken. I wonder why I'm destined to love all the women who're not meant for me. I wonder how on earth I suddenly developed such strong emotions for Chaitali. Was it the forlornness of my new world or just the insecurity that I may lose another woman I'm close to? Why am I always so close to getting what I want, yet so far?

When I think of Chaitali, I think she possesses a rare ability to both invoke sympathy in men as also to be the man in the relationship when needed. She's the most intelligent and compassionate woman I've ever met. Add to this the fact that she's damn attractive physically.

Yes, I am convinced that I love her. The optimist in me thinks I'll still woo her and make her mine. I wonder how and when that will happen. The sooner it does the better.

I'm equally convinced that a more consistent and cohesive Left–Congress coalition is what will serve the country's interests the best.

Brajesh

KALSARP YOG IS AN ASTROLOGICAL DEADLOCK that occurs when all your planets fall between *Rahu* and *Ketu*. This results in failure and dejection. Unexpected impediments ensure that achievements are not commensurate with your efforts. This leads to a feeling of negativity.

Now, you'd wonder what on earth I'm doing, talking about stuff that sounds irrelevant to my existence today. Well, it's not my doing, for sure. Amma called this morning to tell me that she had shown my horoscope to a respected astrologer in Allahabad and that it was this thing called *Kalsarp Yog* that was preventing my marriage. She asked me to plan a trip to Trimbakeshwar along with them, which is where one needs to offer prayers to get rid of this affliction.

Trimbakeshwar is an ancient Hindu temple in the town of Trimbak, in the Nashik district of Maharashtra, some 28 km from the city of Nashik. It houses one of the twelve Jyotirlingas, the extraordinary feature of this Jyotirlinga being that its three faces embody Lord Brahma, Lord Vishnu and Lord Rudra. The temple is located at the source of the river Godavari.

I chuckle at the thought; an interesting connotation arises in my mind. A well-known palmist had once seen my palm and asked me if my marriage had been cancelled once – as in, whether a marriage that had been fixed, had to be called off. I was perplexed as such a thing had never happened – not to the best of my knowledge. That is when I gathered that 'marriage' for Hindu astrological purposes and parlance would perhaps mean a relationship, which among its other components includes a sexual association with the concerned partner. In that sense, I've probably been married thrice. I'm sure some others my age would have thus experienced an even larger number of 'marriages'.

Why then do I need to go to Trimbakeshwar to get maried? I had probably been in a 'marriage' till just about a year ago. And today, my relationship with Shweta is a semi-marriage of sorts. For all of our personality differences, we do have a strong emotional dependence on each other.

Even as I think about Shweta, she arrives. She carries a report prepared by her, which she'd like me to read. She feels it will be of interest to me. If I acquaint you with the content, I'm sure it will be of interest to you as well. It will surprise you to know that a tribe found in the deepest interiors of Madhya Pradesh employs a most radical practice when it comes to choosing life partners. An equal number of males and females are brought together for a week-long fair. The couples are allowed a sort of test drive – they have the right to copulate with their chosen matches and gauge their sexual compatibility before finalizing the arrangement! I wonder if this manifests another paradox in a long list of endless ones that characterize Indian society.

Anyway, Shweta looks a bit off-colour and I ask her the reason. She is evasive initially but later tells me that her friend Sameer has met her a second time to reiterate how much he loves her. Shweta's response to him has once again been non-committal.

To be honest, I'm in a dilemma vis-à-vis Shweta. For all my projected strength, I know I'm emotionally fragile. I know that over the last few months, Shweta has been a big support for me, and I to her. She's taken good care of me – whether it has to do with preparing important documents for me, doing research work, or just giving me company when I have none. She's heard out my musings with patience and contributed to the conversation wherever she could. She's a great friend and in the frame of mind that I'm in, she suits me just fine. I mean, even if the accusation that *I cannot fall in love ever*, is an exaggeration, I would be honest to admit that I'm mostly too pre-occupied with matters of country and career – and somewhat of a narcissist too – to be able to pay much attention to my lady. I can be a passionate lover as well, but Shweta somehow doesn't evoke these sentiments in me. The good thing about Shweta is that she doesn't seem to have too many expectations from me. She's just happy being with me because she likes me a lot.

Why then is she not able to make me fall in love with her? Is it because she's too sedate and simple and that I've got used to expecting more adventure and spice, as with my previous girlfriend?

When you get sucked into some outlandishly exaggerated notions about yourself, you end up creating unnecessary problems. I'm afraid I'm suffering from heightened expectations of myself. What that implies is that if four out of five women fall for me, I will, in all likelihood, go for the fifth. Because the fifth will give me some sense of achievement that the other four will not. Now, Shweta obviously would be among the first four. I can sense she's fallen for me, but the bourgeois trait of glorifying everything with medals of self-dignity would never allow her to spell out her feelings in so many words.

Also, like I said, Shweta, is too sedate and plain. We've been good friends for six months now and it's getting a little tedious of late. I'd have liked Shweta to be a little more adventurous in initiating things between us. My PA and good friend, Bhatnagar, however, tells me that 'adventurous' romances are shortlived. They come as the fresh winds of the spring and disappear soon enough into the hostile summer. My friend could well be right. If I can be blunt about my dilemma – I need a girl who can be both wild and familial in equal measure. It's a tough combination, as unreal as several other expectations of mine are.

I would be lying however if I say I never feel insecure about losing Shweta. At the same time, I'm not prepared to embrace her just yet. What option does that leave Shweta with? I'm inclined to think that she does not dislike Sameer; she just likes me more. For a moment, I wonder if I can bring in her the changes that would make her more acceptable to me. For instance, I'd like to see her a little less in awe of me. I'd like her to shed some of her inhibitions. I'd like her to contradict me more, and then maybe I could derive a sense of challenge and achievement in being able to convince her about my way of thinking.

In almost the same instant, I'm left wondering why I have to expect so much from Shweta? If she likes me the way I am, can't I do the same? I guess this is where I hate my perpetual discontent. I think I'm shying away from her because it hasn't taken me any effort to get her.

I decide to buy time and ask Shweta to take a few more weeks to decide her reply to Sameer. She knows it's actually me who has asked for a few more weeks; it's I who needs time, not her.

◆

It's evening. 7:30 to be precise. I'm in my study. As Delhi is getting warmer by the day, I've donned a white kurta pyjama for a change. I feel comfortable in it, mind you; comfortable enough to make me wonder why I don't wear it more often.

Mr Aditya Samar Singh is supposed to come and meet me. Yeah, you heard right. He should be arriving any moment. Aditya's PA, Yadav, called up my PA, Bhatnagar, two hours ago to fix up this impromptu meeting. Yadav said Aditya wanted to exchange notes with me.

I know what this exchange of notes will entail. Our party is planning to move a no-confidence motion against the government. What has led to this impasse is the government's unnatural alacrity to scotch the Nuclear Deal, ignoring the implications that it would bind us in. To be honest, I'm not anti-deal. I do have some reservations but I quite agree with what Aditya said in his maiden speech – *international diplomacy today is about well-meaning interpretations*. There are no absolute–win situations anymore.' I also do believe that had the NDA government been in power, we'd have bargained better. Dr Manmohan Singh, with all his qualifications, can never be the leader that Vajpayeeji was.

Aditya walks in some fifteen minutes behind schedule. He broaches the issue of the Nuclear Deal on expected lines. He tries to convince me that our available sources of energy are bound to get depleted and that the transfer of nuclear energy and technology is the inevitable way forward. He tells me that the younger leaders should understand this and impress this upon the older leaders. He employs some other logic too, to convince me – he speaks of how opposing the deal would hamper our middle-class vote-bank and that being seen on the same side as the Left would only harm us...

To be honest, I've a taken a liking to this dude. He's not your typical, aloof, legacy-inheritor who doesn't quite belong here. And I can see the effort that he's putting into his new job. If his maiden speech employed great oratory punctuated with well-researched facts that were interpreted astutely, here I see him going a little beyond to execute what one would call Real-politik. Politics, mind you, transcends ballots and speeches. It goes right up to some deft drawing room manoeuvres of the kind that Aditya is here to explore. Just in case the media has already got wind of this meeting and is found waiting outside, don't be surprised if both of us claim this visit was only a 'courtesy call'!

Aditya wants me to convince my party members to re-think the issue and support the government. I know that irrespective of what our official stand is, most of our members wouldn't want a mid-term election. The problem is we've gone too far in our opposition of the deal. I doubt there is a way back that will not dilute our credibility. In my heart of hearts I do not oppose the deal. I see it as a way forward and the way forward is never easy at the start.

I mull over the matter. An idea strikes me. 'What will your government do in return for our support?' I ask.

'What are you expecting?'

'Your government's biggest failure is your inability to combat terror, what with a useless Home Minister in Shivraj Patil. Can your government set up a federal agency to investigate terror attacks and bring back POTA?'

What I say leaves Aditya stumped. I know what I've said is entirely hypothetical – I mean my seniors might just dismiss this bargain idea as crap. My solution, though, is borne out of a positive, well-meaning horses-for-courses approach, which would, by default, also serve our national interest.

Aditya thinks for a bit before he replies, 'Well, to be honest, I do feel a bit disappointed with my government's approach towards fighting terrorism. It's in denial. Let me think about what you've said and also bounce it off a couple of my senior colleagues whom I trust.'

I must confess that Aditya's honesty is quite remarkable. It leads us both to feel more comfortable about our intentions, as well as to trust each other. A common binding factor is the earnest sense of responsibility that we feel towards upholding national interests. And when I say this, let me add that in comparison, some of the older politicians whom I know don't give a shit about important policy issues. They're quite unabashed about their own ignorance – just so long as they manage to stay in power.

After our discussion on the affairs of the state ends, we discuss our personal lives for the first time. Aditya asks me if I ever had a woman in my life. I tell him – they come and go every season – like our Parliament sessions. We laugh. In his laughter, I can sense some pain. I ask him about his status.

He must be feeling low because he talks to me as one would to a friend. He tells me about his ex, Sarah, and more recently about this young political activist he has met.

'Falling in love is the most unpreventable accident, my friend. I'm surprised that just three months into knowing this girl, I feel a very strong attraction for her, like I've felt only once before. I think I really love her.'

'Then what's the problem?'

'A crazy mental block. She's a little screwed up in the head!'

'Oh, you need to be careful then. Such women can screw your happiness,' I advice, with a fair degree of authority.

'No, that won't happen. She's quite sensible actually... Just that at times, she has her own demons to battle. I guess by this age, we've all seen lots of those.'

Later that evening as I am seeing off Aditya I ask, 'Would I know the girl you're seeing? Can I be of help – as in would you like me to speak to her?'

Aditya thinks for a moment.

'Well, she did mention to me once that she knows you.'

I'm intrigued when I hear this.

'But let me handle this on my own. I think it's just too complicated for a third person to understand,' he reasons and then adds a sentence that leaves me confounded. 'It's strange, how things sometimes happen so fast. We'd met on the same day that you and I spoke in Parliament on the Nuclear Deal.'

I freeze when I hear this.

'What's the name of this girl?' I ask, a strange apprehension taking over me.

'Chaitali… Chaitali Sen.'

Aditya hugs me and drives off. I'm left standing under the moonless night, confounded and numbed. My thoughts are transported back nineteen months, to a moonless and stormy night that I can never ever forget.

◆

It had been raining incessantly since evening – and pretty heavily at that. Even as the rain and thundershowers continued unabated outside, I locked horns with this young CPI (M) activist Chaitali Sen, in a thunderous debate that took place in the studio of a leading English News Channel. I had seen Chaitali on TV and the impression that I carried of her was that of a juvenile delinquent. The irony was that she was an immensely attractive woman – more attractive than she looked on TV and definitely the sexiest woman in Indian politics.

The issue on which we exchanged fire was the violence in certain parts of Orissa and Karnataka, where some Christian minorities had been terrorized and churches ransacked:

Sandeep Kishore, IBTV: Welcome to the News@9, Mr Ranjan. Your party shares power both in Orissa and

Karnataka and it is clear from reports that the violence could have been averted had the perpetrators not enjoyed the support of the government.

Brajesh: I think you are being rather presumptuous. Let us not forget that a large percentage of our population is not evolved or educated enough to resist provocation, especially when it concerns religious issues. In Karnataka, we have reports of a concerted plan being employed by the so-called evangelic missionaries to covert tribals. There has been growing unrest among the tribals over this issue for a long time now which has unfortunately taken a violent turn in the last few weeks. Similarly, in Orissa, violence was triggered after a Hindu priest was murdered. Now these are emotive issues which sometimes result in anger and violence. However, we have never supported or condoned violence; rather we condemn it. It would be naïve to accuse our government of supporting the perpetrators of violence or of it being hand-in-glove with them.

(My answer was sufficient provocation for Chaitali to pounce.)

Chaitali: Of course, you are hand-in-glove, Mr Ranjan. Your verbal condemnation in this studio is nothing beyond shedding crocodile tears. By talking about conversions, you are actually trying to deflect attention from the core issue here – your government's failure to combat violence.

Brajesh: No, I'm not, Ms Sen. If you actually read the literature of some of these evangelists, it is disturbing. They show Hinduism in bad light.

Chaitali: Fair enough, but murdering Christians or ransacking Churches – does that show Hindus in any better light?

Brajesh: Of course not.

Chaitali: Then why don't you support a ban on the Bajrang Dal?

Brajesh: Look, ma'am, there are rogue elements in every organization. That doesn't mean you ban every organization. If we start doing that, we might as well ban your party for promoting the 'bandh' and 'violence' culture in West Bengal.

Chaitali: I think Mr Ranjan is just being mean over here. Fact is, Sandip, these people would never think of banning the Bajrang Dal because after all, it's an offshoot of the saffron umbrella. They are hand-in-glove.

Chaitali's aggression caught me by surprise. I wasn't expecting this unprovoked onslaught.

Sandip: Well, Mr Ranjan, I think Chaitali has a valid point. The BJP cannot have a dual approach on such issues and get away with it. If you condemn Naxalite violence and fight it, if you ban the SIMI, then I think you must also be prepared to act against the Bajrang Dal.

(I took me a moment to gather my response. My position was akin to a boxer who had been dealt some heavy punches. This was my last chance to hit back and turn the tables, if at all.)

Brajesh: Sandip, you simply cannot compare the Naxalite Movement or SIMI with the Bajrang Dal. The Bajrang Dal has never advocated secessionism, terrorism or armed violence. Yes, it needs to be less ignorant of the interests of other communities in its zeal to protect Hindu interests. That's something I accept. And of course, the rogue elements within the organization need to be dealt with in the firmest possible manner. There's no denying that.

However, I am amused at my esteemed colleague, Ms Sen's assertion that the Bajrang Dal is an offshoot of the BJP, which it isn't. The Naxal Movement on the other hand is most certainly an offshoot of the Communist movement in Bengal and there are substantiated reports of the Communist government in West Bengal having sheltered Naxals all the time. In fact, in 1969, in the West Bengal Assembly, Chief Minister Ajoy Sen of the United Front, of which the Left parties were a key component, had declared his own government to be uncivilized and barbarous. The CM had even publicly rebuffed the then deputy chief minister and home minister, Jyoti Basu by telling him that the portfolio was given to him for running the administration properly and not for raising funds through paddy. Does Ms Sen need more evidence of her party's complicity in strengthening the Naxal Movement, which is today the biggest security threat to the country?

I am really surprised that Ms Sen, whose party has a history of supporting armed revolution and violence, should point fingers at us.

◆

Established facts are potent enough, not to be undone by rhetoric. By referring to some unsavoury facts from history about the Communist parties' tryst with the Naxal Movement, I had saved the day for myself and my party. Having said that, I would be lying if I said I wasn't perturbed by the violence in these two states. I would be lying if I said that these two state governments had done all they could to curb the violence.

As I was leaving, I spotted Chaitali in the lobby, waiting for her car. We exchanged parting courtesies, which I'm sure neither of us meant. It was still raining and even as I waited for my chauffeur to get my car, I realized she didn't have her own vehicle. A car provided by the TV channel was supposed to drop her home.

I'm sure it was her looks at that point and not her intellect that prompted me to ask if I could drop her home. In the time that she took to think, I re-iterated the offer, leaving her with little option.

In the car we started talking from where we'd left off at the studio but soon discarded political conversation for more interesting personal stuff.

'You guys are damn shrewd. You get away with so much crap under the cloak of nationalism. The problem is for you nationalism is Hindu nationalism. I doubt you realize there are people from other religions in our country as well,' Chaitali said.

Well, I'm sure she did not realize many truths about her own ideology either. But then I was in no mood to remind her of that, in a milieu as sensuous as the one outside. It was still raining.

'But tell me, how did you know about the WB CM snubbing his deputy?' she asked.

'Well, it's as important to know about the history of your adversaries as about your own,' I told her.

'Hmm… so that means I need to dig skeletons out of the Sangh Parivar before I meet you for a TV debate next time,' she smiled.

'Do we need to wait for our next TV appearance to meet?' I asked, surprising her, and myself.

My words, I'm sure, sounded presumptuous. It was just that I found this girl so damn attractive – the sort of wild and sexy intellectual who could send a man like me on a voyeuristic fantasy – frankly, the sort I'd love to spend a wild, crazy night with. Taming her rebel instincts, would give me a sense of achievement. And when I say this, don't get judgmental. I've had a one-night escapade just twice.

I was too enamoured of the rain and my company to sustain a focused conversation. Instead I hopped from one topic to the other. I learned she was staying in a house on Shahjahan Road that belonged to an old, ailing Rajya Sabha MP from Kerala who seldom visited Delhi. She discovered my address. 'You like the rains?' I enquired suddenly.

'Oh I love them.'

As we were nearing central Delhi, I suddenly felt emboldened enough to ask if she'd like to have dinner at my place.

That she didn't instantly reject the offer, made me insist till she accepted. I'm sure she could sense my interest in her. Or else, I'd not have been so generous to her, after a hostile public debate. Another reason she agreed to dine with me might have to do with the fact that unlike me who had my staff to ensure that my meals were duly taken care of, she'd have either had to make her own dinner or to order in. A third possibility was that she too felt attracted to me and saw the meal, as I did – an opportunity to spend more time together.

The eternal optimist in me had me believe it was the last of the three options.

We had a simple dinner through the course of which we talked about everything – from our folks to our personal lives, to likes concerning music and sports. It goes without saying that my attraction now enjoyed a realistic possibility of being accorded the fulfillment it was seeking. I was also glad that on issues not related to politics, Chaitali wasn't the snooty, irascible, pseudo that I'd initially thought her to be. She had a strong opinion on just about everything, and it would invariably be at loggerheads with mine. But that was fine. While I liked to have my way, I also liked to work my way into having it. Women who meekly acquiesced to everything I said did not hold my attention.

After dinner we sat chatting in the dim light of my living room. On not many occasions does it happen that you can't stand someone's political views, but have a superb personal chemistry with the person. We had reasons for this I guess – we belonged to a very small group of new-generation politicians who did not carry a political pedigree.

After chatting for nearly an hour, Chaitali looked at her watch. 'It's past midnight. I think I must leave…'

'I'm sure nobody's waiting for you,' I said.

'Sorry?'

'Oh… w… well… you can be here for some more time.'

'And do what?'

'Keep me charmed.'

'Aha… apart from a shrewd public speaker, you aren't a bad flirt. Anyway I don't do much at nights except battle for sleep.'

'And what's in sleep anyway, except ignorance?'

'Yeah… being a light sleeper, I sometimes get some entertaining dreams.'

'Sure… But they won't be as entertaining as the real thing.'

My last sentence was pointed. But she ignored it.

'Which I'm gonna see now, is it?'

'Well, not quite yet. So, you are an insomniac too?'

'I just end up thinking when I ought to be sleeping.'

The downpour continued.

'How much do you love the rains?' she enquired of me.

'Quite a lot.'

'Come with me,' she said impulsively.

I followed her into the portico and then she surprised me by running out into the open. She flung out her arms and turned her face to the sky, as if romancing the rain. I was mesmerized watching her wet white salwar kameez stick to her skin and expose it. I was a little embarrassed by what my security personnel posted at my gate would think. Chaitali, for her part, had abandoned all concern for such trivial details. Looking at her, one would think she was born to dance in the rains. Her exultation was infectious. I was left wondering once again about the ways of destiny – was this the same girl I was locked with in an unpleasant debate, just three hours ago?

She called me out. I was reluctant to wet my clothes and conscious of what my men would think. But I didn't want to squander this once-in-a-lifetime opportunity. I went up to her. She held my hands and had me virtually perform a rain dance with her. I was overwhelmed by how irresistible she was at that moment. I held her face and kissed her hard. She was taken aback for a moment, then she kissed me back with passion.

The showers accorded a mystical quality to the act.

Half an hour later, we sat inside my living room. Chaitali had changed into one of my pyjamas and t-shirts. She did look a little sheepish about her impulsive adventure and of what followed between us. But I'm not sure if the act was entirely impulsive. For a guy from Allahabad, it takes a litter longer than usual to realize that women can fake. Oh, and how.

It was a quarter past one now and I thought that Chaitali would want me to have her dropped home. However, after our rain dance, she seemed more comfortable about being at my place. She asked me if I could play some music. My taste in music, I have to admit, is a little old-fashioned. You may even call it desi. I opened my laptop and went to a file that contained a collection of some senti, romantic numbers from old Hindi films.

The first song on the collection was a sensuous number from this film called Ghar, released in 1978. The lyrics were – 'Phir wahi raat hai…' Chaitali, apparently found it passé so she opened up her own laptop stopping my song before it ended and played hers – the James Blunt number – 'You're beautiful'… I stopped it mid-way to play the next from mine – 'Dil to hai dil, dil ka aitbaar' from the film, *Muqaddar Ka Sikandar*. She cut it short to play hers – a Bryan Adams number – 'I'm ready'. I stopped that to play mine –a song from the 1970s film *Rajni Gandha* – 'Kai baar yu hi dekha hai ye jo mann ki seema rekha hai…' I thought the song was an apt embodiment of my temptations towards the lady, which were getting more uncontrollable by the moment. She stopped this to play hers – Shakira's peppy, 'O baby when you like that, you make a woman go mad…' I got a bit miffed seeing her truncate some of my best numbers. I stopped her song to play mine. She stopped mine and played hers...

'Listen to the lyrics, Chaitali, they've got real meaning,' I said.

She grabbed my collar and pulled me to her, surprising me yet again.

'You listen to mine – Baby when you look like that, you make a woman go mad. That's how you make me feel at this moment.'

There was a concupiscent glint in her eyes when she said this to me. And in the position that we clung to each other, a more intensive physical indulgence was only natural. It goes without saying that we smothered each other with kisses. And all of it happened on my unsteady bean bag. As I licked Chaitali's neck, buoyed by her husky sighs one of my hands pushed down her pyjamas. 'It has been a very long time since I last did it,' said she.

'Me too,' I said.

I'd have ideally liked to drop Chaitali back after that. I believe that sleeping with someone is fine, but waking up together leads to an emotional attachment, which unless one is sure about the relationship, is best to avoid. But Chaitali was so different from the other girls that I'd met. We ended up talking like pals for an hour after we made love – where she told me about her gay love and I briefly mentioned to her a thing or two about my past. After that I thought it would be unchivalrous on my part to ask the girl to leave. So we ended up sharing a bed. As I lay with Chaitali beside me I couldn't stop thinking about her. She was just the kind of stuff that a thinking man's fantasies are made of, the sort whose physical beauty and intelligence put together would stimulate her partner to madness; she was just as passionate as a truly passionate man would want his woman to be. The only thing that cast some doubt in my mind about her was the ease with which she agreed to have sex with me. It made me wonder if she was this forthcoming with other men as well. Of course, she was entitled to think about me the same way. I felt pretty certain she wasn't really the steady girlfriend or wife kind. Beyond a point, her rebel streak would become an impediment in her playing that role. But why did I need to bother myself with that unwarranted thought at this point? I soon resigned myself to slumber, with the lady for company.

As the rains continued the next morning, one was bound to feel the need to stay in bed. The wetness outside only added to the escape one would want in such weather. Thus I slept longer than I did.

At about a quarter to eight, I was woken up by the gentle touch of a warm body lying next to mine. Chaitali who was still asleep, held me with the abandonment that you feel with someone you trust implicitly. This moment did something to me. I guess it was the innocence of her touch. Her lips touched my neck, her arms and legs, entwined mine. The feel of her breasts against my skin produced a sensation I'd not known before. There was an intuitive inkling in me telling me that this girl was not what her outward appearance made her seem.

She was more the kind I'd like to believe I am.

At that point Chaitali woke up. I was sufficiently aroused by then to kiss her on her forehead, followed by a kiss in the vicinity of her lips. She responded by smothering my chest and abs with kisses. Within minutes, we found it hard to resist each other and made love again.

This time round I held myself back for a moment to quickly don a contraceptive. What impressed me about Chaitali was her ability to take things head on – she ensured an intercourse position just the way she liked it. For once, I enjoyed being dominated.

After we made love we wondered what was wrong with us. Both of us were convinced that the last ten hours had been fated to happen. And since destiny had willed us to exercise physical indulgence, we had resigned ourselves to its wishes. We decided to bathe together before parting. I don't think I really wanted to part from her at all, but then neither of us was in any position to discuss the implications of what was happening – it was all so bizarre and sudden.

Rinsing my lover with soap under a shower is a fantasy I have always had. Unfortunately, I had not been able to live it yet. This time I did. Yes, Chaitali and I bathed each other and felt the lather drip down our bodies. We caressed each other's wet bodies and were so aroused that we ended up making love in the bathtub.

I dropped Chaitali home around noon. It was still raining and we were still too overcome to be able to think about what had happened and what it might lead to. About the only thing I knew well enough was that I wanted to meet Chaitali again. Soon.

As I dropped her I said, 'So when do we meet again?' barely concealing my excitement.

She thought for a moment. I could sense that Chaitali was in some dilemma. 'Do we need to?'

Her answer shocked me for a moment. 'You don't want to?'

'Well, if things happen too often, they become a habit. Some habits should be avoided.'

I didn't quite know what to say as I had no idea what was on Chaitali's mind.

'Bye. Take care,' she said before I could react.

'Bye.'

'Don't call me; I will call you,' were her final words. I wondered why she had to say this.

◆

For the next three days, my schedules were completely impaired – so terrible was my hangover. I could feel every inch of my physical self yearning for Chaitali's touch; for those hours with her that had been gifted to me out of nowhere. I desperately wanted to call Chaitali and meet her again. Yet every time I'd hold myself back as I'd remember Chaitali's nonchalance at the time of parting. Why did she have to reinforce that *she* would call me? Was she into one-night stands? Would she carelessly forget the night that I considered my most memorable night ever?

Four days later, I finally called her. She sounded preoccupied and ensured that the conversation did not go beyond formal queries. I was left wondering this time round if she was actually a very decent girl and was overcome by guilt about what had happened that night.

My restlessness grew by the day. I called her again. This time, she took the call but almost immediately told me that she was in a meeting and would call back. She never did. At times I couldn't help feeling used – Was I just one of her several fuck-buddies who were not meant to be entertained everyday?

Four weeks later, Chaitali finally called and said she wanted to talk to me. We met at the India International Centre, of all places. She told me if we met there, nobody would suspect that we were meeting over a personal matter.

I landed up at the appointed place at the appointed time. I must confess I'd never felt so nervous as I did that day. What Chaitali told me numbed my senses.

'Brajesh, I was carrying your baby. I got myself aborted yesterday.'

'What?' I was dazed.

For a moment I actually hoped that Chaitali would tell me that I had heard wrong. Or that she was playing a prank. That she was unable to look me in the eye confirmed that what I heard was right.

'But, Chaitali, you could have told me,' I reasoned, gathering myself.

'Why? Could we have kept the baby?'

I didn't have an answer to that. But the mention of pregnancy and abortion kind of overwhelmed me. I no longer had any negative thoughts in my mind about her. She could well have been destined to be the mother of my child!

'Brajesh, I'm sorry for not informing you before. I just felt it would serve no purpose. But in the end, I thought it was my responsibility to let you know...' Chaitali explained.

I paused for a moment and then made a monumental declaration. 'Chaitali, I think I love you.'

'What?' She seemed taken aback.

'I love you,' I said again.

She laughed.

'But why? How? When?'

I spoke to her about my state of mind since that epochal night between us.

Her response was disappointing. 'Look Brajesh, I don't believe in love, commitment and all that jazz. Trust me, I can be a very good friend, but nothing beyond that. So you'll have to make a choice.'

This rebellious and defiant sentence of Chaitali's, I guess I took as a challenge. This girl was not like any that I had met. Yes, I yearned for her and even if I hadn't exactly fallen in love with her yet, I was prepared to fall in love with her. It was for me to make her change and come around to the normal ways of the world.

I thus accepted her friendship. In the prevailing circumstances, that was the way out, to stay in her company and to understand the way her mind worked.

Soon, we started meeting more often. We'd meet and have lengthy and absorbing discussions of the kind that we had had on our first night during dinner, before we'd made out. I still hoped to relive our first night again. But Chaitali's indifference on that score made it seem virtually impossible.

Over the next few weeks I found that Chaitali could indeed be very nice company – she was extremely helpful and intelligent and conversations with her were always thought-provoking. That she was extremely fond of me and that we shared a chemistry was something I figured as well. I surmised thus that all these statements – *I don't believe in love, etc.*, constituted a defence mechanism against future despair. Perhaps she was still to completely get over her previous heart-break. Besides, it goes without saying that her pregnancy and abortion, right at the start of our relationship was the worst thing that could have happened.

I was thus hopeful that she would reciprocate my feelings once she was sure about me and about us together.

◆

A month after that, my parents came to Delhi for a couple of days. As always, they carried a couple of marriage proposals for me from well-off families in Allahabad. One girl was a lecturer in home science and the other a dentist. How I wished I could tell my parents that I had graduated beyond these professionals. That I refused them outright triggered off another squabble.

The night before my parents were to leave Amma had a heart to heart with me and asked me if I was seeing someone or had someone in mind. I ended up telling her about my feelings for Chaitali. Amma wanted to meet her. I agreed to call Chaitali home, after specifying that so far my feelings were one-sided.

Amma however, ended up behaving like a potential mother-in-law, asking Chaitali exhaustive details about her family, her hobbies and her plans for marriage. All along I barely managed to hide my laughter on seeing Chaitali's discomfiture. This conversation was bound to leave Chaitali upset.

Next evening, after dinner I took Chaitali out for a long drive, shunning my security cover.

'Chaitali, I'm sorry about yesterday. Actually Amma...'

She cut me short. 'N… no…it's okay. I understand.'

The good thing about being with an intelligent girl like Chaitali was that she could sense exactly what was on my mind. What she said next proved it.

'Brajesh do you really love me so much?'

I didn't have a verbal answer. Instead I played a song out on the car deck – 'Tera mujhse hai pehle ka naata koi, yoohi nahi dil lubhata koi' from an old movie called *Aa Gale Lag Ja*. From her expression I could sense her turmoil. She abruptly stopped the song and turned towards me.

'But why, Brajesh? Do I really deserve this love?'

I played the song again. She stopped it again. This time her reasoning was different.

'Anyway, a Communist and BJP coalition is just impossible,' declared she.

I was amused. Nonetheless, I got down to my part of the talking. I told her what I felt about her – that she too was an emotional girl and loved me, but perhaps the tragedy of her past had left an indelible scar; that the fear of failure had made her erect her own defences so she took refuge in hollow statements glorifying her escapism. I told her that every time we drove our vehicle on the road, there was a probability of us meeting with an accident. Did one give up driving just because of that?

My brainwashing of Chaitali did have an impact on her. She agreed to courtship, but on the condition that it would be on her terms – without any immediate pressure of time, time-frame or commitment, till she came to terms with her own feelings. I considered this a diplomatic triumph. I had managed to make her bend partially from her uncompromising posture.

On our way back, I felt more optimistic about converting those twelve hours of sheer magic of our first night into a life-long engagement. I couldn't restrain myself from telling Chaitali about a lesser-known paradox of Indian politics, which I was sure she wouldn't know: the BJP and the Communists had formed a coalition way back in 1957 in the Delhi Municipal Elections to keep the Congress out of power.

Agreed a BJP–Communist coalition seemed highly improbable, but history does repeat itself.

◆

The time I spent with Chaitali was complete bliss. We both had a mad streak in us which our togetherness brought out. And from experience I can tell you that some of the best romantic moments are those that occur unplanned. Thus, one Friday night, we decided to take off for the Corbett National Park. I have to mention here that my PA, Bhatnagar, is a deft strategist. The VVIP cottage at Corbett was booked in my name and Chaitali curled her hair, sported a pair of dark glasses, and a straw hat. The idea was to have Chaitali pass off as an unknown friend of mine, if at all she was clicked by a snooping reporter. My security thankfully was completely supportive in this plan.

After a full day of driving around the park, we returned to our cottage in the evening. Chaitali went in to take a shower. I discovered that the door wasn't properly shut. As I opened it, the sight of a naked Chaitali under the shower was just majestic. You won't get any marks here for guessing what happened afterwards. The passion that followed went on well up to midnight.

Chaitali looked her most stunning and intense that night. It was a full moon night and the moonlight coming in from the two skylights positioned on opposite walls created an artistic play of light and shade on her body. I have never known a woman to look as gorgeous as Chaitali did that night. I instantly recalled a poem written by Lord Byron that was in our syllabus in class 9 or 10 and which I hadn't thought of in years, but that moment was overwhelming enough to make me instantly recall it in its entirety:

She walks in beauty, like the night
Of cloudless climes and starry skies...

Chaitali listened, amazed, perhaps wondering how much I loved her and why. I went close to her and started kissing the parts of her that lent themselves to the moonlight. Forehead, eyelashes, then the lips and finally the navel.

'I want to marry you, Chaitali.'

I waited for her answer but her only response was to affectionately caress my hair. I knew we were not on the same page yet.

◆

Now each man-woman relationship has a different constitution and a different set of factors working for it. To the best of my understanding there are three essential factors, which in varied proportion, lead to a man and woman coming together: intellectual compatibility, the emotional empathy of a companion/friend and physical chemistry. Of course all of these need to be complemented with a generous dose of unselfishness. Besides, in each relationship, the domination of one of these factors over the others is common.

With time, I was left wondering if physical chemistry had come to assume a disproportionately high importance between Chaitali and me. For soon enough we were to discover that, barring our moments of physical engagement which were undeniably fantabulous, there were far too many temperamental differences between us. Friction soon became inevitable.

One problem was my need to lead a more disciplined life. I had put on substantial weight and everytime I looked in the mirror it would depress me. Now, nothing would have changed for me, had I not cared for my appearance but then the perfectionist in me went that extra mile to ensure that I had a perfect physique as well. Thus, I hired the services of a promising young trainer, Wasim Iqbal.

Interestingly, I met Wasim during my morning jog in the vicinity of India Gate. Wasim stopped me and said he was a great fan of mine. As we got talking he gave me some diet tips which made sense to me. As he happened to be looking for extra work as a fitness consultant, I quickly recruited him.

I was impressed by Wasim's innovative skills as trainer. He'd change the routine every three weeks to ensure that my system didn't get bored and that my body adapted well to the change. Thus three days of the week, he'd train me with weights at the Constitution Club gym, and on the other three days he made me jog. Twice in the week, he'd make me crunch my abs. And mind you, some of these crunches were so barbaric that I'd yell in pain. But yes, in just about a month, I had lost 3 kilos and my muscles felt toned.

After my workout, Wasim and I would have long chats. I was damn impressed to learn that he had done his Masters in Computer Applications and that it was his passion for fitness that had made him a fitness trainer. As we developed a comfort level, I asked him one day what he, as a young Muslim, felt about the BJP.

'Muslims don't dislike the BJP any more than they do the Congress. In fact, the BJP is less hypocritical about being secular.'

His answer surprised me. 'So would you vote for the BJP?' I asked.

'Not just me, a lot of Muslims would have, had the Gujarat riots not happened. After all, Vajpayee had universal acceptance.'

I mulled over his answer. I thought it was a challenge for me and my party to exorcize Gujarat from the minds of Muslims. I took it as a personal challenge to make Wasim change his impression about my party.

What I also liked about Wasim was his objectivity. Unlike even Chaitali – who would see things as black or white and would invariably dismiss the BJP as a party that thrived on communal rioting – Wasim's views were more balanced.

◆

The regimen that I now followed included strict diet control. Hence, five days of the week, dinner meant soup and salad. On one such night, Chaitali took me to her friend Ira's house to bring in her birthday. Since I was determined not to upset my schedule, I avoided both liquor and the main meal. This upset Chaitali, who was by then some three pegs down. In her drunken state, she confronted me with some ridiculous logic.

'Mr Brajesh Ranjan, young, dynamic, dashing MP from Allahabad, you're not planning to strip for the cover of *Marie Claire*, are you?' said she, out of the blue and before I could react, added, 'Then don't throw these tantrums, and eat your food.'

I didn't react there because I didn't want trouble. But Chaitali's behaviour that night deeply offended both my sensibilities and my ego. I wondered whether in her opinion an MP would want to lose weight or be in shape, only when he chose to pose for a women's magazine. I didn't like the way she spoke to me in front of her junkie friends.

Okay, let me introduce you to Chaitali's core depraved circle – Udit was a copywriter with a leading advertising agency, with hair and beard so thick they'd put a bear to shame. Swati was an editor with a publishing house – she was lesbian. Arun and Ira were apparently an on-off couple – both were into theatre, Ira more as an actress and Arun a director.

Oh, yes, I call them depraved because they belonged to another world – loud music, alcohol, and partying all night was their idea of enjoying a weekend – and I couldn't, despite my effort, relate with their notions. There was also some brazen physicality in their body language that made me squirm. For instance, when Udit and Chaitali met, they'd bear hug and Udit would kiss her really close to the lips. You can blame my Allahabad roots for this, but I was still to come to terms with this form of permissive behaviour, even if it was between close pals. And by the way, how would you react if you saw Udit get carried away in his excitement over a joke and pinch Ira's butt hard – and that too in the presence of her supposed boyfriend, Arun?

I did speak to Chaitali about my reservations once. Her response was a bit strange. She said that since we weren't sure about our future, we must give each other a little more space. She also accused me of being a chauvinist. 'You know something, Brajesh, you can be quite an MCP at times,' she chuckled. And sensing my offence added, 'But I like you this way.'

There's a thin line that distinguishes chauvinism from chivalry.

Another thing about Chaitali that I disliked was her going overboard with the 'queer' cause. A project that she undertook, to study the prevalence of HIV among eunuch prostitutes, required her to visit the infamous G.B. Road far too often and that too, late in the evenings. Now in as much as her work aroused my curiosity, I would not do something that went against my image. Therefore, late evenings, when we should have been spending time together, I would involve myself in meeting associates and she'd do her own thing.

One night, after work, Chaitali was supposed to come home for dinner. Instead she arrived with two uninvited guests – two eunuchs who kept ogling at me. Chaitali told me that she'd become friends with them and that she had brought them along as they wanted to meet me. And meet me for what? Well, to acquaint me with some of their problems, but more importantly, because they'd seen me on TV and were my fans.

I tried to be as patient that evening as I could. At night though, Chaitali and I had a talk. I guess she had sensed my increasing discomfiture with her ways. 'Brajesh, we're not like regular people. We've both seen much more of the world. We're bound to be different from each other. We're bound to pursue our different interests and beliefs. Shouldn't this diversity actually be to our advantage? I mean, I like being with you – with all that *is* you. That's all I expect from you.'

It's surprising that when Chaitali spoke like this, or when we made love, the impact was such that it eclipsed all our differences. She had something to say about my other concern too. 'Brajesh, I know you want more reassurances from me. You want to hear that I love you too. But does love have to be accorded vocal expression for it to be real? It's for the first time after a full six years that I'm sharing my life with a man in this manner. Isn't that proof that you mean a lot to me? That, somewhere you might have become a habit for me?'

Somehow this girl had made me weak. I was willing to allow her to have her way. Or maybe I was evolving from being a hardliner to a moderate. I was taken in by her words. I lifted her in my arms and carried her outside. The moon was not full, it was about three-fourths of its size.

Chaitali chuckled, looking at the moon. 'Braj, doesn't that reflect the state of affairs between us? We're three-fourths there, half of it with your effort and one-fourth with mine. That crucial one-fourth is what I need to tread. And your love will make me do that soon.'

Chaitali's words reflected a maturity that made me feel vindicated of my choice. I looked at the moon, hoping it would be a full one soon.

◆

I got busy helping my party plan its strategies for the elections to the Himachal Pradesh and Gujarat assemblies later that year. By default, Chaitali and I ended up giving each other the space that she had asked for. On one occasion I saw her have a heated discussion with Udit on the phone. When I asked her about it, she was dismissive of it. And I let it at that. They were old friends, after all, and problems between friends are not uncommon.

One Saturday night, Chaitali decided to throw a party at her place for Arun and Ira. The two had decided to marry. She obviously expected me at the party but an urgent engagement in my constituency that day meant I would not be back in Delhi before midnight. Besides, somehow I wasn't too keen to see Chaitali with her friends. I think I was quite possessive of her and disliked seeing her with them.

Nonetheless, when I arrived in Delhi some half an hour before midnight, I couldn't resist being with Chaitali and landed up at her place unannounced. What I saw there left me zapped. In the inner room, a lady whose long hair covered the actual act seemed engaged in some intimate activity with Chaitali. On a closer look I realized it was Udit. The two were obviously stunned to see me. I was just as shocked to realize that the two were doped. Chaitali pushed Udit away, as if the act was forced, which it wasn't. I picked up particles of the substance lying on the floor.

'Wanna have some? Wait, I'll prepare it,' said Udit unfazed.

Even as Udit was taking it away from my hand, I furiously hurled the weed in his face. I looked at Chaitali and wondered if she was the same girl whose mind and maturity had entranced me.

'Listen, Brajesh, it isn't what you're thinking. I'll tell you everything,' Chaitali pleaded, her faltering speech making it clear that she was high.

'Do I need to tell you to fuck off?' I turned and snarled at Udit.

He disappeared.

It wasn't as if Chaitali hadn't told me that she had doped in the past. It wasn't that she hadn't told me she'd had one-night stands. But I had a right to believe that they were in the past. I had a right to expect that an imperfect past wouldn't find its way back into her future. Why then had she let me down?

'Brajesh, I swear Udit is just a friend and we've had nothing more between us.'

'How many such dope friends do you still have?' was my next query.

She obviously knew I wasn't going to let her have her way this time.

'You'll have to trust me, Brajesh. Men are perverts. If Udit suddenly developed a fancy for me and started pestering me what could I do? I didn't think he'd come on to me when I was high.'

I had calmed down a bit. But the incident probably made me realize that the differences between us were too glaring to be reconciled.

'No guy behaves that way with a woman unless he gets encouragement, either directly or otherwise. You need to check your behaviour, Chaitali. I hate this pub culture,' I asserted.

Chaitali was stung. 'What are you trying to say? That I give wrong signals to men? That I'm a whore?'

'Well, if you lived in a smaller town and did such a thing, that's what people would call you,' I said and walked off.

I didn't know why I had to say that last sentence. Probably it was my frustration over my inability to make Chaitali change her behaviour. But if so much needed to be altered before things could be 'perfect', was it really worth keeping hope? I regretted my words for another reason: it gave credence to Chaitali's charge of me being an MCP. I would still think I am not one. But yes, I like to uphold certain norms and decorum. And yes, I hate this pub culture of brazen physicality and indulgence. If that qualified me to be called an MCP, so be it.

◆

I've always believed that the death of a relationship is as long-drawn-out a process as getting into it is. And incidents like the dope episode leave a scar that never heals. Somewhere at the back of my mind, the sight of Udit closeted with Chaitali in a doped state would always haunt me. After all, relationships are about trust and once the trust is dealt a body blow, it's only a matter of time before the relationship comes apart.

For the next three weeks, I consciously kept a distance from Chaitali. We met just twice: once in Parliament, where we exchanged formal greetings; and on the other occasion Chaitali dropped in with a cake. She said it was to make me feel good. Out of nowhere, she also mentioned to me that since that night, she had cut off all contact with Udit. I could see an effort on her part to reach out to me. But my hurt wasn't yet salvaged. And since I hardly spoke, Chaitali too kept her distance after that. Chaitali did send me a couple of text messages to enquire if I was well. I did not reply to them.

I would be lying if I said I did not miss Chaitali in these three weeks. I missed her like crazy. I couldn't sleep; I ached for her touch that had made my nights special. There were at least two nights when I woke up thinking she was asleep next to me. And when she wasn't there, I felt bereft. There were times when I started to dial her number, but disconnected mid-way.

Finally one night, I sat in my study well past midnight. I was supposed to finalize a report on the Government's apathy towards the plight of farmers in the Vidharba region, from where an alarmingly high number of farmer suicides had been reported. The report was almost done and I just had to read it once. But I couldn't concentrate. Memories of Chaitali thronged my mind and incapacitated its working.

I realized that the heart need not subscribe to logic all the time. I got up and drove to Chaitali's place that very instant. She wasn't surprised to see me; as though she had expected that I would come one day.

We held each other tight: 'I've missed you a lot, Chaitali,' I said.

I could sense guilt in her. And I felt bad to make her feel guilty. I wanted to tell her that I was wrong in expecting her to change. And that I was prepared to love and accept her the way she was. But she surprised me instead: 'Brajesh, I want to say something to you.'

I looked at her.

'I'm sorry to hurt you. From today, I'll be the woman you want me to be. I'll do everything to give you the happiness that I have deprived you of. I don't know what prevented me from saying this so far, but yes I love you too. I love you more than I have loved anybody else.'

I can't tell you how I felt when I heard this from Chaitali. Her words were magic to my ears. At that moment, I felt like I had achieved everything in life.

The moment led us to bed. Since it was happening unexpectedly I wasn't carrying protection. And the outcome of the previous misadventure made me stop before I went any further. Chaitali surprised me again, though. 'It doesn't matter anymore. I want to carry your baby.'

We made love till the wee hours of the morning. When sunlight and sensation woke us up, our physical and spiritual selves felt a oneness I'd never experienced. I said, 'It's easy to find women to sleep with. The challenge lies in finding someone you want to wake up with. I want to wake up with you every morning of my life.'

◆

One day when we were having breakfast, Chaitali got a call from an NGO. From what I heard, I gathered it had to do with children. It surprised me. But since I too got a call at that point, I couldn't follow more.

'Brajesh, I've decided to sponsor a child,' she informed me later.

'But… suddenly?'

'Yeah… A couple of volunteers from this NGO met me last week. There's an orphanage in Mehrauli that wants people to come forward and sponsor their inmates' education, health care, needs, etc. My friend Monica and her husband too have adopted a baby, though in another orphanage. And I have decided to adopt and sponsor a child too.'

'But you should have informed me,' I responded, surprised.

'I thought you wouldn't like it.'

'Why?'

'You don't quite like the other cause that I support –'

There are times in a relationship where you're suddenly forced to sit up and wonder whether it is your partner who hasn't quite understood you or if it is you who is wanting. There is also a stage when you do things not so much because you believe in them, but because it makes your partner happy. Ideally, I'd have wanted my first child to be born out of us, but then I was prepared to tread that extra mile to see Chaitali happy.

'It's going to be our child,' I reassured her.

Chaitali was jubilant as she probably hadn't expected my support. Now while unofficially I had decided that the child would be ours, practical constraints demanded that the child be adopted by one of us. For, though Chaitali and I had been spotted together in public a few times, we'd maintained that we were just friends.

Next Sunday we went to this Mehrauli orphanage, where we were introduced to twenty kids aged between three and ten. Among them, there was this four-year-old girl called Radha who struck an instant chord with us.

'I think she's the one for us,' Chaitali told me.

I nodded.

While we were formalizing the agreement for sponsoring Radha, we were told about her background.

She was the daughter of a sex-worker. It went without saying that Radha's biological father could be anybody. Luckily, all her medical tests were clear. The information about her past disturbed me. To be honest, for a moment it sullied my enthusiasm for adoption. And I guess Chaitali sensed that. 'Don't worry – that was Radha's past. Even destiny has its law of averages – that's why it brought Radha to us.'

Radha brought some positive changes in our lives. One, she deflected the focus from our internal chaos to make our lives more unselfish. We realized that while education and exposure was meant to evolve us, it also confused people like Chaitali and me. Through our complicated and layered interpretations, we'd ensure that our problems and skirmishes never ended. Radha, on the other hand, needed a very basic enrichment at this point that would make her face the world more confidently.

Almost every Sunday, we'd land up at the orphanage with gifts and food for Radha and her friends. After lunch we'd play cricket or fly kites with the kids. One day when I was playing with the other kids, I saw Chaitali and Radha weeping profusely and Chaitali hugging Radha and trying to soothe her. When I asked her about it Chaitali said that Radha had told her about some unsavoury incident involving Radha's mother. And on seeing Radha cry Chaitali too couldn't stop crying. To see Chaitali be that protective of Radha, moved me deeply.

Then, one weekend, Chaitali brought Radha home to stay with us. Radha slept on the same bed, between Chaitali and me. That night much after Chaitali and Radha had dozed off, I lay awake. I was worried. Chaitali's dependence on Radha had begun to bother me a bit. I mean, as an Indian man with his heart in the right place, I wanted to become a biological father soon. And since I was toying with the idea of marrying Chaitali, a scary thought loomed in my mind: Was Chaitali spending all her emotions on an adopted child? Would she have enough left, when we had our own baby?

I'm not sure whether I was insecure – as Chaitali sometimes accused me of being. But subsequently I cooled off Radha. I immersed myself in work on Sundays too and skipped some of our visits to the orphanage.

◆

About the two really interesting people whom I met through Chaitali were her friend Monica and Monica's husband, Prashant. Monica was Chaitali's bosom buddy from her boarding school days. Chaitali had acquainted me with some of their misadventures together and I was eager to meet the lady. Having done her doctorate in International Politics, Monica now worked as a research fellow with the Institute of Peace and Conflict Studies. Prashant, on the other hand was an IPS officer who headed a special anti-terror cell. His job was to track down potential terror cases, besides finding and busting sleeper cells, and keeping apace with latest Intelligence reports. The fact that he had killed roughly forty terrorists in encounters had listed him among the country's best-known encounter specialists.

I thought the couple made an extremely interesting professional match. Monica's work entailed probing the root causes that led to terrorism and suggesting ways to thwart it. Prashant's, on the other hand, negated the root-cause theory entirely. His was more like an emergency operation – much of it took place in situations after the damage had been done and left him with little choice – either to kill or be killed. One would think that to effectively end the menace of terrorism, both these people and their respective organizations had a crucial part to play. But if one were to sit through an evening with the couple, one would realize just how differently they thought.

When Chaitali and I first met, Monica was away on a work tour of some European nations. Hence it was almost five months after Chaitali and I were together that I first got a chance to meet the couple. Monica had invited us for dinner.

It was a Saturday night. With a couple that was so deeply entrenched into terrorism issues, it was obvious that our discussion would soon veer around to the vexed problem. And, as I normally did, I ended up lashing out against the government's lack of will to fight the menace.

'What we need is an all-out war on terror,' I advocated, mild intoxication making me spin a bit.

Monica looked amused. 'When will you politicians rise above empty rhetoric?' She was a teetotaler.

'Well, while in the Opposition, I can't indulge in much beyond rhetoric. But if we were in Government, trust me, we'd not have sat this helpless,' I shot back.

'You know something. A term like "War on Terror", used injudiciously, simply creates misunderstandings about concepts like "war" and "terror" resulting in ill-advised policy responses.'

I put down my glass to listen to her more intently.

'By definition, *war is violent engagement between two legitimate political entities*. War cannot be waged with an activity like *terror* or with illegitimate entities like terrorist groups. The right term to fight terror is "counter-terrorism".'

'Go on,' I said.

'Terrorism by definition is *the use of violence against civilians by non-state actors to attain political objectives*. Hence, while states are constrained by the principle of non-combatant immunity, terrorists are not. Moreover, the ambiguous nature of terrorists guarantees them immunity, unlike states, from the rules of war as none can be held accountable. For instance, we still know very little about who the Lashkar-e-Hindustan really is.'

'Hmm... I see... And what would counter-terrorism thus mean?'

'Pest control – that's what it has to be like. Search them out and kill them wherever they are lurking – like you kill cockroaches when they enter your house,' Prashant said tersely.

'Oh come on, darling. I've told you before that you mustn't indulge in such discussions when you're drunk,' Monica's voice had an edge to it.

Prashant shrugged his shoulders. 'I need a refill,' he said and left the table. His capacity for alcohol consumption was large. Chaitali joined him.

'You were talking about counter-terrorism steps,' I said, turning back to Monica.

'Yes. Andrew Kydd and Barbara Walters cite five strategic logics and goals of terrorist outfits. The strategic logics include attrition, intimidation, provocation, spoiling and outbidding. Terrorists utilizing attrition advertise to their adversary their ability to impose considerable costs on the target population over a period of time; intimidation is mainly aimed to coerce the target population to support the terrorists' cause; provocation attempts to induce the adversary to respond to terrorist acts with indiscriminate counterforce, resulting in enormous hardship for people. Consequently, the population ends up supporting the terrorist outfits. Spoiling includes attempts by terrorist outfits to undermine any move against terror by moderates amongst the target population. Outbidding aims at convincing the target population that one terror outfit is more credible than others.'

'And what is it that they want to achieve – just death, destruction, or to create a fear psychosis?'

'Well, five principal goals are meant to be achieved by these strategic logics: regime change, policy change, territorial change, social control of the population and status quo maintenance of an existing regime or territorial arrangement. Amongst these goals, the 9/11 attacks were primarily waged by the al-Qaeda to engineer U.S. policy change in West Asia, especially in regard to U.S. troops stationed in Saudi Arabia. The recent terror bombings in India are meant either for 'territorial change' or 'social control.' If the LeT was indeed involved in these, its goal was territorial change in Kashmir.'

'Hmm. And what would you specifically suggest in the Indian context?'

'Well, India's counter-terrorism strategy would require well-coordinated specialized units with superior intelligence-gathering and assessment skills. The government must urgently activate effective counter measures such as law enforcement, covert operations based on sound intelligence against terror networks, and efficient bureaucratic coordination. There has to be a seamless flow of information unhindered by centre-state distinction.'

Prashant walked in at this point, clapping his hands, in mockery. He was drunk and yet not so gone as to lose his train of thought. 'So you agree with this theoretical crap?' he asked me.

'We do,' quipped in Chaitali, exuding some amount of defiance.

'Great,' retorted Prashant, clapping again. 'God bless you all. But I beg to differ.'

I looked at him in anticipation.

'Do you know how impotent I feel at times?' he looked me in the eye and asked. 'All these theories are fine, but how would you feel when you are in a position like mine? If I had my way, I'd have killed at least half-a-dozen of these terrorists in the last one month.'

'Why couldn't you?' I asked, worried that I wouldn't be entirely unaware of the answer.

'I was advised to go slow. One of the suspected terrorists has travelled frequently on a Railway VIP pass issued by an MP. The other suspect's father is an ex-MLA in UP.' Prashant smiled. 'Now Mr MP, you do understand the repercussions of acting against such terrorists, don't you?'

I had no answer. And Prashant had just too much to tell.

'I too love to hear these theories. But my dear, the situation on the ground is just frightening. We're sitting on a time bomb that is about to explode – all thanks to those wretched politicians who have raped this country.'

The level of Prashant's anguish took me by surprise. Even as Monica tried to calm him, he went on:

'You know, Brajesh, we're actually fighting a losing battle. Today, the police and the law-enforcing authorities are fully equipped to wipe out terrorism. But we can't. We can't, because every time we make an arrest, some of these political parties gang up against us and ridicule our motives. Every time we kill a terrorist in an encounter, these jokers called "human rights activists" stage protests.'

I could sense Chaitali's discomfort.

'Tell me, Brajesh, you think we are assholes who know nothing? That we arrest and kill people because we enjoy it?'

Prashant's angst and the unpleasant questions that emanated from it, were in a way directed at me because in this informal, friendly gathering I happened to be the only official representative of the breed called politicians.

'Some of our politicians are indirectly instigating Muslims by repeatedly undermining institutions such as the police force and other law-enforcing agencies. This has to stop. If the politics of this country does not change, a civil war is inevitable.'

Prashant's words were so piercing that they had me in turmoil. It made me realize how we'd failed this country; we'd incapacitated the very system that we were meant to strengthen – all for votes and political survival.

Prashant's uncharitable remarks about human rights activists protesting terrorist encounters had irked Chaitali: 'Prashant, you may not do such a thing, but the fact remains that we have proof of fake encounters having taken place. And worse, some of them had the backing of respective state governments.'

Prashant's vociferous and agitated retort to this almost shook the room. 'What the hell! Okay, agreed, that fake killings have at times taken place, in some cases of innocents too. But why the hell are you building up an atmosphere where a policeman will have to think a thousand times before killing or nabbing even a known terrorist? That's what you people have done. The tragedy of officers like me is that we are not scared of terrorists. We are scared of politicians and people like you.'

Prashant calmed down when he realized his remarks were insulting to his guests. 'You know the biggest challenge today – it is to identify the terrorist. The terrorist could look like any ordinary college student from a good family or he could be working in your office. He is faceless. *Mark my words, Brajesh, you will just be shocked by some of the arrests we make in the next few days.'*

Prashant went off for another drink. I could sense however that he was a defeated and dejected man.

Monica, by the way, showed a remarkably pragmatic approach towards the issue that seemed to agitate her husband so much.

'Terrorism in India is a very complex problem. The kind we see in Kashmir, the kind we see in these sporadic bomb blasts all across and the kind we see in the north-east are all different from each other. It's easier to combat terrorism abetted by outsiders. But where it enjoys local support, combating it becomes far more challenging. It throws up lots of compulsions. That is why policy-makers need to understand where we've failed to keep peace within our own family, our own brethren. We need to introspect on where and how we have failed them.'

Even as I heard her out, Monica made a suggestion that I'd have turned down instantly, had it come from another person. But Monica seemed to be one of the more sensible, intelligent and objective women I had met. 'The ban on SIMI should be revoked. You need to win them over in this counter-terror operation. If you fight them, remember you're antagonizing a sizeable population whose number is only growing everyday.'

I have to admit that I've never met a more terrific couple – each almost an encyclopedia on terror-related issues – one emotional and direct-action bound; the other rounded and strategy-bound. To see a woman expound so well on terror issues, was damn impressive. A passing thought occurred to me: I wished Chaitali was a little less judgmental at times, and more objective like Monica.

◆

My wish was dispelled on our way back, that night itself.

Chaitali sensed that there was something going on in my mind.

'What are you thinking, Braj?'

'I was just thinking about Monica's suggestion to revoke the SIMI ban.'

'Yeah. That should be done.'

There were bigger thoughts floating in my mind.

'Chaitali, why does religion have to be the cause of so many problems in our country? Tell me, has the country failed the Muslims? Or have they failed us?'

When I said this, a sensible girlfriend would have sensed my turmoil. Chaitali to my surprise did not. 'A prejudiced thought process towards them is what has failed them. It's about the way that people like you and Prashant think that has failed them.'

'What?' I asked, shocked.

What Chaitali said thereafter incensed me no end. 'Tell me, Brajesh, can't a Hindu group be behind these recent bomb blasts?'

'Have you gone nuts?' I retorted in anger.

'Why? We have reports that last year in Kanpur some Hindu activists disguised in burqas were trying to plant bombs. In any case, tell me one reason why Hindus can't be terrorists?'

'You give me one reason why they would be? For centuries Hindus have been at the receiving end of torture and oppression in their own country. And you think we'd do this to their own country for no reason?'

'Hindu groups know that nobody will suspect them.'

'You know, Chaitali, you must get your head examined.'

'You know, Brajesh, you're a racist.'

'No, I'm not. You've met Wasim, my trainer. Why can't an Indian Muslim be like him? He doesn't have any bitterness in him. He is a patriot to the core.'

'How many Muslims have you interacted with to know them? I doubt you can do that being in an outright communal party.'

Chaitali's accusations made me livid. 'Fair enough. I am racist! I'm communal! I'm a chauvinist! Does it make you happy to be the girlfriend of such an unworthy character?' I shot back.

If the chaos of that night was any indicator of things to come, I was afraid turbulence was back in our lives. The brief period of peace that we'd laboured for, with Radha's assistance, was in danger.

◆

Next morning, after my jog, I returned home to complete my abs workout in my garden. Wasim joined in to help me with it. However, I remained pre-occupied, thinking about the previous evening and couldn't really concentrate. One particular sentence of Prashant's came to my mind repeatedly – *'Mark my words, Brajesh, you will be shocked by some of the arrests we make in the next few days.'* I wondered what could be that shocking? Who could the person be? After all, the country had really seen so much that even some of the most unthinkable occurrences had lost their shock value.

I went through the motions of my workout and just as I was on the verge of winding up, I saw Prashant walk in with three other cops. I wondered what brought him here.

'Arrest him,' he instructed his junior pointing towards Wasim.

Before Wasim could make a counter move, three cops over-powered him. I was shocked to see this bizarre scene.

'This guy has a big hand in at least two of the recent serial blasts,' Prashant told me.

'What? How can it be?' I queried in disbelief.

'I had told you my friend you'll be shocked… We've been following him for the past three weeks.'

Wasim was taken away. His arrest took away much of my faith too. I knew now why Prashant had been so agitated the previous evening.

Two days later, I was told that the investigation had established that Wasim was part of a terrorist group that planned to eliminate six political leaders, mostly from the BJP, and that included me. His employment as my personal trainer gave him the proximity to study the security set-up of MPs and to meticulously plan the act. I was shocked to realize that my murder was being hatched by a person of whom I was so fond.

Chaitali and I had barely spoken after our fight. However, after Wasim's arrest, she met me. She just hugged me tight, in a yielding manner, as though trying to tell me I had been right all along and that she had been wrong. That was the least of my concerns. I was increasingly worried about our inability to identify this new age terrorist – who might well be your gym instructor or a close associate.

Chaitali, for her part, tried to make normal conversation. 'I'm sorry, Braj. You know, having heard first-hand accounts of the Gujarat massacre I guess I have a bias against your party which I will never be able to overcome. I know your concerns are genuine, you are unbiased…'

'Cut it out, Chaitali. What are you really trying to say?'

What Chaitali said only manifested the confusion that was now beginning to characterize her. 'Problem is Braj… I love you, but I hate your party and ideology.'

'I am not different from my party or ideology,' I asserted.

My firm retort left Chaitali with little option but to accept her folly unconditionally. Nonetheless she put forth a suggestion and made me agree to it. I agreed in the larger interest of our future – if it still existed. We decided that we'd henceforth not entertain any contentious political conversation between us.

◆

One thing that Chaitali never ceased to do was surprise. Once we avoided meddling with our political philosophies, our relations improved significantly. Also, Chaitali, either consciously or naturally, entered a new phase – she said she felt disillusioned with her political existence; that she wouldn't mind quitting all of it if we were to start a family.

Having seen the steep swings in Chaitali's thought process I wanted her to sustain herself in this new state of mind for some more time before I took her seriously. But yes, to see her make this effort evoked sympathy in me. I guess hers was in some way a case of *past imperfect, future tense*. It made me realize that I needed to be more patient with her.

Three weeks later was Chaitali's birthday. I decided to follow a slightly different approach in her case. Much of her problems in life emanated from the fact that her life was largely devoid of real love. I decided to surprise her on her birthday by proposing marriage. And I planned to do this in a secluded milieu away from the city – in a restaurant on the Delhi–Jaipur highway.

But alas, my plan was truncated as on the appointed evening when I was driving my lady out, a series of blasts rocked Delhi, killing some fifty people.

No, we weren't affected by the serial blasts so much as by the explosion it triggered between us.

I vented my anger on the terrorists; Chaitali did so on the 'communalists' who bred terrorism. Since I've already told you about this clash, I will avoid re-living it. But yes, the level of our animosity that night still amuses me; it amuses me more than it did then to think that I had actually asked Chaitali to leave the country.

I can't help laughing about it when I think of it now. We knew from then on that it was a matter of time before we would not be able to stand each other. Our relationship seemed afflicted by a fatal disease and only a miracle could have cured it. Could Radha be that miracle? I doubted it very much.

Over the next few weeks, our conversations dwindled. It was like we were serving a notice period before bidding the final adieu. On one occasion, I saw Chaitali talking to Radha's mother, Shanti. She had found out about Shanti from somewhere and wanted to visit Shanti in the red-light area. On another occasion, when we were having dinner she got a call from Sid. There was something he wanted to discuss so urgently that she excused herself from the table to talk to him.

It had been sometime since we had met Radha together and I was feeling bad about this. Then someone from the orphanage called to say that Radha was missing us and acting difficult. We had decided thus to set our issues aside and visit Radha the coming Sunday. Chaitali came home for dinner on Saturday night. Even though conversation between us was not to be expected to be like before, I'd say we behaved ourselves. After dinner, I lay on the couch and Chaitali came and rested her head on my chest. Parting was tough and it was a good thing that we were trying to make it more cordial.

I suddenly got an unexpected call. It was a call of duty from the party headquarters.

'Chaitali, I won't be able to make it tomorrow,' I informed her. 'I have to go to Gujarat to campaign for the Assembly elections.'

She was upset. 'Brajesh, you can push it to day after.'

'I'm afraid I can't.'

'Oh, so it's more important for you to campaign for that *merchant of death* than it is to be with your daughter?'

I was livid. I was simply amazed at how Chaitali could use an onerous term like 'merchant of death' so frivolously. Looking straight into her eyes, I acquainted her with facts she'd ignored:

'16th August 1946 was declared "Direct Action Day" by the Muslim League to achieve Pakistan. The then Muslim League CM of Bengal, Hassan Shaheed Suhrawardy, purposely declared it a holiday so that the administrative control became ineffective. This move ensured the unabated killing of countless innocents and goes down in Bengal's history as its darkest day. I would consider the perpetrators of this violence and their allies in government to be "merchants of death".'

I then took out a file and hurled it at her.

'Read this. On the night of 19 January, 1990 the whole of Srinagar reverberated with incendiary exhortations to bring in the new dawn with the imposition of an Islamic order. Here, read these three slogans that were played all nights from the mosques: "Kashmir mei agar rehna hai, Allah-O-Akbar kehna hai" (If you want to stay in Kashmir, you have to say Allah-O-Akbar); "Yahan kya chalega, Nizam-e-Mustafa" (What do we want here? Rule of Shariah); "Asi gachchi Pakistan, Batao roas te Batanev san" (We want Pakistan along with Hindu women but without their men). Can you believe that people killed their own neighbours, gouged eyes and gang-raped women? That all this would not have happened, had the administration of Farooq Abdullah not been a silent supporter throughout? Well, the perpetrators of this violence were "merchants of death" in case you still don't comprehend what the term means.'

I was violently agitated.

'Braj... I'm sorry,' Chaitali said, mellowing down.

'In 1984, after Indira Gandhi's assassination, Rajiv Gandhi had callously dismissed the pogrom by saying, *"When a big tree falls, the earth shakes."* Have you ever heard a BJP leader say such a thing? Then how can you call us "merchants of death"?'

'Braj... I said I'm sorry.'

Chaitali seemed more repentant now. This change though didn't make any difference to me.

'To hell with your sorry. The problem with pseudo-intellectuals like you is that you have a short memory. You neither know nor recall anything prior to 2002.'

'What?'

I don't know whether I had begun to derive some kind of sadistic joy from this conversation by now. But there was so much more that I had to rub into Chaitali and so I did.

'Besides, you have a psychological disorder that makes you invite chaos and trouble all the time. Why do you have to meet Radha's mother now? And what makes you keep in touch with Sid and have these long conversations? Is he really gay or is that another lie?'

'Enough, Brajesh, enough. The problem with me is that I've been far too honest with you,' Chaitali shot back.

'No, Chaitz, You've been honest enough to tell me only half-truths, which I consider dishonesty. The truth is you've had an entangled history of grass, men, queers, controversies and a pseudo intellect that has screwed up your brain. There are far too many skeletons in your cupboard.'

The intensity of my outrage surprised me as much as it did Chaitali. It was an explosion of the frustrations that had been piling up inside me for far too long. And I was yet not done with them.

'My tragedy is that despite you having done everything to hurt me, I could not find a better woman to love. My tragedy is I loved you.'

To which Chaitali responded with words that I can't forget:

'You really think you loved me? That's your misconception, Brajesh. You loved *yourself*. You are too obsessed with yourself to be able to ever love anybody else.'

That night was a no-moon night. It was symbolic as we seemed to have wiped out the entire distance that we'd traversed together. Our relationship died that night. In its death though, it was made to carry an unwanted burden – of those last words of Chaitali – '*You are too obsessed with yourself to be able to ever love anybody else.*' Those words would haunt me at all times – often keeping me awake till the wee hours of the morning. Those words would also make me fear something I hated to think – was Chaitali the only girl who really knew me, maybe better than I knew myself?

◆

I had not seen Chaitali since then. We bumped into each other at the India International Centre on the evening of what was the coldest day in Delhi last year. Chaitali proposed coffee.

As soon as the waiter left Chaitali said, 'Brajesh, I've been missing you a lot. Can't we give it another try? Can't we meet again like we met the first time? Can't we forget all the problems that happened between us and start afresh?' she almost pleaded.

I am a little more pragmatic than Chaitali. I know that some moments were meant to be lived only once and when they were destined. They couldn't be re-ignited and re-lived by conscious, mutual planning. I tried to convey the same to Chaitali. She was heartbroken. I still cared for her. I didn't want her to be shattered again. I knew that even if we re-lived our moments of ecstasy, our moments of chaos would eclipse them soon enough – so irreversibly different were we.

I'm surprised though at destiny's astute designs. Chaitali, after she met me, met Aditya on the same evening and at the same venue. And soon a new story started – a story which though it doesn't have me playing a central part in it, doesn't free me from its folds either.

◆

Trimbakeshwar, North Maharashtra

It's six in the morning and dawn is just breaking. I'm about to take a dip in the chilly waters of the Godavari. Yes, I have acceded to my parents' exhortations to perform the rituals necessary to get myself rid of the Kalsarp Yog and possibly pave the way for my marriage. I take the dip, which I'm told is meant for 'purification of the mind and soul'.

My parents are there too to oversee the rituals. Also present is my PA, Bhatnagar, who has become a good friend. Bhatnagar's responsibility today is to ensure that the operation remains completely hush hush – that nobody from the media or my political colleagues or adversaries learns of it. And to be honest, being in the position in which I find myself today, it feels as if an intensive operation is being performed on me by priests substituting as doctors. It doesn't take much time for a local cable channel crew to arrive on the spot. Fortunately, I'm whisked away to a restricted area where the crew is not allowed.

From here begins the most comprehensive set of rituals that I've seen, forget participated in. I'm asked to worship Lord Mrityunjay before the main ceremony begins. Then, to expiate me from all the sins committed by me, I'm asked to make a donation to the spiritual guide; we have brought a goat for this purpose. As I make the donation, I'm not feeling good at all. If I had my way I'd still have stopped it. But the hope and devotion I see on my parents' faces make me feel helpless. I decide to not think and go about the rest of the ritual in a mechanical manner.

The main ceremony begins with the worshipping of Lord Ganesh. After the Ganesh Pujan, I perform a Lord Varun Pujan, also known as Kalash Pujan. This follows the worship of Goddess Durga, Lord Shiva, Rahu Kaal (God of time) and some other gods, godesses and deities of whom I haven't really heard. These rituals are finally followed by a 'havan'. As I sit through the most laborious worshipping (read atonement) exercise of my life, I can't help battling a whole gamut of emotions that I experience at this point – I mean the whole paraphernalia is so intimidating that it does something to you.

The situation compels me to think why I, an elected member of my country's Parliament, have to be in this pitiable position. Why couldn't I get what I deserved in my personal life, just like I had on the professional front?

After the exhaustive ceremony, we drive down to Mumbai. Another round of emotional cajoling is about to start when I gesture to my parents to just let me be in peace for a while. They take a flight to Lucknow where they'll stay with relatives for a day. I fly back to Delhi.

My flight back is full of rumination. And I have for company Bhatanagar, who at 43, has seen a little more of life than I have.

'Brajesh, I think you should marry Shweta. You've seen all that one should of bachelorhood.'

I just nod. Not that Bhatnagar has said something that hasn't already crossed my mind; but it's reassuring that he understands my state. He has seen me with Chaitali to know what I might be missing in Shweta. 'Shweta will make a good wife,' he says more indulgently.

'I know.' There's a pause before I add, 'Just that, apart from a good wife, I'd ideally want my wife to be a friend and perhaps a more passionate lover.'

Bhatnagar smiles. 'Chaitali was all that, but as you found out, she wouldn't be a good, stable wife.'

I think I agree with him.

'You know what, Brajesh, for all your zeal on the professional front, you're quite a conservative guy when it comes to women. And right now, with all the changes that your life has seen in the last few years, you're fighting different forces within you. It makes sense in this situation to go for someone simple who supports you, rather than someone who adds to your chaos.'

I think Bhatnagar has summarized the situation just the way I'd do it. I feel tired of being a wanderer at thirty-two. I deserve to be taken care of. Besides, I remember one of the few things worth remembering that Pitaji had said to me on the subject of choosing a life partner – *go for someone who loves you more than you love her*. It may sound clichéd and often repeated; but it is true.

As my flight prepares to land in Delhi, I've made up my mind to ground my wandering as well. To my surprise, the moment I land and turn on my cell, I get an sms from Shweta. She tells me she's come to the airport to pick me up. I think this is telepathy. I'm surprised at how things seem to have begun falling into place in the last few hours. I wonder if this is a result of prayers to get rid of Kalsarp Yog. But yes, this seems like magic. I think I should respect my parents' counsel a little more.

◆

I meet Shweta and we drive to an Indian restaurant in a five-star hotel not very far from the airport. This restaurant plays old Hindi songs at low volume and that only adds to my exhilaration. I can't believe I'm actually going to talk marriage to Shweta – to someone, I'd always tell myself I was not in love with. But then matches are made in heaven. I'm surprised at how I am able to see her differently. She's looking a lot more gorgeous today, a lot happier. I am beginning to like her a lot more.

'Shweta, I have to tell you something,' I tell her excitedly as a south Indian dish is laid out before us.

'Really? Me too,' she says.

I can't believe this. I knew there was always a lot on her mind; that Shweta always wanted to profess her feelings for me, but could not for fear of disappointment; I am amazed at how everything falls into place when it has to.

'Tell me na, Brajesh. What is it you want to say?'

A thought occurs to me. I have never been formally proposed to by a girl. I have just been too reserved to give girls I do not like, that leeway. Now is the opportunity for me to soak in another prized feeling. Yes, I'd like Shweta to propose to me. I'd like to see how she does it. Besides, I've always thought she needs to be more articulate. Today, she might well be that.

'No. Ladies first,' I sit back, smiling in my heart.

'Brajesh, I've decided to marry Sameer.'

'Sameer?' I ask, the incomprehension apparent in my voice.

'Yes. I realized he loved me a lot. And it makes sense to go for someone who loves you more...'

I find it tough to conjure up a semblance of courage and equanimity to be able to congratulate her. I tell her that I am happy for her.

'Now you tell me. What did you have to say, Brajesh?'

A song from an old seventies' movie *Rajnigandha*, plays in the background at this point – 'Na jaane kyon hota hai yeh zindagi ke saath... achanak yeh mann, kisi ke jaane ke baad, kare phir usko yaad...' I wonder if the song is talking to me. Shweta is excited and asks me again what it is that I wanted to say.

'Just what you told me. That you must get married to Sameer at the earliest,' I say with a smile on my face and tears in my heart.

◆

Ghulam Mohammad Saab can be a good agony uncle as well. His wife is out of town. Over dinner at his place, he gives ear and support to Aditya and me. Aditya's relationship with Chaitali has grown even more chaotic now. He is in love with Chaitali and wants to marry her. Chaitali perhaps is still in love with her ex-lover, i.e., me. Aditya doesn't know the identity of this ex-lover. It's as complicated a situation as can be.

'You know the difference between your generation and ours – why our relationships and marriages worked and yours don't?' Ghulamsaab asks and then answers the question himself: 'We basically looked for sex and procreation in marriage, whether we admitted it or not. Nowadays there's no dearth of sex without marriage. So you people look for ever-lasting companionship in marriage – which is hard to find.'

Aditya and I hear him out intently.

'I mean, you get bored being with a single friend all your life, unless the friend re-invents himself, evolves constantly, and is able to match you step for step. Both partners have to match the pace of evolution or else one surges ahead and the other is left behind.'

A pause precedes his stark conclusion. 'Our generation was lucky. It's very tough to make relationships work nowadays.'

At this point, one of Ghulamsaab's peons comes in and tells him that Ghulamsaab's brother has called from Jammu. Ghulamsaab excuses himself.

I look at Aditya. I can sense the turmoil in him. I'm not sure if he'll ever know that Chaitali has wreaked so much turmoil upon the both of us. I don't know what it is about her that made us both fall in love with her. I'm not sure why Chaitali hasn't mentioned the identity of her ex-lover to him, if she could tell him other details about her relationship. Why do I need to be mentioned as a friend? Women fake and how! Does she really love me even now or is it, as in my case, that she's probably realized the worth of someone after losing the person? Human traits and psyche, after all are not too dissimilar.

Out of friendly concern, I ask Aditya about the latest on his romance. His response puts me in a messy spot.

'Dude, I think, I'll need your help finally,' Aditya tells me. 'I think you'll have to talk to Chaitali on my behalf. You can do it as you're a common friend of both.'

I wonder why life has to be so cruel to me. I want to tell Aditya that he mustn't expect this from the person responsible for Chaitali's indifference towards him. But I can't.

Right then, Ghulamsaab walks into the room. His sombre expression gives an indication that something is terribly amiss. 'I've just got news from my staff that a terrorist encounter took place near Noida about an hour back. There's some very bad news...' He switches on the TV with the remote. The image that I see is probably the worst way to end an already chaotic day. Prashant Singhal is no more. He was shot at and killed in the encounter.

◆

The next morning is witness to a grim spectre. Hundreds, including the Prime Minister, the Home Minister and the Chief Minister converge upon Prashant and Monica's Dhaula Kuan residence to pay homage to the brave cop. I am present. So is Aditya. So is Chaitali. Later in the day when the sun sets and Prashant's body is consigned to the flames, I'm reminded of Prashant's outburst on the evening I had dinner with him, nearly a year ago. I remember each and every word like it was said yesterday – so telling they were. I wish his death had been less cruel than his life had become.

It's darker now. A few friends and close family members are left. I can spot a significant change though in the physical positions we occupy. Aditya seems more aligned with Chaitali. I give my shoulder to Monica.

Chaitali

WHEN I AM REALLY HAPPY OR SAD AND HAVE nobody with whom to share my joy and sorrow, you know whom I fall back on? I snuggle up with my teddy, Tequila. He is warm and he is non-judgmental, unlike the men of today.

Now you'd be surprised why neither Brajesh nor Aditya have ever mentioned my fascination for soft toys.

Brajesh didn't, because he found my fascination for soft toys 'childish'. Frankly, Brajesh never really appreciated the simple joys of living. He couldn't, because he had gifted himself the illusion of inflated self importance. He had started believing that only he had a sense of purpose in life; all lesser mortals were rudderless and frivolous. I'm afraid I can't conceal my bitterness when I talk of Brajesh. And I would rather not, because I'm a normal, lesser mortal with no illusions of forced propriety.

Aditya didn't, because Aditya likes things to be underlined or specifically stated. Therefore, his quandary over whether we were or could be a couple made him overlook many of the subtler things that fascinated me the most.

I have to tell you here that both these men had something in common – an uncanny lack of understanding of a girl's psychology.

When we spoke last, I was reeling under the trauma of not being able to get over my love for Brajesh. I made one last attempt to get my love back, and failed. Whether on the rebound or otherwise, I got into a hasty relationship with Aditya. You might think it's an enviable position to be in – one hunk goes out and the other comes in. How I wish matters of the heart were that simple. I'm afraid they aren't that straight for an Indian girl, who for all her outwardly appearances, is conservative at heart; and for whom people and relationships matter a lot.

Brajesh accused me of dishonesty; of telling him half-truths. I can reciprocate the honour, but I won't. I won't because I like to think that often dishonesty (read half-truths) carries the best of intentions. If inconsequential, it is meant not to hurt the person you love. Besides, we seldom speak the whole truth, do we? Let me tell you something interesting – what a person shows about himself or herself to the world is not the truth; what a person hides of himself or herself, definitely is.

I'll tell you why precisely Brajesh and I could not be together.

Brajesh, for all his projections of a cool, modern, pragmatic dude is a chauvinistic Allahabadi at heart. It is one of life's biggest paradoxes that it sometimes throws you into situations that are diametrically opposite to those that you anticipate. Therein, lies the biggest challenge to your personality. Some take the situation in their stride; some keep being a doubting Thomas.

Man-woman relationships follow different patterns – some start off with companionship and friendship and only much later develop into something not platonic. In other cases, things start off directly in fifth gear – as it happened with us. I guess a lot of things that happen in life, happen because of an unknown number of disparate factors converging to make them happen – in our case for instance, I didn't have a car that night; it was raining cats and dogs; Brajesh offered me a lift which I accepted; and both of us were attracted to each other.

For me, it remains the best night of my life – a night that I'll cherish for a lifetime. The best of things happen when your expectations are zilch. It is when expectations creep in between two people that things begin to sour. I would be a moron to suggest that relationships should not carry expectations. The important thing is to know the point at which your relationship is ready to bear the load of expectations. If you rush things, the magic as you call it, gets impaired. And worse, if you don't realize what impairs this magic, salvaging the situation becomes increasingly difficult. I think this is where Brajesh faltered.

To be honest, neither Brajesh nor I would have anticipated on our first night that we'd even enter into a relationship. I was too unconventional for him and he was too perfect and upright for me. Besides, I'd somehow formed the notion that I could never fall for a guy again. That I was not a lesbian, made matters worse. I guess when Brajesh and I gave in to our passion that night, it in some way signified our mutual submission to each other. I was pretty sure I would not relate with him beyond that first night; I was sure he would not want to meet me again.

I don't know if it was my touch – my *sparsh* – as Brajesh called it, that made things happen but by next morning we felt differently about each other. The forging of our body and mind made us realize that we were probably not as alien to each other as we thought we were a night ago. I would not have given in, had there been no mental connect between us; despite what Brajesh said, I am not a whore.

I'm sorry to harp on that word but aside from those magical moments of love and love-making, if there is one thing that refuses to fade from my memory it is Brajesh's acerbic dismissal of my character. His words to the effect that *if I were in a smaller town and behaved the way I did, I'd be called a whore*, still ricochet in my ears; it mutes out all the good things that Brajesh may have ever said to me.

You'd ask me why then did I go back to him?

Let me confess – somewhere, I wanted to be like him – perfect, and in full control of things. I know I am too imperfect and with little control over myself. I took drugs more frequently than I let Brajesh know. And substance abuse invariably leads you to be friends with similar escapists. I didn't hide this information from Brajesh for any other reason than for our good. His presence in my life only made me more aware of my failings. I wanted to stop doping. I wanted to be more disciplined. I wanted to be half as correct as him. To that extent, he was perhaps right. I saw a panacea in him. I thought he'd bring focus to my life.

If rape is the worst physical assault on a woman, to be called a 'whore' would be the worst verbal assault. The emotional turmoil of the victim is worse when the assault is wreaked by the person she loves the most. I'm not sure whether that assault was a blessing in disguise, because I haven't once done drugs after that.

Now, every saint has a past and every sinner a future. Brajesh, unfortunately does not realize this. When he saw

Udit trying to kiss me, that moment became the indelible defining moment in our relationship that put everything else under the scanner. Brajesh hence always suspected our first night – *was he the only man I'd had that escapade with, or was he one among several? Did he live the best night of his life with a whore?* Of course, I am within my rights to have similar doubts about Brajesh. After all, I have information that he has in the past, made a pass at one attractive journalist at least, that too at a party. When the journalist clarified that she was committed and not available, Brajesh is said to have told her that her cleavage and body language suggested otherwise.

Does *that* give you an idea of how Brajesh's mind works?

He accused me of belonging to the 'pub culture'. Well, what is that? Yes, I like to wear short dresses to house parties. I find them comfortable and cool. I'd have worn them to pubs too if I were not into politics.

I like to hug close friends, including guys, and if I'm really happy or excited, the hug tends to be more robust. I drink, sometimes to consciously escape thinking. I like to dance and at times my dancing partners have been men I didn't know – the criterion of my choice was their ability to match my steps and spirit. I do smoke, though I am not a chain smoker. And yes, in the past I have doped on grass and weed, with a phase in between when the doping was more frequent. I have had sex with four men in all and kissed two others. I believe in that thing called love. I believe in commitment. I believe in an institution called marriage. I crave motherhood.

I'm still clueless about what exactly Brajesh meant by this 'pub culture' and why I was accused of belonging to it. I am an ordinary girl, who unlike Brajesh, entertains no desire to be seen as being more correct than everybody else.

After the 'whore' episode, I had serious doubts about our future. The more logical thing for me to do would have been to back off. Yet, I knew how lonely Brajesh was. I knew that I meant something to him. From that point, I don't really know why, but I took it as a challenge to belong to him.

Brajesh will not tell you this: on the day that we patched up and he woke up in my house to say *that he'd like to wake up with me every morning of his life*, something else happened soon after on the breakfast table.

'Braj, can I suggest something?' I'd said with childlike innocence. 'Let's get married, yaar...'

The shock of my words made him choke. 'You serious?' he asked.

'Of course, let's go this Sunday to the Akshardham temple and get married... What's the fun if we plan everything to the minutest detail?'

Brajesh's ambivalence did not leave him with the words to reply. From his expression, though, I knew he wasn't prepared to unconditionally embrace me just yet. He wanted time to be fully convinced that I was not what that fateful doping night had him believe. He wanted to be convinced that I no longer belonged to the 'pub culture'.

But does love really have to be conditional? I mean there were times when Brajesh's obsession with himself bored me to death. It amounted to egocentricity of an intolerable kind. Yet I accepted him with his flaws. Why couldn't he?

My decision to subsequently adopt a child was borne out of my own desperation to prove myself different from what Brajesh perceived me as. He surprised me by joining hands in the venture. And though, in hindsight, I regret trying so hard, at that point Brajesh's support meant the world to me. I guess I was weak. His reassurance, albeit superficial, was a pillar of strength.

And yet when things are not meant to be, they're not. For one, I couldn't stand his ideology – especially when it came to religion and terrorism. In so much as he tried to project himself as a nationalist, I could sense a racist streak in him. I could sense a bias that would stifle me. And just as, when things are meant to happen, many factors converge to create synchronicity, similarly, when things are meant to go haywire, many factors converge to cause doom.

And so, apart from our ideological clash, our contrasting temperaments made the conflict more insoluble. Nonetheless, today I will reveal some truths to you. I will tell you why I engaged with Radha's mother, Shanti and my ex-boyfriend, Sid.

Sid and I had not really been in touch after I came back from London. We did meet once when we attended a common friend's wedding in Delhi. Other than that it would be an occasional birthday or New Year's message. Around the time that my relationship with Brajesh was mired in turbulence, Sid re-established contact with me. One evening, I was surprised to get a call from an unknown number from abroad. That it was Sid calling me after so many years surprised me. But what he said shocked me. He wanted an unusual favour from his ex-girlfriend.

Sid was in a relationship with this new guy, Sam. And the two wanted to start a family; they wanted a baby. Adopting one surely was the most feasible and easy solution. But they wanted to experience purer joy. Sid wanted to donate his sperm to a surrogate mother to bear his child. It would surprise you to know that surrogacy norms are the easiest in US and India; India tends to be the preferred destination for such couples, as it is relatively inexpensive. My task was to scout for a surrogate mother for my ex-lover.

'Chaitali, I know it's weird to expect this from you, but the thing is I've snapped ties with my family and can't let them know. I asked two other friends to help me with this but they ditched me. I can't trust anybody more than you,' Sid had pleaded.

I was troubled all that night. I kept thinking that if God were a script-writer, he'd win many awards – so convoluted were his plots. I mean, logically, if I think of it, had Sid not been gay, his sperm would have been in me. Now, I had to search for my surrogate. My feelings for Sid had ended long ago. But I knew I would have to do his bidding. I could not turn my back on the only favour he had ever asked of me.

Thus began my search for a surrogate mother. Around that time I was meaning to meet up with Radha's mother, Shanti. I thought the meeting would help me understand Radha better. When I finally met Shanti in the red-light area in Mongolpuri where she stayed, I thought I had serendipitously discovered the surrogate mother that I was scouting for.

Shanti was a commercial sex-worker past her prime. She'd get a client once in two days and that didn't pay her much. Besides, Shanti herself was thoroughly disappointed with her profession. 'Didi, please get me out of here. I'll work in your house for free but I just can't handle this any more. I feel like killing myself.'

I told her about the proposal to bear a surrogate child. Of course, she would qualify for it only if she was medically fit. Though it went way beyond my proscribed responsibility I negotiated a deal between Sid and her. She was to be paid what she'd make in three years. Besides that, it was agreed that she could also be the baby's nanny in London, if she agreed never to let the child know she was its biological mother.

And what reward did Brajesh give me for this? Another acerbic taunt for my obsession with the likes of Shanti, besides the insinuation that I had lied to him about Sid being gay? I thought this was the last nail in the coffin. When Brajesh said – *'My tragedy is that despite you having done everything to hurt me, I could not find a better woman to love. My tragedy is I loved you'* – I decided I ought to leave him for him to be happy.

Yes, I left him because I loved him too much to see myself be the cause of his unhappiness. I left him because I didn't want to be his failing, in the otherwise exemplary success that he enjoys. I left him for his good and mine.

But did I really leave him?

I tried to.

Even after six months of being away from him I missed him still – so infected was I with him. It took me an unplanned conference with Brajesh to know I had to re-learn to move on. And then, on the same fateful day and venue that I discovered that Brajesh was no more for me, I met another man – Aditya.

◆

Today, I'm in an unenviable and peculiar position. I can say with certainty that I don't miss Brajesh. Aditya, on the other hand, loves me for who I am. Why then am I holding myself back? You know something – it's so strange but your feelings towards someone are influenced more by the state of mind you are in at a given point of time, than by the attributes of the person. Aditya has everything that a woman would seek in a man. He's intellectually strong, a good compassionate human, a caring friend and perhaps as good as Brajesh in bed. I would like to think it is a matter of time before I can give Aditya the happiness that I couldn't give Brajesh. I fear though that having failed twice, the process will be that much more arduous.

Hmmm. Brajesh and Aditya add up to what I always felt was a life less ordinary. I wonder why it is so difficult for either of the three – Congress, BJP and the Left to be at peace with each other.

My pondering is hampered by some breaking news I see on TV – a Hindu group is reportedly involved in the Malegaon blasts. The first important arrests have been made – of Sadhvi Tapasya and Col. Anshuman Agnihotri. More arrests, including one of a senior army man are expected.

I am not too surprised. Malegaon has a dense Muslim population and I had long suspected that such a place could not be the target of known terrorist groups. Now, my worst fears have come true. I'm glad that right-wing nationalists will realize the futility of linking terrorism with religion. I'm sure it's a slap in their face.

What surprises me more is the name I see flashing on my mobile screen. It is Brajesh.

◆

The unearthing of a Hindu terror group has left the country dazed. In as much as we suspected its presence, its unearthing has been a shock. Brajesh had called me last night. I could sense the torment in his voice. He said he wanted to meet me. I didn't ask him what it was for. I guess I wanted to fantasize about the reasons that had made him call me suddenly. He'd called me only once after our break up. Though he said he wanted to know how I was, I knew he was terribly depressed about something. We were to meet in the evening at the Constitution Club café. I could have easily asked him the agenda. But I didn't. That's the difference between him and me. I don't think meeting an ex ought to have a reason.

I scan the morning papers. Well, well, well... every perpetrator is loaded with a justification for his doing! Col. Anshuman Agnihotri has his. And as I read the report, I can't help thinking about the fight I once had with Brajesh and his asking me – *'You give me one reason why a Hindu group would be involved in terror? For centuries, Hindus have been at the receiving end of torture and oppression in their own country...'*

I think Col. Aginhotri might hold the answers to many of our unsorted conundrums. I read his testimony with a growing sense of horror:

Denouement of a Hindu Terrorist

Have you ever thought why Nathuram Godse, a well-educated young man, belonging to a scholarly Brahmin family had to kill Gandhi? Well, Gandhi is called the 'father of the Nation', but in reality he ought to be called the 'father of Pakistan'. For, it was his policy of consistent pampering and acceptance of the nuisance of the Muslim League that eventually paved the way for the desecration of our motherly land and the creation of a theocratic state called Pakistan. Despite the fact that from August 1946, allies of the Muslim League had unleashed a rampage in the country killing, raping and looting Hindus at will, Gandhi's attitude towards the League was pacifist. His acceptance of the partition of the country called the bluff of his much hyped weaponry – his inner voice, his spiritual power and his doctrine of non-violence – all of it evaporated in the heat of Jinnah's determination.

Sixty years after Independence, the country is still paying the price for having bred a Gandhi. His policies that have since been imbibed by subsequent generations have made Hindus defensive and apologetic about their religion. Where does Hinduism preach non-violence as a response to oppression and use of force by the enemy? Ram killed Ravana to relieve Sita. Krishna killed Kansa to end his demonic acts. Arjun killed several of his own relatives including Bhishma, as the latter was on the enemy's side. But Gandhi's non-violence was beyond comprehension. Worse, its repeated failure did not deter him from glorifying his idiosyncrasies – 'A satyagrahi can never fail'. Gandhi's satyagraha amounted to cowardice and inaction.

The same vices were adopted by the subsequent governments of the country – it is not difficult to decipher their source of inspiration. Why does our secular country end up pampering Muslims to the hilt? Why does India have to be the only secular country to dole out a Haj subsidy? And if so, why aren't we given subsidies for the Amarnath Yatra or the Vaishno Devi pilgrimage? Why does Kashmir have to be accorded special status? Why can't Article 370, which abets its alienation, be repealed?

All these questions have a common answer – it's the fight to appease and grab the Muslim vote. The facts that I tell you now will make you realize why this vote share is so important.

The percentage population of Hindus in Pakistan today is a tenth of what it was at the time of Independence. Concurrently, the percentage population of Muslims in India has grown unimaginably. And mind you this is not due to the effects of family planning or of the lack of it. Muslims are systematically being pushed into our country through the Bangladesh and Nepal borders and of late, through sea routes. Then there are these buses and trains plying between the two countries, which under the cloak of friendship bring in unwanted problems into our country. Those from our side, who go there, come back; those who come from there have every reason to want to stay back. That country sucks. It's a failed state that is finding it difficult to retain its civilized façade. Why would they want to go back? Then, they are sent here on the pretext of watching cricket matches between India and Pakistan. A good number dodge our security agencies to set up sleeper cells here. All this happens with the support of our political parties who purposely turn a blind eye to the problem, lest they antagonize the community. If that is not all, some of the shrewder Pakistanis hook up with Indian girls on matrimony sites. That provides them a more legitimate means to become Indian nationals.

In addition to all of these, in some of the states that have a denser Muslim population, young boys are encouraged to woo and marry Hindu girls. That is another systematic ploy to alter the demography and increase their strength. Besides, in some states Hindu Dalits are systematically being indoctrinated to convert. In *one of the recent bomb blasts, the two main accused were Hindu Dalits who had only recently converted to Islam. What is worse is that our government always fudges population figures and under-reports them; this to ensure that they continue to reap the benefits of being in minority. The Muslim population in India today is anywhere between 25-30%, as against what the government might want us to believe. Their ever-increasing population has emboldened them to carry out serial blasts on an alarmingly regular basis and get away with them. In fact, India, between the start of 2004 and March, 2007, lost more lives to terrorist incidents than all of North America, South America, Central America, Europe and Eurasia put together. All these places put together lost a total of 3,280 lives in terrorist incidents between January 2004 and March this year. India alone lost 3,674 lives over the same period of three years and three months. Unlike other countries, India does not seem to realize or recognize terrorism as the major problem. Needless to say, our government perhaps thinks that non-violence (read inaction) of the kind that Gandhi propagated, can in some strange way, automatically solve the problem.*

We beg to differ. We can't sit idle; for if we do, they will soon outnumber us and make India an Islamic state.

India is secular because it has a Hindu majority. It's the Hindu tenets of acceptance and tolerance that make us put up with a lot of crap. But when the situation goes out of control and endangers the survival of the country, it becomes the moral and religious responsibility of every true Hindu to take charge and correct wrongs. We at Hindu Rashtra Samiti have the courage and the selflessness to sacrifice our lives for the good of the generations to come. Violence needs to be answered with violence. Fear needs to be responded to, by inflicting bigger scars and fears. We will devastate their ghettos with explosions that they would never have imagined. We will organize training centres for suppressed

Hindus in Bangladesh to prepare them for armed struggle. We will re-incarnate our motherland into the rightful Hindu Rashtra that it was always meant to be, by killing them or packing them off. There's no stopping us anymore….

◆

I meet Brajesh in the café of the Constitution Club. He comes fresh from a shower after his workout. He smells of a deo that is different from the one he used before. I'm not surprised. Consistency, other than in his political beliefs, is something I have not known him for. I am curious, though, to know what he wants to talk about.

'So how you been, Chaitali?'

I wonder why conversation has to become this formal when you are not seeing each other. Fifteen minutes of stilted conversation later, Brajesh and I are joined by his protein shake and my iced tea. Yet conversation is sparse.

'You wanted to talk about something?' I ask him finally.

'Yeah…' he says, rather incoherently and then adds, 'I was feeling bad. I mean, so many of our arguments had to do with issues concerning religion and terrorism. Perhaps, you were right. A Hindu can be a terrorist too.'

'I was just reading the Colonel's statement on what made him a terrorist.'

'It doesn't matter. Nothing can justify the violence. And yes, I'm upset that my party has not been as vociferous in condemning terrorism this time round.'

I admire Brajesh for this. Not many would accept their folly with their heads held high. Brajesh can. No wonder I found him different from the rest. But I think

I've known him well enough to know that there is more to this meeting than what it appears. Something else is bothering him. And since I haven't known him to be as articulate in personal matters as he is in politics, I coax him on. 'So, what's new on the personal front? Are you dating someone?'

He shakes his head, even as he sips his shake, surprised at my rather unprovoked query.

'I am,' I say.

'I know,' he says.

'Oh yeah? I heard Aditya and you are friends.'

There's a pause. Surely something consequential seems to be floating in his mind. Oh, he speaks:

'I'm happy for you, Chaitz. So when does one hear the announcement?'

'Not till I'm sure I am ready.' As I say this, I have an inkling this is what Brajesh would have wanted me to say.

'And what prevents you from being ready? Me?'

I wasn't expecting this and don't know how to respond 'You know something? I really, really like Aditya. He's the best thing to have happened to me.'

Brajesh has a studied expression on his face.

'Actually I want to talk to you about something.'

Brajesh pauses again. I am surprised. What is it that has pulverized his prized confidence? He is rescued by his phone ringing. By the time he is done with the call, his focus has shifted. 'Listen, Chaitz, I have to be in the Party Headquarters at 7 for something urgent, can I see you again later?'

'Sure... but it's only 5:30 now.'

'No, I need to be in the right frame of mind for this conversation. Let's do it some other time.'

Brajesh's confusion leaves me just as perplexed.

For the next few days, I don't call Brajesh and he doesn't call me. My equation with Aditya, as you know, is already a bit strained. We meet once in a while for dinner. But beyond that we know that any proximity will only lead to disappointment. There is an expectation mismatch. I think he still loves me and would want a yes from me to go ahead with our relationship. I'm just not up to it yet – we haven't had sex in the last few months. This physical distance is obviously designed to reduce the load of expectations, but Aditya I know is still optimistic. I wonder if it is my holding back that accords me invincibility and makes me more alluring. I wonder if like Brajesh, Aditya too wants to possess his women completely. I wonder what is it that attracts people and entangles them in relationships? Why do we sometimes go around in circles?

◆

Just as the indictment of the Hindu groups in terror attacks and his party's cavalier response to it shook Brajesh, my faith gets further shaken by two unsavoury incidents that have generated a lot of heat.

The first is Ratan Tata pulling the Nano car project out of West Bengal. It hurts me when I hear the oft repeated accusation that 'the Communists killed industry in West Bengal'. The Nano, I feel, was our best opportunity for redemption. Instead of thwarting Mamta Banerjee's stance and providing the Tatas the reassurance they needed, we've goofed up big time. That the Nano project should go to our *bete noire* Narendra Modi is a slap on our face. That getting the Nano into Gujarat might help erode the memory of the Gujarat riots – for which Modi was hitherto infamous – is a travesty.

Around the same time, the WB CM, whom I admire greatly, issued a statement saying he will ban 'bandhs' in the state. His statement draws such huge criticism from his own party cadres that he has no option but to withdraw the statement. As a young Communist, I am embarrassed.

These incidents only reinforce what has been on my mind for sometime – the Communists in India need a vision. And that vision ought to extend beyond BJP-bashing and anti-establishment antics. If it doesn't, our future is bleak.

What doesn't make me feel any better is the mob violence that breaks out in Mumbai. A regional party demanding better opportunities for the *Marathi manoos* has indulged in unthinkable violence and arson that has led to the death of three innocent people and brought the entire city to a standstill. Their uninhibited ransacking of cabs and public property has killed the spirit of the financial capital and brought shame to the country. I am disgusted. My disgust is also on account of the fact that the CPI(M) refrained from even making a statement on the issue.

◆

It's been almost ten days since I last met Aditya. He was busy starting a programme in his constituency. He called me an hour ago to say he'd be coming over. I've personally prepared kadi chawal for him. He loves the dish. And I love him – as long as he does not clamour for the clichéd reassurance of a 'committed relationship'.

Aditya comes in and to my surprise he appears hassled and annoyed.

'What happened? Did all go well in your constituency?' I ask.

Aditya nods and mutters a monosyllabic 'yeah'. He gets up abruptly and walks to the window. I am concerned. I haven't known him to behave churlish before. I wonder what makes people behave so uncharacteristically of late? Me?

I hold myself guilty for Aditya's intemperance. I think he is just disillusioned with my inability to commit. I'm not sure if it has to do with Brajesh's veiled admission of guilt but I'm feeling a lot more confident about myself now.

Brajesh was a man who did not value my love, despite me giving him my all; while Aditya is a man who gives me his all, but whom I've invariably let down. I want to hug Aditya tight and apologize. I put my hand on his shoulder. He turns. He sees the emotion in my eyes. He pulls me roughly towards himself and kisses me hard. His lips bruise mine. I'm left wondering if it is love or anger that triggers the act.

And then, he extricates himself almost as suddenly, as though realizing his folly. He turns around and almost bangs his hand against the wall. I am about to say sorry to him, when he speaks out.

'Chaitz, you are half Bengali, half Tamil and have lived in at least four different cities of the world.' I wonder why he says this, but don't interrupt him. 'I am half Rajput, half Muslim – both my parents had roots in

Gujarat and the undivided Madhya Pradesh. I have lived in as many cities.'

I wonder where this is going.

'Have you ever been asked in any of the cities whether you are a native of that city?'

I shake my head.

'Then why is this parochialism being allowed in Maharashtra?'

'Well, your party can stop it if it wants,' I tell him.

'Exactly. But it doesn't. And that's what hurts me. To be a centrist does not mean you have to accommodate everybody's idiocy! But that's what my party is doing now and that's what it has done in the past.'

I am shocked to hear this from Aditya.

'Chaitz, this policy of covert appeasement towards divisive forces will have to stop. When Brajesh accused my party of being responsible for the Punjab problem by encouraging Bhindranwale, I was livid. But when I see my party become a mute spectator to all the mayhem in Mumbai, I am left with no answer.'

For the rest of the evening, I soothe Aditya – as a caring semi-girlfriend ought to.

That night, I'm left alone with my own thoughts. I am left to think how the weakening of ideological convictions can make those driven by them so utterly rudderless. That it impacts their personal relationships and bonds is something you'd know if you've followed our trials and tribulations.

◆

Aditya, Brajesh and I are in a bizarre, unenviable situation right now. In as much as we feel disillusioned by the personal complexities between us, the fact that we now see chinks in our political beliefs too, adds to our turmoil. We're not whom we used to be. I can smell the change. I can foresee re-alignments. I can see fundamental shifts in our thinking and policy. Our past has been horribly imperfect; it's only setting up the tension for an uncertain future – a future, where nothing is ruled out and anything is possible.

My pensiveness at this point reminds me of what a friend had once said in a rather matter-of-fact way. He'd said, 'I wonder why people crib about politics and politicians. There's more politics between a man and a woman in a relationship, than anywhere else.'

I can't agree with him more. Envy, control, confession, denial, acceptance, rejection, empathy, indifference, feeling, not feeling – at times they're all triggered to manoeuvre a favourable response from our partners and to put ourselves in the controlling position.

I wonder why there's so much politics in love.

Or is it love in politics?

◆

Two-and-a-half weeks have passed since I last met Brajesh. I am still to figure out what he really meant to talk about that evening at the Constitution Club cafe. However, his behaviour of late, has led me to entertain expectations yet again.

We've spoken a few times since our last meeting. We've even shared stuff about our lives like pals do. Brajesh has shared his disappointment over his party voting against the government on the issue of the Nuclear Deal. He confessed to me that he was glad the government survived the vote. I do relate with him. My party too withdrew its support to the government on the same issue. But my point, as also I'm sure Brajesh's point, is simple – what significance does the Nuclear Deal have for the common Indian voter? Most people don't have a basic idea of what it entails. I think Brajesh's concern about national interests is more real than that of his other party members. He is convinced that the deal will benefit the country. Brajesh has been equally patient, listening to my rants against my party's failures.

This revived communication between us has led me to entertain a fifty per cent possibility that Brajesh and I might get back together. As for Aditya, the status quo remains. He loves me; I like him. He expects more that he gets from me; I am more than happy with what I have got from him. I consider him my coolest buddy – something I do not consider Brajesh.

Aditya thinks of me as his girlfriend. The mismatch makes us converse about everything under the sun, expect us.

◆

On the professional front, my disillusionment with my party seems to be growing rapidly. I'm beginning to find its entire approach unconstructive. I mean, for four years we supported the government, despite opposing most of the economic reforms and policies of the government. When the government repeatedly raised the price of petrol and kerosene, we led protests against it, yet could do nothing beyond that. Through all our disapprovals, we continued to support the government just because we wanted to keep the BJP out. Then why didn't we join the ministry as a coalition partner and contribute to things the way we wanted?

I do remember that in 1996, after a hung Parliament verdict, an offer was made to Jyoti Basu to head a coalition as PM. The CPI(M) had immediately turned it down. Basu was later to describe this missed opportunity as a historical blunder. When I think of it now, it may just be my present state of mind, but I feel all we've done so far is commit numerous historical blunders. To support a government from outside and yet rip it apart at every given opportunity amounts to craving for authority without responsibility. This I'm afraid is not what people expect from us. And that explains why we've never grown beyond our citadels in Kerala and West Bengal.

I need to fix my personal life. I need to fix my political life as well. Fixing the former I surmise might be easier to start with. Don't really know what it is about Brajesh that does something to me every time we communicate. I feel a rush of adrenalin every time he calls me. And then till the time I call him next, I keep wondering which way his heart is leaning.

In the last one year since our parting, we hadn't met Radha together even once. I'd visited Radha quite often. And as had been decided between Brajesh and me, I'd told her that were both '*katti*' and that we were no longer friends. But I wanted Brajesh to come with me to the orphanage once. I wasn't sure that he'd agree.

But he agreed readily.

On Wednesday we decide to meet Radha in the afternoon after her classes are over. All night, though, I'm left rekindling memories so vivid they seem to have occurred just a few hours ago – my first night with Brajesh;

his longing to meet me after that and my brushing him off; my telling him that I'd had an abortion; his virtually calling me a whore; our adopting Radha, spending some terrific moments together, almost like family, and then parting. All these memories leave me with a terrible feeling of guilt. The guilt emanates from my dishonesty. Yes, I have once indeed been grossly dishonest. My dishonesty has been grave. And no, it is not inconsequential. Perhaps our whole relationship was triggered by this one lie – *I was never pregnant and had no abortion.*

Now you'd wonder why I'd do something so juvenile. Well, Brajesh's persistence after our first night had more or less convinced me that sex was all that he had in mind. I'm not sure whether I'd overestimated my sexual attractiveness or underestimated my other attributes. But that is the notion that I'd formed. And the whole story about pregnancy and abortion was a strategy planned by Monica and me, over a transatlantic phone chat. I wanted to see the dude's reaction. I was sure that he'd run a mile. But his reaction had stunned me. This guy had a sincerity about him that was just so other-worldly. A sense of responsibility that made him feel guilty about my pregnancy and abortion.

At various points in our time together I had wanted to tell him that it was a prank. And at every point, I waited and played along – he was just too good to be real. Even after our courtship began, my cynicism had me believe it would not last. And hence, though I did mean to tell him the truth, I didn't feel any pressing need to do so immediately. It was when he started to snub me for what was wrong in me that I realized I did not mind being controlled by him

Brajesh, however, took everything far too seriously. And as I got to know him better, I knew he'd be outraged if I told him that my pregnancy and abortion had been a farce. This guilt made me compensate to him in every way I could.

As I think about it, I feel it's time to cleanse myself of my guilt. I decide that after we've met Radha, I'll tell him at the orphanage itself that I've lied to him on something very crucial and that this lie had, by default, been the foundation of our relationship. If I know him, he'll appreciate my coming clean. He might feel more inclined to give our relationship a fresh start – laying its foundation this time round on absolute truths.

After playing with Radha for nearly an hour, we leave her to play with her friends. Brajesh and I decide to take a stroll around the place. We move together with uncertain steps, looking at each other, starting to speak, and then looking the other way. Just as I turn towards him to tell him the truth, I find he too has something to say...

'Chaitali, I want to tell you something.'

Oh, how my ears yearn to hear those three magical words he'd said to me almost two years ago.

'Chaitali, you must start afresh.'

'Yes, we must.'

'Yes, so will I.'

I'm dying to hear what he has to say next. But what he does tears me apart:

'You must go ahead with Aditya. He loves you a lot.'

I had no idea that my man had come to endorse his new-found friend to his ex-girlfriend! I am left numb!

'You know, Chaitz, it's important for you to be in a relationship with someone who loves you for who you are. Aditya does that. I couldn't. I have a feeling both of you will make a very happy couple.'

It takes me a while to gather myself. And then, all I can tell Brajesh is that I really appreciate his concern. Brajesh misses the sarcasm, just like he has overlooked so much else.

◆

It's fairly dark by the time we reach home. Aditya's car is parked outside my house. 'Hey, good to see you both together,' he greets us warmly and then turns to me: 'Well, I'm supposed to leave for a sudden trip of Chattisgarh tomorrow morning. I thought I'd surprise you by dropping in. But you were out.'

I'm left in a slightly awkward position. I wonder why Aditya is not surprised to see me with Brajesh. He appears a bit aloof, as though making a conscious effort to hold himself back. Would Brajesh by any chance have told him about our past?

Brajesh takes his leave and Aditya stays back to have the kadi chawal cooked by me. Even as I set out the dish and chat with Aditya, I realize I'm feeling miserable. I hate myself for living in a fool's paradise. My hopes of being loved by Brajesh are nothing more than me chasing an illusion. I was spot on when I'd concluded that Brajesh could never fall in love with anybody except himself. I hate myself for having loved him, when all he could give me was disappointment.

And tonight, I shall do Brajesh's bidding.

Aditya seems to be in a talkative mood.

'You know, Chaitz, I'm worried about this classification of terrorists into Hindu terrorist and Muslim terrorist. It's going to set a very bad precedent.'

But I'm too preoccupied with more personal stuff to be involved in the discussion. Aditya realizes this.

'What is the matter, Chaitali, what are you thinking?'

I fumble for words.

Aditya's anticipation grows.

'Aditya... I... I want to apologize.'

For a moment, Aditya doesn't quite realize what I have said. And I repeat. 'I'm sorry about the way I've been... I'm ready for you.'

Even as I say these words, Brajesh's words – *'Chaitz, it's important for you to be in a relationship with someone who loves you for what you are. Aditya does that. I couldn't'* – ricochet in my ear and anger me.

To my surprise Aditya appears less ecstatic and more dazed.

'You know, Chaitali, I'd given up on us. It's a pleasant surprise...'

From Aditya's expression however it is clear he is more confused than happy. Maybe he is skeptical about my sudden about-turn.

Aditya hugs me hard. Even as we embrace, I'm hoping that my tribulations may finally have ended. I'm wishing that henceforth I'll be less differentiating about the fine line that separates a best buddy from a lover. I am hopeful that in the course of time I will be able to reciprocate Aditya's love in equal measure. I had better do that, or else I'll have to spend the rest of my life struggling to pay back an increasing debt.

Unfortunately, our moment of togetherness is abruptly cut short by a national calamity. Aditya gets a phone call, after which he rushes agitatedly to the television and turns it on. What we see, keeps us awake the entire night: *Firing by unidentified gunmen has been reported in two or three places in Mumbai.* Casualties are mounting every minute. In less than an hour, we learn that Mumbai has been hit by the worst terror strike in its history and that the city is under siege.

I'm left wondering how God can sometimes pack in so much in a day.

◆

It's Sunday. Three days have gone by since the ghastly attack on our country. The last of the terrorists was felled last morning by the NSG commandos after two days of intensive battle. A pall of gloom has descended upon the country and is hard to dispel. We're feeling livid, helpless, frustrated, despondent and terribly humiliated – all at the same time. Nearly 200 people have been senselessly killed; like there was no worth attached to their lives. A war has been waged against the country and we were caught unaware, and unprepared.

India has only once suffered defeat at the hands of an external aggressor. In 1962, China inflicted defeat upon us, decimating much of the confidence and belief of our young nation. I was not born then so I didn't get a sense of the national opprobrium the nation must have felt, but Ma told me that she had seen my grandfather, who had been a freedom fighter, weep profusely; the sight was so pathetic that Ma could never forget it.

This armed aggression by some ten, militarily-trained Pakistani juveniles, upon the heart of our financial capital, was no less an indelible insult. It put our intelligence-gathering mechanism under the scanner; it raised doubts about the sincerity with which our sea borders were being patrolled; worse, it manifested some of our worst fears – there are domestic sympathizers who may have provided logistical support for such a heinous act.

The feeling of collective gloom is overwhelming.

Incidentally, Aditya, Brajesh and I have been in constant touch since the time the mayhem broke out. We've shared our sense of anguish.

Aditya gave vent to his anger by writing a column in a newspaper that was critical of his own government. He wrote, '...What is even more unfathomable is the amateurish approach and virtual abdication of responsibility by the union home ministry. How many times have we heard the Home Minister say: We had intelligence inputs, which we had forwarded to the state? The home ministry of the concerned state is known to respond in predictable fashion: we had general information, no specific information.'

It goes without saying that Aditya was reprimanded by his party for the extra courage shown by him in being honest.

Brajesh added on his blog, 'Can a country as progressive as ours, be run by politicians whose naiveté would put schoolboys to shame? Even the student councillors and group heads in schools show more enterprise and responsibility...This attack has set a dangerous precedent. Tomorrow, God forbid, terrorists may zero in on a building that houses Indians in some other part of the world, just like they zeroed in on the Nariman House this time round. The last thing that we can do in this fight against terror is duck for cover and get defensive. In fact, if this attack cannot substantiate the need for collaboration between India, US, UK *and Israel to wipe out the menace of terror, nothing else can. So far as the Indian scene is concerned, all it needs is political will power and integrity and our erudite PM would do well by starting off the exercise by removing a grossly incompetent dummy from the office of Home Minister.'*

In the wake of the despondency that prevails upon the entire country, Aditya and I have quite naturally, not had the time or the inclination to think about what had happened between us just moments before the news of the attack first broke. My giving in to Aditya seems undone by the overbearing impact of the terrorist attack. I think thus that we are still where we were – maintaining a status quo. What surprises me a bit is that Aditya hasn't quite shown the joy I'd expected him to show when I consented to our relationship. I wonder why this is so.

In the meantime, I did call and tell Brajesh about the development between Aditya and me. Brajesh felt Aditya must know now about our past; Aditya getting to know of it from some other source could create problems between Aditya and me. I couldn't agree more. I know though that this can wait till we are in a calmer state of mind.

◆

Aditya today called me early morning and asked me if we could meet over brunch. I have no reason to decline. We meet outside.

Much of our initial conversation centres round the sharing of mutual angst. Aditya again seems somewhat aloof, like he was the last time we met. I ask him the reason. He is evasive. I'm surprised when Brajesh joins us.

'I'd called over Brajesh too. I hope that's okay with you,' Aditya tells me.

'Yes, of course,' I say, concealing my discomfort. I can sense that Brajesh too has no idea of of my presence here.

Soon, the three of us let loose about our political parties. Both Aditya and Brajesh seem very agitated and I wonder if I've actually been involved with two alter egos instead of two different human beings; they can be so similar at times.

'Yes, my party's government has been an absolute failure on terrorism and I accept it,' laments Aditya.

'My party shouldn't have tried to en-cash on the issue in the ensuing assembly elections. It's so insensitive,' rues Brajesh.

Looking at Aditya, I can sense there is something going on in his mind. And it doesn't take long for it to come out.

'Why did the two of you have to do this to me?' Aditya asks abruptly, suppressed anger evident in his tone.

Brajesh and I are taken aback, wondering what is on Aditya's mind.

'Why did you have to hide your past from me?' Aditya gets more direct.

The query puts both Brajesh and me in a spot. It's Aditya instead who does the talking:

'A journalist told me about the two of you some ten days back. And it didn't take my PA, Yadav much time to dig out the facts. Chaitali, when I suddenly landed up at your place on Wednesday night it was to tell you about what I had learnt. I was shocked, first, to see the two of you return together and then shocked again when you said you wanted to be with me. I'm just confused. What's going on?'

For the next half hour, Brajesh and I tell Aditya all that he may have wanted to know about us. Aditya wonders why neither of us had so far told him about our past. Brajesh does the explaining.

'Look, Adi, I just felt the information could become an unwanted deterrent between the two of you. Trust me, the only reason that I didn't tell you was because I wanted your thing with Chaitali to work out.'

It's my turn. 'Adi, I just felt the identity of the person was unimportant, but I did tell you about my relationships.'

I sense some relief in Aditya. It's like a thing that had been bothering him for sometime had been sorted out. I know now why his reaction when I acceded to him on Wednesday night had been devoid of joy.

For the next few minutes our conversation is tumultuous– it's about us, about the latest news on the Mumbai attack, and about this massive non co-operation movement that the junta is planning three days later, on Wednesday. All three of us have something in common: we share an immense dissatisfaction – both personal and otherwise – that's simply tearing us apart.

And then Aditya gets back to the topic we've been trying to avoid. 'Chaitz, I'm sorry, I just don't feel for you the way I did before.' The abruptness with which he tells me this, is intriguing.

In a way, I also feel relieved to hear this. I'm not sure whether I was really convinced about being with Aditya. I guess I was trying to absolve myself of the guilt of being unable to reciprocate Aditya's sentiments. I'm glad if less is expected of me now.

'And how did this happen?' I ask him.

'I'm not sure. I guess it's the evolution of my thoughts, I have realized that if I had to try so hard to make things happen, they will perhaps not last.'

'Or has it to do with the information that I've been in a relationship with your friend?' I insist on asking.

Aditya isn't quite sure about the answer. 'Not really. It's just a whole chain of events. I think I'm happy with your company the way it is.'

Brajesh, who has been a quiet spectator for sometime, now joins in: 'Or maybe forbiddance makes a thing more desirable? And when you get it, you realize you were fighting the forbiddance more than loving the person?'

'Maybe,' Aditya laughs off Brajesh's suggestion wryly, only to deviate to a topic more impersonal.

Neither of us wants to talk about our relationships any more. We talk instead about stuff that concerns the country. The fact that we've been losing faith in our political ideologies, as much as we have been getting skeptical of our personal preferences, leads to a rather unlikely development.

◆

Three days later, on Wednesday the 3rd of December, Aditya, Brajesh and I, along with Monica, actually join some 1.5 lakh people at the Gateway of India in Mumbai, to protest against our apathetic and indifferent political leadership.

Each one of us is aware of antagonizing our top leadership.

Yet, it's an inner voice that propels us to own up to our failings.

Hordes and hordes of people walk the stretch from the Regal Cinema in Colaba to the Gateway of India shouting '*Bharat Mata ki Jai*' and *Vande Mataram* and castigating our politicians and Pakistan in equal measure. Seldom has the country been more livid and seldom has it seemed more united: people of every religion, caste and region are there, all proud to be Indians and furious at being betrayed.

Even as we march I can sense that this movement will lead to change.

And that the change, this time around, might well be for real.

In the midst of this movement, what doesn't escape my notice is the bonding between Monica and Brajesh. They seem to be getting along well. That the four of us should join hands, heralds a new order for us too.

Jai Ho!

Spring

Aditya

TWO-AND-A-HALF MONTHS HAVE GONE BY SINCE
the Mumbai carnage. The catastrophe ironically brought
Brajesh, Chaitali and me closer, as it must have done
countless scores of fellow Indians. It made us sit up and
think about what ailed our system. Our ruminations were
bred out of a shared disenchantment with the manner in
which everything around us existed. We acknowledged
that a fundamental change or thorough cleansing of the
system was perhaps the only way out.

An inner voice told us that we might have to tread
that extra bit and be the initiators of this change. At that
point, though, there were some attendant self doubts that
left us in a quandary.

The 26/11 carnage, ironically, got me out of the
unending disappointment that engulfed my relationship
with Chaitali. If knowing of Chaitali's past with Brajesh,
who has come to be a very dear friend, had lessened my
interest in her, the Mumbai carnage eroded whatever
remained of it. The collective sense of loss that was to
descend upon the nation, made lesser personal issues
seem unnecessary. And yes, I no longer felt for Chaitali
the same way. For the first time Brajesh, Chaitali and I
could chat as colleagues and friends with many things
in common.

The first step that needs to be undertaken in the process of ushering in a 'paradigm change' is to acknowledge the failings of existing thought. Thus, in one of our late evening discussions, barely a couple of weeks after the carnage, Chaitali came up with an interesting suggestion.

'You know what, let us probe the way we've thought so far. Let us step into each other's shoes.'

'And what would that entail?' queried Brajesh.

'Look, we are all strong believers of a defined thought process or ideology, which in turn has influenced our political affiliations and choices. What if, for the next few days, we put our beliefs under the scanner and start acknowledging the merits in each other's beliefs?'

I quite understood what Chaitali was trying to say. Ideology is akin to religion. So strong is its mooring. Nonetheless, extraordinary situations demand extraordinary steps. Realizing that a paradigm change in the country's policies would not be achievable without us shaking up our existing beliefs, I acquiesced to the exercise.

Brajesh suggested that I go on a tour of Assam, where serial blasts in Guwahati, just a month prior to 26/11, had claimed nearly a hundred lives. He wanted me to educate myself about the problems of the land. Assam, no doubt, is close to Brajesh's heart, considering he has worked there.

I did go on a tour of Assam. My findings were startling. In fact I've assembled them into a report that I intend to discuss with Brajesh and Chaitali, whom I will be meeting for dinner this evening. I will come to my Assam visit in a bit.

Our government, in the meantime, has finally done a few good things to combat terror – like setting up a federal agency called the National Investigative Agency. Interestingly, some of the provisions are reminiscent of POTA, which does make me wonder what was the need to disband POTA in the first place? Agreed, its misuse had to be prevented, but I would accept the criticism that not having a special law to deal with terrorism gave some sort of a leeway to the terrorists. The absence of a law, coupled with an indifferent and ill-equipped Home Minister had surely emboldened the terrorists. And I have to concede that we were living in denial – like we've invariably done through history.

For the moment, I would think though that we've done pretty well on the diplomatic front too. By providing Pakistan a dossier containing evidence of its nationals' involvement in the carnage and exerting unrelenting pressure upon it, we have made Pakistan own up to the involvement of its nationals. Pakistan's admission last week, after a string of obstinate and puerile denials, has been a victory for us. What worries me is the news that came in last evening of the Pakistani Government having succumbed to the Taliban and allowing the Shariat Law to prevail in the SWAT region. This, it is believed, is Pakistan's desperate bid to buy peace with the Taliban.

Pakistan today is characterized by chaos and anarchy. Its Nuclear Proliferation records would embarrass any responsible nation. While the terrorist groups operating out of its land, with their connivance with the Taliban, pose a threat to civilization, its own army's links with the Taliban can't be ignored.

As an observer of what I see happening across the border, I am perturbed. Perturbed, because while it is not within our rights to choose our neighbours, any sensible, well-meaning country would always wish its neighbour to live in peace. For, anarchy, especially when it is laced with religious fervour, spreads faster than wildfire. It is unfortunate that Pakistan's wisdom made it think otherwise. Its ploy of fomenting trouble for its neighbours has backfired to hit it with savage intensity. Today the Taliban, which would not have achieved this strength without the backing of the ISI, threatens the very existence of the country.

I'm often constrained to wonder how twins born of the same mother can grow to be so unlike each other, as India and Pakistan are today. Sure they were never identical twins – the very fact that religion was the basis of the birth of one of them, ensured that some differences were imminent. But that one should constantly bay for the other's blood, without provocation, is what makes the situation implausible. In the sixty-two years of our nation's existence, almost all our problems concerning internal security have been triggered by our neighbours – be it the problem of terrorism in Punjab and Kashmir and now the north east, the three wars that we fought against them, or the whole issue of the proxy war that Pakistan unleashed upon us by aiding local terrorist modules within our country. If we were to seek compensation for the harm that our sibling has inflicted upon us, it would run into several hundred billions.

The present situation, as I perceive it, is explosive to say the very least. They say that the 26/11 attack was just a trailer. India is high on the Taliban's hit-list. India's economic strength and its patronage by the US, at least till George Bush was president, account as being the main reasons for it.

If India does not immediately brace up to fight this menace, then anarchy, similar to what we see in large parts of Pakistan today, will be knocking at our doors in the next few years.

Why is Pakistan what it is today? And why is India, for all its advancement, still found wanting where it matters the most?

The answer cannot be found in isolation of the blunders that were committed sixty-two years ago. And when I talk of blunders, I'm not exactly referring to the partition of the country. The question – *who was responsible for Partition* – has never ceased to be a topic for debate among the intellectuals and ignoramuses alike.

My genuine, well-meaning intentions, I'm afraid, will make me travel back a few decades. I would hold the aggressive and uncompromising posture of the Muslim League, which later assumed a violent form in June 1946, in response to Jinnah's call for 'direct action' for the creation of Pakistan and caused unthinkable bloodshed across the country, to be the prime culprit. The British are about as much to blame, as they abetted the Muslim League in every which way.

I would go a step further today to re-phrase the oft-repeated question slightly, so that it reads – *who could have prevented India's Partition?* There are only two people, if at all, who could have done that. One was Gandhi, who enjoyed a status bigger than his party. The other was the Congress leadership of the day, which had at its forefront Nehru and Patel. While nobody doubts Gandhi's efforts in preventing the vivisection, the other Congress leaders in comparison were found to be less resolute.

The reasons for their lack of resolve could be varied: a genuine weariness from the prolonged freedom struggle and a desire to see the country free sooner; or it could have been a genuine belief that Partition was the only way out of unending communal tension.

Which of the two reasons is more likely, is a matter of conjecture as well as perception. But I'm inclined to think that Nehru being the visionary that he was, could well have envisaged the dangers of co-existing with the Muslim League. I mean, a force that thrived on the coercive exactation of its whimsical demands, rather than on electoral realities and which always pursued a divisive agenda, would have posed a huge threat to our new nation. If Nehru, in acceding to the Partition, actually had the peace and good of the larger geographical portion of the country in mind, then Partition ceases to be the big blunder which it is otherwise perceived to be. The dominance of fascist elements would have lacked the liberal outlook that was quintessential for nation building. At the same time, to have allowed the Muslim League to rule the country without mandate, simply as a desperate bid to prevent Partition, would have been counter-productive and led to endless communal clashes.

While Partition thus can be reasoned for, the abrupt manner in which boundaries were re-drawn by a select minority was to lead to unmitigated butchery and barbarism. Never in history have so many people been killed or displaced as they were by this event. None of those involved in executing this hasty operation can escape the responsibility for the loss to humanity inflicted thereupon.

I would think that Partition, if seen as a blessing in disguise, gave us a fresh, unpolluted milieu to raise and groom our infant nation the way we wanted. This is where the identity of the child became all the more important, considering the chaos that preceded its birth.

And appellations, in as much as we may want to wish otherwise, do play a significant part in establishing identity.

I'm thus inclined to question why my country was named India and not Hindustan. A single name 'Bharat' was given to the whole territory from time immemorial. The *Vishnupurana* has devoted a whole chapter for eulogizing the name and special quality of this land. It says, '*The country which lies to the north of the seas and south of the Himalayas is Bharat and inhabitants of this land are Bharatiyas.*' Bharat was subsequently named 'Hind' by the Arabs, who referred to the inhabitants of our land. 'Hind' it goes without saying, was derived from the language Hindi. Hind was to become Hindustan, via a Persian coinage.

It was the British who gave us the name 'India', which is derived from the river Indus. Now, the contribution of the British in helping us see ourselves as a cumulative whole by the name of India cannot be disregarded. After all, what is India today would quite possibly have been some 100 independent countries had the British not ruled us and united us by default. That, however, should not have prevented us from assuming a new identity post Partition. Why did a country that had a population of eighty-five per cent plus Hindus, have to be so apologetic about its composition being reflected in its name?

To my thinking it perhaps had to do with the disproportionately high importance that is attached to Hinduism being a religion, for convenient political purposes.

In the first place, Hinduism is a religion only by default. It is a culture or a way of life, influenced and guided by countless scriptures where the espousal of 'truth' and tolerance hold utmost importance. One can argue about the whole concept being ambiguous. This ambiguity, on the other hand, confers vast freedom of thought and action. Individual interpretations thus have every reason to be varied. Hinduism reverses what many other religions preach. It believes there is a God in each one of us. The quest to invoke this God/Godliness is what many interpret as Hinduism. Hinduism never forbids any one to question its fundamentals either. Mahatma Gandhi had maintained that an atheist can be a Hindu. Similarly, scholars who disregarded the existence of Hindu Gods and Goddesses are as much Hindus. Hinduism is about adaptability, tolerance, pluralism and the quest for truth.

I deduce thus that local inhabitants of this ancient land who followed practices contained in this definition and who did not subscribe to any other organized or known religion, were called Hindus. If this is what a Hindu is, then the leaders of the country had no reason to be unduly wary or apologetic about naming our new country Hindustan. In fact, the usage of 'stan' itself is a Persian contribution and what could be a more secular name than one that blends two cultures?

And mind you, this is being espoused by Aditya Samar Singh – who had a Muslim mother and has read both the Gita and the Koran. Irrespective of whether you consider me a Hindu or a Muslim, I have absolutely no qualms being called a Hindu. I would like to think that anybody who understands the essence of Hinduism would agree with me. And since I have gone this far, let me go a step further. Assuming that 'Hindustan' would have had us referred to as a Hindu State, why could a Hindu state have not been a secular one? The USA after all is seen a Christian state and is the best example of secularism.

You might wonder why I'm harping so much on the name of my country. It is for want of a clearer national identity to be projected to the world. This identity becomes all the more crucial as India and the world face their biggest security challenge ever.

Does my last sentence surprise you?

Well, it should not. It would not, if I now enlighten you about the findings from my recent trip to Assam.

◆

Assam has a 272 km long border with Bangladesh, which is only partially fenced. Moreover, the Border Security Force (BSF), like other institutions, is not immune to corruption. There are reports of BSF professionals having allowed Bangaladeshi nationals in for bribes as low as Rs 500. Interestingly, the Border Security Forces worldwide are known to succumb to such temptations. A friend of mine, who happens to be a defence expert, recently told me that even the forces patrolling USA's border with Mexico are known to indulge in similar malpractices.

I visited three of Assam's border districts that are worst-affected by the menace – Dhubri, Karimganj and Cachar, besides the state of Tripura. I have little hesitation in accepting that the demography of these places has been altered irreversibly by the influx. The vast stretch of Assam's forest land across its border with Nagaland, has disappeared. The entire area instead is full of illegal migrants. Worse, many of these illegal migrants carry ration and voting cards that have been provided to them with unusual promptness. Ironically, many of the Indian locals are still to obtain their Voter Identity Cards.

Now, lest you suspect I am turning communal, let me set things right – I have no issue with Indian Muslims in Assam producing more children compared to their Hindu counterparts or them migrating to Assam from other parts of the country. The issue here is that sustained infiltration of illegal migrants into Assam and other Indian states right from the time that India became independent thwarts the very rationale on which India was created. I mean, if people from the two Pakistans (west and east) had to be pushed into our territory then why did the land have to be divided in the first place?

I was shocked to discover my party's complicity in encouraging this menace. This scourge which the Supreme Court declared as 'external aggression' would not have been possible had my party which has ruled independent India for the maximum number of years, had shown the character to stop it. Instead, I suspect that the government, by tacit means, allowed illegal migration. What else should I infer when I read about the amateurish provisions of a flawed law called the Illegal Migrants

Determination by Tribunal (IMDT) Act – the only law that was in place to curb the menace?

According to this law, the onus was on the complainant (in this case, India's security agencies) rather than on the accused (the illegal migrant) to prove that the accused was not a citizen of the country. It goes without saying that the law was a farce. The actual number of people deported out of the country was less than one per cent on whom enquiries were thus initiated. Besides can anything be more unthinkable than a Pakistani passport holder fighting Assembly elections in Assam? As an Indian, I feel ashamed, but this has actually happened.

Indian history has a particularly condescending reference to a wily, avaricious trader called Omichand whose duplicity aided the East India Company in the Battle of Plassey. This win was to alter the history of our land. I'm forced to wonder today if my party has been a modern day Omichand. Haven't we after all been trading the interests of our country for votes?

Even as I pitch forth this analogy, I cannot completely negate the presence of some pro-migrant sentiment among a small minority of locals, which I personally find amateurish. A businessman in Cachar reasoned that the presence of Bangladeshis had ensured cheaper labour and migrants were more hard-working than the locals. A doctor in Dhubri pointed out that almost the whole of the public transport system and the supply of essential commodities would collapse if Bangladeshis were to be evicted. He in fact equated the situation with the influx of migrants from UP and Bihar into Mumbai. I would completely discard that reasoning. One, because our

Constitution confers upon every citizen the right to live and work in any part of the country. Two, elements in UP and Bihar are by no means being indoctrinated to wage a war against Mumbai.

There are no concrete figures on just how many illegal migrants are staying in the country at this point. However, even if some of the rare admissions by government sources are any indicator, one is forced to wonder if we are fighting a lost battle in the North East.

A report submitted by Assam Governor, General (Retd.), S.K. Sinha in 2005, states, *'This (Indo-Bangladesh) border is one of the world's most fluid borders, crossed daily by some 6000 Bangladeshis who come in search of work, often staying to join the estimated 20 million illegal immigrants in the country.'* On 15 July 2004, Sriprakash Jaiswal, Minister of State for Home Affairs, stated in the Rajya Sabha that, *'1,20,53,950 illegal Bangladeshi migrants were residing in 17 states and Union territories as on 31 December, 2001.'* The Minister had to retract his statement.

Of course these are just the figures for Assam. The problem is no less menacing in West Bengal.

I am not in the least suggesting that all these illegal migrants are terrorists. Only a fool would say that. Hunger is a much bigger concern for millions than religion can ever be. In all likelihood only a very small percentage would be terrorists. But the point is not that.

If these figures are even partially true, it provides ample evidence of just how the demography of 'Hindustan' has been purposely tampered with for decades, for electoral gains. I wish to question the authenticity and credibility of our population data when the government is clueless about illegal migrants. I'm inclined to wonder what assurance there is that this change in demography will not lead to newer demands for more partitions of our country.

I say this because I find a significant likelihood of this migration being backed as a policy by Pakistan and Bangladesh. History provides a precedent for this. Way back in the pre-Independence period, the Muslim League had resorted to a policy of pushing Muslims from East Bengal into neighbouring Assam, which had a Hindu Assamese majority. The act had a vicious design attached to it – to have Assam included in Pakistani territory at the time of Partition. Eventually though, only one district of Assam – Sylhet – went to Pakistan, where migration had achieved its desired impact.

Besides, there is little reason for a nexus to not exist between jehadi terrorist groups across the subcontinent. After all, they have a common enemy. Therefore while HUJI is the recognized terrorist group operating out of Bangladesh, its infrastructure is being used by Al Qaida and LET to enter India.

What surprises me about our leadership is its sheer indifference. The Assam problem, if left ignored the way it has been thus far, threatens to alter the map of my country yet again. And God forbid, if it happens this time round, the responsibility shall entirely be on my party – the Congress.

Much like I probe the role of my predecessor generations for problems that exist today, I'm sure someone will be doing the same on us sixty years hence. I'm afraid I will then not escape from being held responsible for many of the ills that are being allowed to exist today. After all, I am an elected representative of my country and I acknowledge the gravity of the problem.

I discuss my thoughts with Brajesh and Chaitali, whom I'm meeting after almost three weeks. They are surprised to see the change in me.

'Now that's what a paradigm change is – a Congressman speaking so unlike one,' remarks Chaitali.

'You're shifting your loyalties right-wards,' Brajesh tells me in lighter vein.

I take a pause and with a fair amount of thought, tell him, 'I think I'm getting closer to being a truer and more concerned Hindustani.'

◆

It's 11:30pm and I can't sleep. I think of my whole journey thus far, as a reluctant politician. I think of my evolution and transformation from the fateful night in Manhattan when this journey began. I think of what I've gained and what I've lost and wonder if I can correctly distinguish between the two. At this moment, I miss my Dad like I've never ever done. I'm perplexed and torn apart. I wish I could have a chat with him and sort out some of the conundrums in my mind. After all, my political beliefs have largely been imbibed from him.

Two days later, I'm in Haridwar, one of the holiest cities in India. I'm here for what in Hindi is called 'Pind-daan' or a donation to the poor in my father's memory. It is my father's birthday and I have decided to feed a thousand poor. Yadav, I have to acknowledge, has gone out of his way to organize this ritual. He came here a day before me to take care of all the arrangements.

The ritual takes place at an ashram that we have hired exclusively for the purpose. In a huge list of responsibilities that I have come to shoulder, I'd much rather consider this a duty. I remember Dad doing the same for his father when I was a kid. I've seen the way Dad worked for the alleviation of poverty. That he can feed the needy even when he is not around, I'm sure will bring peace and solace to him, wherever he might be.

In the evening, I spend some quiet, meditative moments at a pious spot, on the bank of Ganges, called Har Ki Pauri, which means God's footsteps. My security guards have ensured a quieter corner for me, away from the crowds. This place is regarded as the most sacred ghat of Haridwar. Thousands flock here everyday for that holy dip that helps them attain salvation; so it is believed. My mind is still loaded with all the dilemmas that the developments of the last three months have brought to it. After the hectic activity during the day, I am finally beginning to feel the emptiness that enters me when I'm left alone. At sunset my mood is sombre.

My state of disquiet suddenly makes me venture forth and take a dip in the Ganges. So unprovoked and impulsive is the act that it surprises Yadav and my security. Irrespective of the discomfort of being in wet clothes, I feel light. What an escape it is! As I stand up after taking a dip I spot a white lady to my left, in a sari. To my surprise she looks like Sarah. She stands barely a few feet away and pushes a burning diya into the river, just like a devout Hindu woman would. I know I am going crazy. I seem to be hallucinating. Next I might see Chaitali swimming in here.

After a pause when I turn again towards the white lady feeling sure that she won't be there, she turns and reveals her face before she leaves. Yes, it is Sarah. I am just numb. I call her name.

She is as shocked to see me as I am to see her.

'Sarah!' I say, panting for breath.

She shakes her head.

'Sita' is her faint retort. 'That's my name now.'

I grab her arm and Sarah passes out.

◆

It's been a week now since Sarah (Sita, as she now calls herself) has been staying in my home. I've given her the guest room. She's sleeping at the moment. I look at her and wonder why her woes never cease. I can sense the hand of God in most of what my life has seen these last couple of years. There can't be a bigger manifestation of the powers of destiny than Sarah's re-entry into my life at this juncture, and in Haridwar of all places.

Sarah's journey to Haridwar was of course as heart-wrenching as most of the other events of her life have been. When I think of what she had narrated to me, on the banks of the Ganges, it still freaks me out.

'Francis Aemilio was a bloody fraud, Aditya. He had a family back in Nairobi and two teenaged children. His wife had apparently left him as he was having an affair with his maid. Besides he had some petty criminal cases against him.

'I left Francis and went to my cousin. She had attended these spiritual discourses and yoga classes at Rishikesh by a new-age Indian guru Yogdas. She was mighty impressed and suggested I try them out. There was no way I could think of going back to my parents. Hence I came down to India.'

'And how long have you been in Rishikesh? And did you benefit....?'

'Y...y... yeah... it was good. Yogdas' ashram had about 25 pupils, all foreigners, mostly Americans. Yogdas taught us about Hindu Scriptures in the morning and trained us in yoga by the riverside in the evening. He told me about Ram, Krishna and Shiva. And all of us were given Hindu names.'

I knew now how Sarah had metamorphosed into Sita. As she said this, I could sense that all was not well at the ashram either.

She continued: 'But Yogdas was a creep. He encouraged opium consumption after the yoga classes and in fact recommended its usage. He said the "trance" that opium leads to is very effective for meditation.'

It was obvious that Yogdas made a lot of money from the sale of opium and was probably part of a nexus. I heaved a sigh and wondered why Sarah had to experience everything wrong on this earth. I asked her if she wanted me to drop her back to the ashram.

'I've run away from there,' she shocked me yet again. 'Everyday Yogdas chose one pupil for an advanced yoga session. This pupil would have to perform yoga without their clothes on, with Yogdas monitoring muscle movements and employing something called "touch therapy" wherever needed. In certain cases, if Yogdas found the pupil stimulating, he would go all the way.'

'What? But didn't you tell your cousin about this?'

'I called her. She said the exercise was therapeutic and I must take it in the right sense. I'd feel spiritually enlightened if I acceded to Yogdas. I had already thwarted Yogdas' designs twice. This time, he employed force. I managed to kick his balls hard, and run. I've been in Haridwar since yesterday. I've been following Hindu rituals in the last few months. I didn't want to discontinue a practice I had been following – of floating a burning diya into the river every full moon night. This is what I was doing here when God finally took pity on me and sent you here.'

I'm not sure whom God had taken pity on. I still held myself guilty of a whole chain of unsavoury events that Sarah's life had fallen into after my abrupt exit.

Sarah's re-emergence in my life at this point, gave me an opportunity for redemption. I did not want to add to my list of losses; hence I grabbed the opportunity.

A vacuum had been forming in my life. Taking care of Sarah seems to have filled that up. In my interaction with her I sense a calm in her that she previously lacked. I like coming home to her. Sarah, I realize now, is a deeper part of me than I had thought. Circumstances had conspired to draw us apart and circumstances have conspired yet again to bring us together.

I thus leave it entirely upon the will of destiny to chart a course for our future, if any.

◆

In the meantime, I'm excited about tomorrow. Tomorrow is Holi and I've invited Brajesh, Chaitali and a few other friends. This will be Sarah's first experience of the festival of colours.

Next morning we play one of our most colourful Holis in the last few years. Chaitali walks in with a new friend of hers, Prakash. Brajesh walks in with Monica, only to leave within moments of greeting us; Monica understandably isn't playing.

What holds my attention through the morning is Sarah's fascination for the colours. With child-like excitement, she paints all my guests. I decorate her with dry colours, like I would a baby. The moment reminds me of Christopher Columbus' epochal remark on discovering America – 'The more you go East, the more you are assured to come upon the West.' I wonder if today Sita makes me reverse the statement and if I can safely alter it to say, 'The more you go West, the more you are assured to come upon the East.'

I feel a deep sense of oneness with Sarah. It swells me with a feeling of fulfilment and almost makes me forget the other thing that is bothering me.

But that too has to be addressed.

In the evening, when I meet my party president to greet her on Holi, I carry with me something other than the expected colours; it's my letter of resignation from the Congress party.

Brajesh

ONE OF THE MOST CATACLYSMIC INCIDENTS, which caused an unmitigated angst in me, was the anti-Mandal agitation of 1990. A self-immolation bid by Rajeev Goswami, a Delhi University student, was to lead to a series of such acts across the country. Worse was the government indifference towards it. A leading newsmagazine had aptly titled its story on the Mandal agitation, 'New Delhi Fiddles Even as the Country Burns.'

The agitation was re-enacted to a lesser degree, years later in 2006, thanks to HRD Minister, Arjun Singh, who since the time of Narsimha Rao, had become increasingly frustrated due to the death of all chances of him becoming PM. So he ordered the implementation of educational reservation to the Other Backward Classes, Scheduled Castes and Scheduled Tribes to the level of 49.5 per cent seats in India's premier, centrally-sponsored institutions. Prior to this, students belonging to SCs and STs already enjoyed 22.5 per cent quota.

What the government proposed thus, was to bring OBCs too under the quota regime by giving them 27 per cent reservations. So with this new move, the total reservations for OBCs, SCs and STs would stand at 49.5%.

The issue expectedly led to huge student unrest. It perturbed me as it had, way back in 1990. This time round, though, as an MP, I was in a better position to make my voice heard. I'm not sure how other MPs perceived it so, but personally, I attached a lot of significance to my first speech in Parliament. I thought of it as my vision statement for the country. Accordingly, my parents and a few close relatives had come down to witness my first speech from the visitors' gallery in Parliament.

Of course much of what I had intended to say was eclipsed by the issue of Reservations, which had sullied the atmosphere in the country at that point. I think I have a copy of my speech. Let me take it out.

Okay, here is how it went:

Sir, it is believed that when the Aryans arrived in our subcontinent from Central Asia, they established a caste system in which they placed themselves in the highest league.

The largesse offered by our flawed social equality policies today, I'm afraid might soon start a reverse trend – a clamour to be allotted the privileged 'OBC'/SC/ST status. The Gujjars have taken the lead in this in Rajasthan by demanding that they be included among the ST. Marathas too want them to be included in the quota. I'm afraid many more communities might follow suit. The tragedy today is that since the backward castes constitute half of our population, none of our political parties will be audacious enough to oppose the reservation policy.

Sir, if democracy and the apolitical credentials of our army have been the key factors in our success as a stable, progressive nation, the biggest impediment for us has been our flawed reservation policy. In our society, barely does a child start school that he gets to be aware of his caste. While we may project ourselves as practical and progressive, the ingrained prejudices resulting from caste differentiation, coupled with deprived opportunities resulting due to reservation in education and jobs later on, do not allow us to stand united as a society and nation.

Sir, critics of Hindu philosophy might argue that the caste system and resultant disparity it created is espoused in religion. This however is a myth. The caste system was merely an anachronistic social practice. Then again, castes did not constitute a rigid description of the occupation or the social status of a group. This is corroborated by the observations of Fa Hein, a Buddhist pilgrim from China, who visited India in the fifth century. He could not find evidence of any biases resulting out of the caste distinctions, except only in the case of 'chandals'. It is noteworthy here that the history of the period affirms the existence of several brahmin and a few shudra kings as well. I would thus infer that class and caste distinctions were more for practical purposes of reference, and not prohibitive or restrictive.

Let us for a moment assume that we were to follow the same 'unrestrictive' practice today as they existed 1500 years ago. Let us for the sake of our convenience confine our study to say, a state-of-the-art heart hospital. In this case, the entire set of doctors would belong to the 'Brahmin class' – the most accomplished ones belonging to the highest caste categories, as compared to junior doctors or pathologists; the security apparatus of the hospital would be manned by 'kshatryias'; the accounts and finances would be handled by 'vaishyas'; the sweepers and attendants would be 'shudras'. Thus, in today's context, there is every likelihood of a Paswan or a Shinde being a leading cardiologist and hence a Brahmin; similarly there aren't too many reasons why a Tiwari or Mahajan cannot be a scavenger and hence a shudra.

We can employ the same classification in a mall, in air or rail services and several other places. Thus, class distinction, the way it was conceived, was a rather convenient device for providing an easy reference of people, based on their 'work'. If we are to follow that, a brahmin, by birth can be a shudra by his work and vice versa; similarly a kshatriya by birth can be a vaishya if he chooses to pursue a business and vice versa. Therefore, the very fundamental of our present day reservation policy which is based entirely on caste, is flawed.

However, I have to admit that my theory is far-fetched and utopian. I would not be too far off the mark, if I attribute the acute caste discriminations that we see in our society, partly to the British. Since British society was divided by class, the British attempted to equate the Indian caste system to their own social hierarchy. They saw caste as an indicator of social standing and intellectual ability. Our caste system was to thus become more rigid during British Rule, when the British started to enumerate castes during their ten-year census and codified the system under their rule. This obviously led to vast social inequalities, for which our age-old caste system bore the blame.

Our Constitution, to correct these ills, rightly pledged 'equality of opportunity' for all citizens. A policy of reservation in jobs as well as educational institutes was thus pursued for a period of ten years to address these disparities. Sir, it has been nearly six decades now. Instead of providing equal opportunities, what our Reservation policy has done, is killed merit and divided people. Besides, what is the credibility of a policy, which for the basic purpose of defining 'OBCs' has not followed any authentication of their socio-economic standing in decades? Sir, the British followed a Divide and Rule Policy. And we, more specifically leaders like Mr Arjun Singh follow ours. We stand a divided and weak nation today, all thanks to our indigenous Divide and Rule Policy.

Sir, till the time that the present reservation policy is not replaced with a policy that is based entirely on 'economic status'

*and has no reference to caste, I'm afraid it will remain a façade
and defeat its very purpose.'*

My speech was epochal. It ruffled many feathers.
I had dared to flow against the tide and put myself in
an unenviable position. Yet I did it because that's how
strongly I felt about the issue. My reward was a severe
reprimand from my party's high command. Nonetheless,
truth and courage I realized drew its own supporters.
Overnight, a few million youth in the country started
seeing hope in me. That's when I realized I had cultivated
a constituency of my own – of aware youth who supported
truth and courage, irrespective of which party or individual
was to be its torch-bearer. This constituency was far too
potent to be squandered away. That's what had made me
start my own blog. I must have been among the first MPs
to do that. Omar obviously is the other politician who
has used the internet to good impact.

Anyway, the reason I recall this speech today is
because it gives me the courage to replicate things more
audacious now. My anger against the present set-up is just
as strong and the sense of helplessness as pronounced.
Aditya has done his part of the 'unlearning' by visiting
Assam and redefining his thinking. It is my turn to pursue
my unlearning.

The process takes me south, to Karnataka and then
east to Kandhamal in Orissa. I have an unlikely partner,
this time round – Monica Bhardwaj.

◆

Much to my surprise, Monica and I have been bonding
well. And as bonds in metros start nowadays, we've been
meeting for coffee every few days. I have realized that

what I like most about Monica is her assured objectivity – something that I had been hunting for in Chaitali and Shweta. Monica shares my concerns over national issues. She listens to me like Shweta did. But, after hearing me out, Monica gives me her perspective – albeit with such calm subtlety that I don't take offence. Monica helps me see issues in a more holistic fashion, rather than simply through the prism of my party's ideology. This is where I think Shweta failed. She did not have an opinion of her own and even if she did, she was never articulate enough to express it. At times, Shweta would almost give me the impression that she listened to me just because she didn't have much to add. As far as Chaitali goes, I think she just loved to rub me the wrong way. In hindsight, sometimes I wonder if all that excited me in the relationship was 'taming' her.

When I mentioned my proposed trip to Karnataka and Orissa with Monica – the two states that have seen the maximum attacks on minorities in recent months – she readily offered to join me. She decided it could double as an official trip; this was after all another zone where her role of conflict management would come in handy. I would have loved to believe that there was more to her willingness, but on second thoughts I concluded my assumption was premature.

In Karnataka, a large number of churches had been vandalized recently by the Bajrang Dal and in the violence that followed a large number of people had been injured. The attacks were reportedly provoked by factors like forced conversions and the distribution of obnoxious literature denigrating Hindu Gods by New Life Church – a fringe Protestant group operating in the state. Similar charges had also been levelled against some other churches in the region.

Now, for someone who has imbibed a Jesuit education in his formative years, the issue puts me in a difficult position. For that matter both Monica and I had studied in schools run by Christian missionaries. And neither of us could recall any instance of our institutions or of the missionaries running them showing any disregard for Hindu religion. We are inclined to deduce thus that the the New Life Church is a fringe, irresponsible, reactionary group among Christians, just like we have our black sheep. But to paint the entire community as villains and to ransack more than twenty churches across the state, by no means befits a Hindu. That the State Government run by my party was soft on the Bajrang Dal, is a fact that cannot be wished away.

Monica and I decide to meet up with Father Joseph Asthana in Mangalore and discuss the entire issue of conversion. The priest condemns the activities of the New Life Church:

'I will not deny that as a policy we'd like to have more followers of our religion. Which other religion would not want that? But the issue of "forced conversion" is false propaganda, meant only to unleash violence on us. No true believer of God will ever do that,' he asserts.

'But, Father, I have a query. Social work for the good of humanity is something every religion ought to undertake. But is it right to attach a price to it – conversion?' I ask him.

'Well, life is about choices. I am an orphan, who was adopted by the Church when I was three. I could well have spent all my life begging on the streets, like one of my friends still does. The Church, by adopting me, gave me a new life. It gave me learning, which helped me evolve and help others. It made me what I am today. Does the Church not have any right to expect something in return? Trust me, for all that the Church and the missionaries have done for me, I'd have anyway embraced Christianity voluntarily. It's really not as big an issue as you right-wing groups make it appear.'

Father Asthana's reasoning leaves us wondering. I mean he has a valid point. And he is not yet done.

'There have been other instances when we have made alcoholics give up their addiction and borne the entire expense of their rehabilitation. There are instances where we have borne the treatment expenses for cancer patients. Yes, as a policy we do expect them to convert. And there's a reason behind it. We want them to imbibe the same vocation of selfless missionary service towards the needy with which we have served them. Religion here plays an important role in binding their philosophies together.'

'Hmm…'

'Besides, if you feel that religious conversion is depleting the numbers of your community, why don't you bring laws to ban conversion? Since we will anyway remain committed to social work, we shall continue with our social work.'

Father Ashthana's reasoning acquainted us with the other perspective. Later in the evening over yet another coffee, Monica offered her observations:

'You know what, the problem is far more layered than it appears sitting in Delhi. We just cannot deny the huge service that Christian missionaries have done for the needy.'

'Yes, but that shouldn't give them the right to disrespect other religions,' I tell her.

'Absolutely. And that's where a distinction needs to be drawn between the truly evangelic churches and those who are indulging in nefarious activities. The situation is quite akin to people associating rogue right-wing groups like the Bajrang Dal, Sri Ram Sena and Durga Vahini with the BJP and the BJP getting painted black, isn't it?'

She is dead right.

'And what's the solution?' I ask.

'Well, one, your party needs to be more vehement in criticizing the actions of these rogue groups. What you guys normally offer is token condemnation which only gives credence to the perception that you guys are hand in glove. Besides, it's your party that rules the state. It's all the more important for the government to deal with these violent acts with an iron hand.'

It's surprising but I find Monica complementing me. She fills in the blanks in my reasoning process and makes my thinking more rounded. I find it stimulating to interact with her on some of the more contentious topics. Unlike Chaitali, she gives me a sort of cushion before altering its placement. I stand corrected in the end. And yes, I think I've started missing her when she's not with me.

After spending three days in Karnataka, Monica and I travel to a place called Kandhamal in Orissa, where communal clashes are said to have claimed 35 lives and resulted in the shameful rape of a nun. Before I come to Kandhamal, though, I will need to travel a decade back to an incident that took place not very far from Kandhamal, in a village called Manoharpur in the Keonjhar District.

The incident had brought shame not just to the country, but to humanity.

On the winter night of 22 January, 1999, an Australian missionary, Graham Staines and his two sons, Philip (9) and Timothy (7) were burnt alive by a group of militants, led by one Dara Singh. The perpetrator had links with the Bajrang Dal. The reported provocation for the heinous act was not very different – forced conversions and propaganda against Hinduism.

This time round, when violence broke out on two occasions – first on Christmas in 2007 and then more recently in August, 2008, the provocation seemed similar. In August last year the provocation was bigger – the murder of Swami Lakshmanananda Saraswati, who had started a tirade against conversions. It is noteworthy here that what started off as a communal clash, later became a caste war between two tribal communities – the *panas* and the *kandhas*, who've had a history of hatred. Thus, most of the killings that were reported as 'communal killings', were in reality, probably the result of clashes between two age- old warring tribal Hindu communities. That of course can't wipe out the shame of a nun having been raped. Nor can it make us forget that in one of the villages around forty people who had converted to Christianity recently, were forcibly converted back to Hinduism. They were forced to undergo a purification process that included bathing in cow urine and consuming cow-dung. Besides, there is evidence that in some places people were issued death threats – to either convert back or get killed. In some other places, houses were indiscriminately burnt.

The sheer scale of violence makes us accept that 'forced conversions' is a bigger issue in the tribal districts of Orissa, than it is in Father Asthana's Karnataka. Moreover it's not a problem that has erupted overnight, but one that has been there for a long time now.

◆

Three days in Orissa leave us sombre. We've been acquainted with the vast potential that misplaced religious fervour carries, of triggering violence and bloodshed. On the one hand we're fighting religion-provoked terrorism from external enemies, while on the other we have to cope with our very own indigenous fascists who are no less in wreaking terror. Monica and I wonder if internal terrorism is any less a devil compared to external terrorism.

This obviously leads me to question where my party stands on the issue.

Yes, we condemn the violence, like we condemn so many other ills in society. But what happens beyond that? When existing laws fail to solve a vexed problem, the onus for solving it shifts upon the legislature. Why have we never defined 'forced conversions' and made the practice unlawful yet? Even if we assume that 'forced conversions' take place it doesn't give anybody the right to ransack and vandalize churches or rape and burn people alive. This act of violence amounts to 'internal terrorism' and should be defined as such.

Monica shares most of my views. She adds an interesting thought.

'Religion carries very little charm for poor tribals, for whom food and health is all that matters. Obviously, if someone is willing to take care of those survival needs of theirs, they don't really mind shifting their faith.'

'Hmm… besides, they don't even know the shape or size of our country. So, there's no reason why they should bother about demography.'

'And why does the demography bother you and your party so much? Is it because of the fear that the size of your voters is dwindling?' she asks me.

I am too weary to answer. It has been six days of a stark unlearning experience. Instead I hold Monica tight. The act is spontaneous. It's meant to seek Monica's empathy and support, which it surprisingly gets. I feel her for the first time. I like the warmth. I feel less weary. We stay in this position for nearly two minutes before we retreat to our rooms.

Once back in Delhi, I feel a change in me. The unlearning has altered my perception of things. My party ought to do more to curb 'internal terrorism'. It ought to have a clearer policy towards banning conversions rather than allowing the likes of the Bajrang Dal to do things their way.

My getting back to Delhi coincides with a not-too-pleasant development. Keshavnath Tripathi, one of our senior members, has resigned from the party. Keshavnath, an ex-IAS officer of the UP cadre had been sidelined for sometime. He was reportedly unhappy over the way the party was being run lately. In private conversations, he is supposed to have said that the party was no longer the 'party with a difference'.

In his letter of resignation, he has listed several issues on which he felt betrayed by the party's stand. I read his letter, which he has made public. *'The party with a difference has become a party of hypocrisies and differences…'* That's how he starts it.

'How can a party that prides itself to be a crusader against jehadi terrorism suddenly do a volte-face when the involvement of Hindu Groups is exposed in the Malegaon blasts? The party president says he will consider the sadhvi innocent till she is proved guilty. Isn't this stance the absolute opposite of what the party had stood for, so far? I'm afraid the party's ill-advised reaction on the issue has exposed our façade. We no longer enjoy the moral high ground over the Congress on the issue of vote-bank politics.'

Tripathi goes on…

'This is not the only issue. On the one hand we talk about public funding of elections, whereas on the other we are found to be most corrupt. Years ago, our party president was found accepting cash on camera. Just two months ago, 2.5 crore gets stolen from our party headquarters and we do not even file an FIR. Is this how we choose to live up to the ideals of Pandit Deel Dayal Upadhyay?'

And it goes on…

'On the one hand we talk of an influx of Bangladeshis into India. On the other, may I ask how many illegal Bangladeshis did we deport back to Bangaladesh during our time? How many fake ration cards and IDs did we confiscate? On the one hand we talk of bringing uniform civil code. On the other, we only extended Congress' minority appeasement when we were in power. Haj subsidy was increased massively. Financial assistance and jobs for Muslim youth were announced at will. How different does that leave our "genuine secularism" from Congress' "pseudo-secularism"?'

And Tripathi's angst in not yet over:

'We make tall claims about our nationalist credentials. It is strange that forget Pakistan, even when Bangladesh had brutally murdered 15 of our soldiers and then threw their bodies back into our country way back in 2001 when we were in power, *we could do nothing. Why could we not snap all diplomatic links with them till they apologized? Over the years and with experience I have realized that our nationalism is more a rhetoric and that in reality we are not really different from the Congress. Maybe our dressing sense is different, but our sensibilities I'm afraid are similar.'*

◆

There are times when you are aware of certain things yet you tend not to take cognizance of them simply because you fear the discomfort of altering an existing order. And then when you read stuff of the kind that Keshavnath Tripathi has written, you are almost forced to sit up and wonder if someone else is speaking your mind.

Keshavnath's outburst perturbs me. It puts me in quandary because I cannot disagree with what he has said. My rumination leads me to write a rather audacious blog, which I fear could have some unsavoury repercussions:

While Keshavnath may not be with the party anymore, the issues raised by him cannot be wished away. In the early nineties when the BJP first emerged as a viable national alternative to the Congress, we had all hoped that it would be a matter of time before we win a majority on our own. The rise of the party in many ways symbolized the resurgence of voters who had long been betrayed by the Congress. Today, nearly two decades later, neither has our vote share increased, nor have we made any significant inroads in newer states, barring Karnataka.

The issues raised by Keshavnathji thus are significant in understanding our failings. Have we failed to live up to all that we had promised two decades ago? Can we really boast of being a party with a difference anymore? We need to a reality check ASAP if we are serious about winning the elections.'

My blog, expectedly, creates a stir in political circles. Not that I had not anticipated it; it's just that I find it difficult to hold myself back anymore. My party issues me a show-cause notice. I do get support though – from my supporters spread across the country, as also from Aditya and Chaitali.

The one person whose support most comforts me is Monica. She hugs me reassuringly. It gives me courage. I'm realizing that a contentious posturing, in as much as it brings isolation, brings in newer supporters. Monica's hug has magical powers – I feel more convinced about my blog now than I did a few hours ago when I wrote it. I kiss her on her forehead.

No sooner has the word of my party issuing me a 'show-cause' notice spread that I get a call from Sitaram Yadav of the Janta Morcha. He insists on dropping in to meet me. So persuasive is he that I can't refuse him.

Sitaram is what in contemporary political jargon is called a 'back-room operator'. He has never contested a Lok Sabha election, but with his clout, influences the destiny of several lesser mortals contesting them. His party symbolizes what can be aptly described today as the growing menace of 'promiscuous' regional parties. In this era of coalition politics, his party with its 35 odd MPs enjoys a very crucial position in making or breaking governments. His party swings either way depending on which way it stands to benefit more, with absolutely no attendant burdens of ideology or conscience. In a political sense therefore, it would not be wrong to consider his party a 'bisexual'.

For obvious reasons, therefore, I was not too keen on meeting Sitaram. But then my PA informs me that he has arrived to see me.

'It takes a lot of courage to speak the truth. Since you have that courage, our respect for you has gone up manifold,' Sitaram tells me.

I take his words with a pinch of salt, anticipating the crap he's sure to come up with.

'We'd like to field you as our party's candidate from Gandhinagar against Advani. With our support, I'm confident you will win,' he tells me, with unwarranted optimism.

I can't help myself from breaking into a smile which soon transforms into loud derisive laughter. My laughter extinguishes Sitaram's smile.

'What happened? If you're not comfortable with that, we're ready to field you from any other seat of your choice,' he tells me.

I take a deep breath before I get down to my part of the talking.

'How old are you, Sitaramji?'

'62-63.'

'You are three decades older than I am. I've heard you joined politics during the JP movement in the seventies and have also spent a few months in jail during the Emergency.'

He looks at me uncertainly.

'Is this what your politics has come to? Is there absolutely *nothing* that your party has to offer by way of policy or ideas?'

He pulls himself together and tries to sound unfazed:

'I'm telling you this for your benefit. After being in the BJP, nobody will respect you in Congress. On the other hand, our party will give you your due.'

I take a pause, which is meant to contain my anger. I fail in my attempt.

'You may leave,' I tell him.

He looks shocked.

'I respect your age; hence I'm being polite. Please go away.'

I walk off. The dazed expression on Sitaram's countenance affirms that not many have rebuffed him in this way.

I don't in the least regret having done so.

I spend the evening sitting in my garden with Monica. We're there till past midnight. Surprisingly, this time round, there are long stretches of silence between us. We realize that silence sometimes speaks louder than words. I can feel her empathy with me. I can sense a unity of thought between us, which needs no verbal reiteration. She knows that the next morning is going to be very crucial for me. I know I can count on her to be by my side in the most difficult hour of my political career. For the moment, we just hold hands and look at the moon. It's almost a full moon. The realization of it being a full moon accords a greater tenderness to our actions. Things, I realize, have just begun to happen, as much for me on the political front, as on the personal one.

◆

Next morning, I hold a press conference. A big crowd of journalists has assembled to cover the event. I've never felt more uneasy. The moment takes me back five years. I'm reminded of the time I'd convened a similar press conference at Guwahati and announced my decision to quit the IAS. This time round I'm quitting the

BJP. Time has come full circle for me, and done so pretty fast.

My announcement stuns everybody. I'm bombarded with questions. I feel diffident and uneasy answering them. I think it's a very unusual sort of feeling. I would think, to be quitting the party on a note of rebellion amounts to some kind of blasphemy. I do feel guilty as well. I want to flee from here. And then I see Monica standing at a distance. She's come here to give me the support I so badly need. Her presence does something to me. I'm not going anywhere now. This is not a hasty decision after all, but something that has been arrived at with a lot of conviction. I need to explain my position, lest I be misunderstood. And I better do it the best I can.

'People and thoughts evolve with time. In 2004, when I joined the BJP, I strongly believed that the BJP was best suited and equipped to serve our national interests. Hence, I joined the party. Today I don't feel the same anymore, hence I'm quitting.'

More questions are hurled at me. They ask me if I'm joining another party and my response is a firm no. They are extremely curious about my future plans and almost act as if I'm hiding something from them.

'I've always believed in addressing the present. The future, in that case, is a natural consequence,' I tell them.

I'm not sure if it has to do with the reassuring expression on Monica's face, but I tend to get carried away: 'We keep saying that we need an Indian Obama. Such coinage is actually an acceptance of our failings and limitations. Why can't the U.S. ever say, we need an American Rahul, Omar, Aditya, Brajesh or Chaitali? We must strive for the day when Indian leadership becomes the benchmark for the world.'

In mentioning Aditya, Chaitali and myself together, I think I may have abandoned all circumspection and inadvertently set speculation mills turning. My divulgence was not planned. It was something I felt naturally at the given moment.

Monica and I drive home together. The moment we enter the house I hold her tight. This time though, the progression is deeper. I kiss her. She doesn't show any surprise and responds passionately. Monica spends the night at my place. We lie in each other's arms and don't know when we drift off to sleep.

I wake up early. The developments over the last forty-eight hours and the sight of Monica sleeping next to me, leave me wondering about a lot of things. I saunter out to watch the dawn break. I look at the rising sun and hope that it marks the advent of a new chapter in my life. To my surprise, Monica stands next to me and holds my hand. The natural light casts a majestic glow on her face. As we hold hands, I realize this is the touch that I had long thirsted for. Apart from love, companionship and lust, it carries a credible, reassuring promise that the lady is prepared to walk that extra mile with me.

Chaitali

I'M AT SANAND, BARELY 30 KILOMETRES FROM Ahmedabad. And no, I'm not here in connection with the Gujarat riots. Sanand, as you know, is where the Tatas have set up a plant to produce their magical Rs. 1 lac car, the Nano. I'm not sure whether this car plant shifting from the Marxist ruled West Bengal to the Capitalist Gujarat carries some sort of a metaphor. But, I think I'd be naïve if I negate the symbolic significance of it.

Oh, and by the way, Prakash is with me on this tour. In fact, he was instrumental in bringing me here, for my 'unlearning' sojourn. Before I get back to Sanand, let me acquaint you with him.

Prakash and I met less than two months ago – on my flight back to Delhi from Kolkata. I'd gone to Kolkata to spend New Year with Ma. I stayed with her, my stepdad Adarsh and my 15-year-old stepbrother Aryan, for four days. I realized something in those four days: time changes everything. And when I say everything, I mean it changes even the way you feel about things. It reminded me of the time nearly two decades ago when I'd spat on Adarsh's face – an act that had ended my stay at home.

Yet, when I met him this time, we met like old relatives who weren't really close and yet were well disposed towards each other. My anger at Adarsh in the past had to do with the fact that I had seen him as the villain in my parents' marriage. I had held him responsible for all the misery that Baba was going through.

It is strange that just as you evolve in personal thoughts and opinions, so you do in terms of political thinking. My party had expected me to link my trip to Kolkota with a couple of meetings with party colleagues in the state. I consciously skirted the issue. On the car journey from the airport at Dum Dum to Behala, I saw innumerable CPI(M) flags, symbols, posters, wall campaigns, etc. They just didn't evoke the enthusiasm in me that they had in the past. I wondered all along if this was symptomatic of bigger changes that would usher themselves into my life.

The pleasant part of my stay in Kolkata was my meeting with my half brother, Aryan. I've always had a soft corner for him. And this time, I actually helped him prepare the 'dialogue' to propose to his girlfriend. We did this on a lunch out. Buoyed by the positive end result, Aryan offered to strategize for my 'love life'. I had to turn him down with a polite *no thanks*. I doubt my 'love life' can be ever repaired.

On my flight back, I met this ultra cool dude, Prakash, who occupied the seat right next to mine. He was quite an extrovert and wasted no time in exchanging introductions. While I confined mine to my name, he was more forthcoming. Prakash Karunakaran, I was to discover, was the scion of a wealthy Malayali industrialist family. They had business interests in hotels, chemicals and pharmaceuticals. The business was spread across at least five states. Don't know if he divulged all this to impress me, for I was in no mood to be impressed.

However, on getting to know of his business, I had an obvious query.

'So your business brought you to Kolkata?'

'Nah… you must be kidding,' he said and went on to add things more rude: 'West Bengal is not the place for businessmen. It's the place to be if you are a trade union leader or activist.'

This was an opinion I was familiar with ever since I was a kid. But for a young guy to say this, it seemed like things hadn't really changed in all these years.

'There's something else I like about Bengal though – its women. They're just so attractive. In fact, I came to meet up with a special friend,' he went on, of his own volition.

Prakash had an easy informality. Within minutes, he pulled out a couple of imported soft porn magazines and started going through them. He seemed at absolute ease, unmindful of the company. Even as he looked at them, he'd turn and look at me rather purposefully. When he did that twice, I checked him.

'Ever thought of modelling for one of these magazines? You've got the looks…' he asked me, unfazed.

I was sure he did not know who I was.

'Excuse me! Politicians in this country are expected to maintain a code of conduct.'

It was now that he realized who I was. He said he'd seen me on TV once but never expected that I'd be the same Chaitali.

I took the liberty of asking him a couple of shockingly personal queries as well. 'Dude, how many women have you slept with?' I asked rather abruptly.

Prakash gave me a sheepish grin and then an answer that dazed me. 'You really want to know the number?' he asked and when I nodded he said, '149.'

'You've had that many girlfriends?' I asked.

'Wait I'll give you the breakdown,' he said and took out his Blackberry.

He opened up a file and pitched forth the statistics.

'Okay, of these 149, only 3 were serious girlfriends, 45 were short term flings ranging from 4 months to 4 days; some of these flings taking place concurrently. 12 were friends and the rest were all one-night stands. Of these one-night flings, almost 50 per cent were with commercial sex-workers in places ranging from London, Dubai, New York, Morocco and of course, Bangkok. Some of my escapades were also with air hostesses or hotel receptionists whom I took fancy to.'

I was obviously left dazed.

'Hey, don't worry. I've got myself medically tested thrice, whenever I had the slightest doubt, and I'm safe.'

'How old are you?' I asked him.

'Twenty-six.'

Prakash was nearly four years younger than me, but in terms of experience, he was 400 times more brazen.

'And what makes you experiment so lavishly with sex?' I asked out of curiosity.

'Adventure.'

'For which you don't need emotions?'

'Well, the only time I had emotions was for my first girlfriend, Darthy. We were in class seven and we knew we were in love.'

'And what happened to her?'

'She drowned in a river on our class eight picnic.'

'Oh. I'm sorry.'

The thought of Darthy changed his expression. 'She died because of me. I'd persuaded her to come away with me towards the fast flowing side of the river. I knew how to swim. She didn't. She was drowned because I didn't have the courage to risk my life to save hers.'

'Oh. That's really sad,' I empathized, discovering how life can script a different story for each person.

'From that day, I've never felt emotional for a girl because I still yearn for my Darthy. Yes, sex has become an adventure, a need. It's some sort of a reassurance. That's probably why there was a phase in between when I wanted to sleep with all my female friends.'

I heard him out intently. He smiled and added, 'And yeah, you inspire me to ask you to be my 150th partner.'

'You're mad. You're perverted.'

'Okay, forget it. Let's be friends.'

'With the hope that I'll be one of those friends of yours whom you eventually convert into your sexual ally?'

He laughed. 'I certainly won't mind that.'

At that point, I felt certain I'd never want to meet this man again. But the stuff that I got to know about him, in the remainder of our journey, made me have a change of heart. Prakash's family business had been going through a particularly bad patch when he had joined it three years ago after doing an MBA from abroad. His father had died and the business had incurred losses of almost 50 crore. At that point, Prakash had the option of selling off the business to an investor. Instead, with his back against the wall, he worked relentlessly to change the fortunes of the company. Finally, just two months ago, the company had managed to recover all its losses. The other thing that impressed me about Prakash was his philanthropy. Prakash was actively involved with an NGO for schoolchildren and destitute women down south.

By the time the flight ended, I realized I didn't really mind keeping in touch with him. Prakash lived out of a suitcase. His business interests had him travelling across the country. And since one of his new units was being set up in Faridabad he ended up coming to Delhi almost every ten days. Every time he was in Delhi we'd meet late in the evening, and hang out in a pub till the early hours. He was a late riser. And since I was no early riser myself – except for a brief period when I tried being one for Brajesh – I had no problems with the arrangement.

Prakash was fun to be with. He could match steps with me on the dance floor, like few men could. When we talked, we talked like bosom buddies. He'd share some of his more intimate experiences with women with me. And, surprisingly, I quite enjoyed listening to his escapades. Such was the comfort level that we shared, that on one occasion, in a disco, I challenged him to bed a Russian chick who displayed her cleavage generously. To my surprise, Prakash actually took up the challenge and vanished with her. I didn't hear from him till the next afternoon.

Prakash would flirt with me as well, even though he knew I wasn't one of those who would oblige him. As our friendship grew he became privy to matters that were more personal to me. I shared with him the cynicism that I and my friends were experiencing post 26/11.

One day Prakash came up with an interesting proposition.

'Want to come with me to Gujarat?' he asked.

'For what? I have been there an endless number of times,' I said, rather indifferently.

'The Gujarat of 2009 is very different from the one of 2002. I am setting up a small chemical unit close to Ahmedabad. We've identified two locations. I'll be going there next week. If you come along, it will be great.'

I guess if the same offer had been made to me two years back, I'd have spurned it without a second thought. For me, Gujarat embodied the death of secularism and democracy. This time round, I was prepared to look at the state beyond the prism of 2002.

And so I am here, in a state that prepares itself for its tryst with history. A huge 1100-acre area has been set aside for the car project. While work inside is on full swing, the entire area around breathes a palpable excitement. The energy and anticipation that one sees all around is comparable to what one might see in a family preparing for the marriage of its daughter.

We are introduced to a gentleman called Rajubhai Kanodia. Rajubhai is a farmer turned small-scale industrialist. He was in the news recently for having sold 50 acres of land to the government at almost half the market price, so that the land could be used for the car project. I ask him about the loss that he has incurred and he laughs it off.

'Chaitaliben, you have to lose some to gain more. I was a small farmer and never quite expected to have all that I have today. Today at 65, it's my turn to pay back.

This car plant will bring employment to thousands of my brothers and sisters. What more do I want?'

Prakash and I are both touched by Rajubhai's larger concerns – something you don't easily get to see in people nowadays.

'Not only me. At least twenty people in this area have sold a part of their holdings. All of them did so voluntarily and at a very low price,' he tells us proudly.

'And what really makes you do this?' I query.

He flashes a positive smile and points towards a hoarding that has the Chief Minister congratulating himself for one of his achievements.

'That man,' he says. 'The Gujarati community was always a very enterprising community. But that man has re-instilled confidence in us. He has made us believe that, irrespective of global conditions, through our sheer will power, we will continue to prosper. Narendrabhai inspires the youth of Gujarat like nobody after Gandhi and Sardar Patel has. What we've done has just helped in realizing his dreams of making Gujarat more and more prosperous.'

I chuckle at the irony that life always seems loaded with.

I think I know Modi enough to realize what lies beneath the façade of 'economic development' that he has relentlessly been trying to project. It helps in deflecting attention from the heinous activities that he has been associated with in the past. As we walk away I feel even more incensed at how this bluff about prosperity is being successfully employed to make people forget the carnage.

'Prakash, don't you think all this is a bluff? They say more than 12 lakh crores worth of MOUs were signed at the Vibrant Gujarat Global Investors' Summit recently. You think that much would ever materialize? Besides, Gujarat has always been a prosperous state.'

'Well, that figure could be inflated, just like the inflation rate projected by the government today is miraculously low on the eve of elections,' Prakash avers.

I think Prakash understands my dilemma for him to add what he does:

'You know, Chaitali, I think you want to believe that all this talk about prosperous Gujarat is a lie. And I don't blame you. But I can tell you this prosperity is as real as the riots were. I can tell you from my personal experience that bureaucratic corruption and red-tapism is non-existent here. Besides, the man takes decisions like he were running a corporate house.'

'But does that absolve him of 2002?'

'Well, the question of being absolved arises when guilt is proven.'

'Oh come on, Prakash, you're talking like a BJP guy…'

'I'm not. Every coin has two sides. I'm just helping you see the other side.'

I don't feel up to arguing. Prakash may well have a point; or maybe I trust him enough to give him the benefit of doubt.

One of the other persons we meet at Sanand is Asgar Patel, a Khoja Muslim. He runs a small welding unit and seems equally upbeat about the opportunities that the Nano plant will generate. Asgar incidentally has an interesting story to share. He, along with his family, had fled to Mumbai when the 2002 riots first broke out. In fact, an acquaintance of his had died in the riots. For a few years thereafter, Asgar worked in a similar unit in the Sewri area of Mumbai. He returned only in 2006.

'I would have been a loser had I continued to be away from this place. This place has changed so much. There is a renewed surge towards enterprise and entrepreneurship. The government is extremely supportive and we feel encouraged,' he tells us with a smile.

I don't know what to say. Well, Ratan Tata had said something similar sometime back – *'You'd be a fool if you are not in Gujarat.'* I had thought that Tata could afford such rhetoric as he wasn't affected by the riots. But to hear this sentiment from a commoner makes my head spin. I wonder if a fascist can become acceptable, if he brings economic gain? Are we really that selfish a society?

'You know something, Chaitali, the per capita income of Muslims is the highest in Gujarat, compared with any other Indian state,' Prakash shares a mundane academic statistic that I don't want to hear. There's already enough that I'm finding hard to absorb.

A day later, on the 28th February, the death toll in the Gujarat riots goes up by 228. Yes, as per law, seven years after people go missing, they are officially declared dead.

We happen to meet one of the ill-fated mothers, Moshina Bano, whose thirteen-year-old son went missing on that ill-fated night, never to return.

'It's a relief. I've gone mad trying to search for him everywhere. At least, now I know where he is.' She sounds half dead herself.

I'm choked when I hear this. Something in me propels me to ask her a tough question.

'Is there something you'd like to tell the CM if you happen to meet him?'

She looks at me wondering why I am asking this question, before she responds.

'You think that man who doesn't have children will understand what the pain of a mother is? I won't insult myself by even talking to him.'

She breaks down.

Even as Prakash and I console Moshina, we can't help looking at each other in utter bewilderment.

What or who is the real Modi?

Is he what Rajubhai or Asgar would want us to believe or is he what Moshina would think he is.

How I wish that this economic prosperity of Gujarat had come about without the riots. This duality about Gujarat is what baffles me. To be honest, somewhere I want to admire the CM for what he has done after 2002. Yet, 2002 was just so excruciating that I doubt if its echoes can ever be silenced by history.

'Prakash, if the riots hadn't taken place, you think Modi would still have been so popular?' I ask.

Prakash too doesn't seem certain about the answer. He pauses and then says with rare honesty, 'In that case, maybe Modi's popularity would only have been only marginally higher than the other successful CMs – those of Delhi, MP, Chhattisgarh and Orissa.'

I wonder why in life, when you get down to probing things, instead of finding answers, you are confronted by newer, ever more complex conundrums. I'm surprised though, at my dependence on Prakash. I think he talks sense. He accords a high importance to logic. I guess I kind of relate with him in the same way that Brajesh told me he's begun to relate with Monica.

Strangely enough, I realize something common between politics and love – the journeys in both cases can be uncannily serendipitous. And if you learn to take the hurt in your stride, I can vouch you'll enjoy this journey much more.

Anyway, my journey with Prakash extends from the richest part of the country to what probably is the poorest one – the interiors of Vidharbha, in Maharashtra. I wanted to see the contrast between boom and despair.

I'm 200 km south of Nagpur, in Kosara village in the Yavatmal district of Vidharbha. In spring itself, a hostile heat wave blows across the place. This village alone had reported some 50 farmer suicides last year. The last suicide, we're told, took place only last week: a hapless farmer Madhav Gire, committed suicide by consuming poison.

It will shock you to know that from 1997 on some 200,000 farmers have committed suicide in our country. For 2007 alone the death toll was 16600, of which nearly 25 per cent were from Maharashtra. And this part of Mahrashtra, where we stand now is the worst affected in the country.

I wanted to speak first-hand to a victim's family. And so, here we are. Sharda's husband killed himself two years ago realizing that he'd never be able to pay back a debt of Rs. 75,000. Now that figure has increased to a lakh. Sharda works as daily labourer earning a measly Rs. 45 with which she feeds her family of four daughters. Her condition is deplorable to say the least. Even as we talk and a crowd gathers around us, Sharda goes hysterical and threatens to immolate herself. It's only after Prakash promises to adopt her family and to pay back her debt for her that she calms down.

We realize though that taking care of one Sharda will make scant difference to a region where there are thousands of Shardas, all dangerously close to pushing the suicide button. What is equally appalling is another heart-wrenching story that we are told.

Just two months ago, in a neighbouring village, two brothers had actually fought bitterly among themselves, both volunteering to commit suicide. The brothers understandably loved each other a lot; hence the fight to sacrifice self before the other. The idea was that the compensation that the act would get, would sustain both families for sometime… When no resolution was possible, one of the two brothers ended up killing himself and the other followed suit within hours. It goes without saying that the amount obtained by the families was hopelessly inadequate in filling up the personal human loss.

We can't stay here any longer – it's that disturbing for me. I feel like I am in a graveyard. We make a hasty departure.

Now there are several factors that can be attributed to this pathetic state of affairs of our farmers. First and foremost and the most generic one of course is that right from the Nehruvian era, we never really accorded the attention and planning to the agricultural sector that it deserves. This is strange considering that 60% of our population still depends on agriculture for their livelihood and that agriculture contributes 25% to our national income. Therefore, the unabated farmer suicides, is perhaps as serious a problem as terrorism and AIDS put together. However, unlike the two other scourges, it does not directly affect the urban population and hence continues to be ignored.

The basic cause of indebtedness among farmers, as I understand it, is the inability to recover costs from the ever decreasing size of individual farm holdings. Being in debt makes them lose whatever land they owned and throws them into irrevocable despair. The situation interestingly is slightly different in the Vidharba region. Here, farmers preferred cultivation of the high-risk cotton crop. First, quality seeds were not available and then they were not able to afford the high quality BT cotton seeds that promised high yields. In other cases where they somehow managed to use these BT cotton seeds, the seeds failed to deliver in the parched climate of Vidharbha. And this only entrenched them further in debt and doom.

◆

It's evening. I'm sitting with Prakash over cups of green tea in our hotel at Nagpur. It's been an immensely distressing and draining day for us. Prakash tells me about a new initiative of the Gujarat Government: *E gram vishwagram* (E village; global village), which aims at providing broadband connectivity to all gram panchayats of the state.

We grapple with the dichotomy that is India and everything Indian. The Congress and the BJP have clear pros and cons attached to them. And where does this leave the Left? Oh, Yechury and Karat have been travelling across the country trying desperately to cobble together an opportunistic, unreal 'Third Front'. If not about anything else, my 'unlearning' sojourn has made me clearer about one thing: Marxism in India is a myth and a hallucination.

Prakash is off for a work-out in the hotel gym. I share my thoughts first with Brajesh and then with Aditya, engaging both in lengthy conversations on the phone. At the end of my chats, I feel a lot lighter. Brajesh and Aditya share my conviction about the three of us getting together. Well, if all goes well, in less than a week, we might be in the news for something big.

Prakash in the meantime is back. He steps into the bath and removes his tee-shirt. I stand right behind him, watching his sweaty physique intently. He sees me. I walk up to him and hold him from behind. The act embodies a craving that both have started to feel.

I let Prakash make love to me. I think I need this indulgence to put one part of my life behind me and prepare for the new. Prakash, I know is someone I'd like to preserve for life. In as much as he may not say this, lest it kill his playboy image, I'm quite convinced he feels differently about me too.

Our conversation after sex, by the way, is quite amusing.

'Hhhh... so you got me finally?' I say.

'Had to,' he retorts in a cocky manner.

'Yeah. But not as your landmark 150th partner. My bad luck.'

'You bet you're my 150th woman,' he asserts rather triumphantly.

'What? You mean you didn't do it with that Russian chick? Nor with anyone else in these two months?'

'Nope.'

I'm surprised.

'From the time that I first met you on the flight, I've only wanted you. You made me realize 149 is sufficient. I don't mind freezing the count at 150.'

◆

Exactly a week later, Aditya, Brajesh and I meet at the Neemrana Fort Palace near Delhi. I have, in the meantime, quit my party.

This six centuries' old fort turned heritage hotel, I'm sure, has witnessed many a turbulence in the past. Today, it is to be the launchpad of the biggest battle of our lives: the battle to be able to stand up for what we believe in. Aditya has come here with Sita who will be taking down the minutes of our summit. Brajesh is with Monica. Prakash is by my side.

Our meeting, which starts around dinnertime, continues through the night. It's only around eight the next morning that we are finally convinced we've sorted out most of the issues to our satisfaction.

By this time, we're told that the media has learnt about our meeting and has gathered in huge numbers in the hotel lobby. Aditya isn't too keen to speak to the media right away. Brajesh and I think otherwise. We feel that we'd sound our most passionate right now, just after our marathon session. And so we are speaking to the media – all impromptu:

'We've decided to float a new party,' Aditya announces to them.

'It's called Nation Building & Development League,' adds Brajesh.

'As the name suggests, the party will strive to re-construct a strong national identity with its pro-active policies and a dynamic approach,' I interject.

Monica and Prakash add their bit:

'We intend doing this by judiciously empowering and enhancing the credibility of state institutions…'

'…And by eliminating all roadblocks that hinder development.'

Based on our collective pursuits in the last few months, we spell out a list of immediate concerns that our new party will espouse.

More announcements follow, impromptu again. Brajesh, by virtue of his seniority, is to be the president of our party. Aditya and I are the general secretaries. Both of us will double as the party's spokespersons for now. Prakash, for his ability to bring in the funds, will be the party's treasurer, whereas Monica will look after organizational matters.

Oh, it's finally over and what a coup it has been! Our announcement causes flutters in Delhi's corridors of power; we're already getting calls from all the three major national alliances approaching us for 'discussions'. I don't think the Neemrana Fort minds another tryst with history: this time for being the venue that started an unusual contemporary revolution in Indian politics!

The six of us decide to shun our cars and instead travel together back to Delhi in a hired bus. We need this time to further cement our strategy once we're back in Delhi.

Never have we felt so inspired in our political careers, as we do now. With every inch that we cover of the 122 km journey back, we can hear a historic phrase echo more resoundingly in our ears – *Ab Dilli door nahi!*

Jai Hind!